T0270415

KAITLYN'S WHEEL

A NOVEL

bancroft
press

CHRIS HALVORSON

Bancroft Press' Other Fine YA Books

Cover Design: Christine Van Bree Design
Interior Design: TracyCopesCreative.com

Kaitlyn's Wheel Title Info
978-1-61088-552-2 (HC)
978-1-61088-553-9 (PB)
978-1-61088-554-6 (Ebook)
978-1-61088-555-3 (PDF)
978-1-61088-556-0 (Audiobook)

Published by Bancroft Press
"Books that Enlighten"
(818) 275-3061
4527 Glenwood Avenue
La Crescenta, CA 91214
www.bancroftpress.com

Printed in the United States of America

For my father, Larry, a kid from the projects

who grew up to become a lawyer,

taught me that the streets often deliver

more justice than any courtroom,

but fought the good fight anyway.

FALL

001

The lights first appeared in the sky the night Kaitlyn Stokes' father died in his sleep. For the previous several months, he'd been fighting cancer with chemotherapy and radiation, his body decimated by the so-called treatments. Despite the endless prayers from Kaitlyn and her mother, his suffering finally became too much for any human being to endure. That's why the angels from heaven came to take him. At least that's what Reverend Jacob said at the funeral on Sunday. But Kaitlyn believed something else—that the lights in the sky were from aliens coming to collect her father's soul, now in the form of energy.

"That's just crazy talk," said her mother, driving their car past a long stretch of cornfields on the county highway.

"It's not crazy," said Kaitlyn, a high school senior with her father's raven hair and curious green eyes. "It's even in the Bible—Ezekiel's wheel. He was a prophet, you know."

"He never mentions little green men in flying saucers," said her mother.

"No," said Kaitlyn, "but he talks about creatures with the likeness of man, who come flying down in wheels with brilliant lights. They take him away to a temple in the sky. It was like being lifted away by the hand of God, he said."

Her mother gazed out at the highway, her brown eyes squinting into the sunlight, which turned her auburn hair red. "It's normal to have these kinds of thoughts right now," she said. "We're both experiencing a lot of grief and depression."

Kaitlyn felt a surge of anger. "You mean it's *not* normal, but you want to tell me in a nice way that I'm crazy."

"I never said you were crazy."

"You just said Ezekiel's wheel was crazy."

"Talking crazy," said her mother, "and *being* crazy are two completely separate things."

"I'm not the only one who believes this," said Kaitlyn. "There are modern-day scientists who call it ancient astronaut theory."

"Just like Bigfoot and the Loch Ness Monster are real."

"Maybe they are," said Kaitlyn. "You know, for hundreds of years, people didn't believe in gorillas—that an ape could really be that big. They began believing in the early 1900s, when a German military officer 'officially' discovered one in the mountains. Before that, anyone who claimed to see one was nothing more than 'delusional.'"

They passed a scarecrow in the field, its straw tattered by wind, sleet, and rain of many Iowa winters. "I'm glad you're reading so much," said her mother, "and not just wasting time on social media."

"I know what I saw, Mom," said Kaitlyn. The wheel in the sky reminded her of a Ferris wheel at night, its lights flashing green, red, yellow, and blue as if transmitting some type of signal. Awakened by its force in the early hours of darkness, she'd actually felt the spaceship hovering over their house before spotting it from their front porch moments later. "And please, stop telling me I was dreaming," she told her mother, "or reminding me I used to sleepwalk when I was little."

Watching the road, her mother sighed. "I think we should make an appointment with Dr. Spalding again." Dr. Spalding was their family grief counselor. For the past several months, he'd been helping them "cope" with her father's illness and death.

"He's a waste of money, Mom," said Kaitlyn. Even with their health care insurance, her father's hospital bills had nearly bankrupted her parents.

"I have a job," said her mother, "so let me worry about that." They would now have to survive on her income from the country feed store, where she managed the inventory and handled bookkeeping. The pay was nowhere near her father's salary as an agricultural sales rep, selling tractors and farm equipment to everyone within a hundred-mile radius. People loved and trusted her father, which was why they continued to buy from him over the years.

"I can't even begin to explain this void I'm feeling," said Kaitlyn. "Not to you, or Dr. Spalding, or anyone. It's beyond grief, and I—" She choked up, her mother reaching over to take her hand.

"Oh, honey, I'm so sorry," she said in a tired voice. After crying all week, her mother's tear ducts had nearly gone dry, and her face had turned puffy with reddened eyes. "We're going to get through this, you know. By staying strong for each other."

"I know, Mom, I know," said Kaitlyn. Face wet with tears, she squeezed her mother's hand. Mom was doing her maternal best, but she could never truly understand.

Her father was out there somewhere.

Zachary Taylor wasn't intentionally named after the twelfth president of the United States of America. One of the most forgotten presidents in history, he never crossed the minds of Zachary's parents in choosing their son's name from a website of popular boys' names.

Not that Zachary himself was any more popular than the forgotten president. In fact, he was nicknamed the "Invisible Creeper" by his twin sister Hailey, senior class president at Walter S. Lemley High School. It wasn't that Zachary was unattractive, or shy, or lacked wit and confidence. He could have easily followed in his sister's footsteps (she was born first), but he simply had no desire to be part of that institutional madness.

"I'm thinking of working for Greenpeace," he announced to his parents at the dinner table, his sister away at either homecoming court rehearsals or a student pep rally. He couldn't care less.

His parents exchanged an awkward look. His mother was a former clarinet player in the marching band at Washington State University, where she'd met his father, an ROTC officer in the Cougar Battalion. They'd first intersected at halftime on the field.

"Greenpeace can't pay much," said his father. His former military haircut was now mostly bald from hair loss, and his bushy eyebrows had turned gray.

"Probably true," said Zachary, "but that doesn't mean it's not rewarding."

"What about college?" said his mother, her graying brown hair cut shorter than her marching band days when she was twenty pounds slimmer and devoid of any worry lines.

"Have you even started your applications?" said his father, wanting both him and his sister to attend his alma mater.

"I have until February," said Zachary. "That's like five months away."

"Why procrastinate?" said his father.

"Unless you plan on retaking the SATs," his mother hinted.

"I scored 1300," said Zachary. "That's in the eighty-sixth percentile, you know."

"Not as good as your sister," said his father, referring to her score of 1550, which was good enough for Harvard. "But not horrible either."

"You're just as smart," said his mother. "You just don't apply yourself."

Zachary couldn't argue. "I just don't know about college," he said. "I mean, what's the point?"

"So you can someday find a decent job," said his mother, whose finance degree put her in charge of lending at their family-owned auto dealership.

"But we're going to be replaced by robots," Zachary said. "By the time I'm your age, there won't be any jobs, and with climate change, it's going to get even worse. We won't be able to grow food in many parts of the world. Mass shifts in population will lead to tribal wars and anarchy. We'll be hunting our neighbors' dogs and cats for dinner, and once they're all gone, we'll be eating rats and squirrels, followed by our neighbors. So why bother with college?"

"Can we not talk about cannibalism at the dinner table?" said his father, picking meat from his teeth as if it were a piece of Mr. Jones next door.

"Do you think you might be depressed?" asked his mother in concern.

"Of course I'm depressed," said Zachary. "Did you not hear a word I just said?"

"I don't mean about the planet," said his mother. "I mean about you."

Setting down his fork, Zachary sighed in frustration. It was pointless. After all, his parents sold massive SUVs which burned fossil fuel at alarming rates. So long as their vehicles passed state emissions tests, his parents could fool themselves into believing they were environmentally friendly.

"You must have some interest in girls," said his father, stabbing his baked potato with a fork.

"But it's also okay to be gay," said his mother with a reassuring smile.

"Thanks, Mom," said Zachary, "for welcoming me into the twenty-first century." He didn't feel like telling them how his hormones were going crazy for the girls at school. But he had nothing in common with those girls. They talked about football players and hip-hop stars they would never meet, and spent all day on their phones, texting and sharing TikTok videos of teenagers dancing and lip-synching to silly pop songs. It was all so meaningless that he felt both bored and frustrated.

Which explains why Zachary skipped school the next day, spending it by the river in their little town of Lemley, Washington. Nestled in the Cascade Mountains, Lemley was built on coal in the early 1900s, though the last of the mines finally shut down not long after Zachary was born. With a dam built upstream, the hydroelectric plant now supplied the town with power and jobs. It was far cleaner than coal, for sure, but Zachary still didn't agree with the town leaders bragging about their "renewable energy" when the flooding of lands destroyed forests, wildlife, and agriculture.

Solar energy would be far better for the environment, but with a thick gray mist rolling in, the future looked as bleak as the dystopian teen novel Zachary was reading on the grassy riverbank. Its story of zombies surviving in the post-apocalyptic world reminded him of high school, with its mindless followers roaming the halls. Halfway through the final chapter, his eyes grew tired, and he dozed off without realizing it. If not for the cold, damp air seeping through his jacket, he might have slept longer, his mind as foggy and still as the weather. Surprised to see the time on his phone was after 2 p.m., he stuffed the book in his backpack and headed off for home at a time when school usually ended. Just in case one of his parents had come home early from work, they wouldn't suspect he'd ditched the day's classes.

The next morning, however, Zachary found himself in the principal's office, where he now had to explain his unexcused absence. "I was abducted by a UFO," he said, the first thought that came to mind.

"A UFO?" repeated Mr. Klausen, raising his triangular eyebrows like

Count Dracula, which the students secretly called him behind his back.

"Yes," said Zachary, his humor so dry he seemed serious. "I was on my way to school when the aliens abducted me to run some experiments. By the time they dropped me off at my house, classes were already over. But I'm fine, so thanks for checking on me."

Mr. Klausen, the slightest of grins curling on his lips, seemed to find the story amusing. "Very well then, Mr. Taylor," he said, "I hope our alien visitors provided you with some valuable knowledge you can someday share with our human species."

"Yes, Mr. Klausen," said Zachary, taking a sudden liking to his school principal.

"Now, get to class before you're late."

"Yes, sir!" As Zachary turned and left the office, he passed the school secretary, Mrs. Wilmer. Overhearing the conversation, she was already texting her daughter Layla, a freshman at the school.

Within a few minutes, Layla had posted the story on Instagram, along with a photo of Zachary that appeared in the school yearbook. Through Facebook and Twitter, she quickly spread the gossip to friends and family across the nation, including her favorite grandmother living at the Desert Springs Retirement Community in Scottsdale, Arizona.

By lunchtime, everyone in the school was buzzing about Zachary's abduction. At Desert Springs, the story was far more exciting than the usual conversation at Thursday afternoon bingo, and the senior citizens in turn passed the news to their massive network of Facebook friends. No matter the age, everyone loved a good old-fashioned tale of flying saucers, especially when the abductee was so good-looking.

By dinnertime that night, the first local news van was pulling up to

Zachary's house.

Alone in her room, Kaitlyn was on her phone, searching a UFO Sightings Map for activity in her area. Last month, a trucker in Des Moines witnessed a glowing pair of orange triangular crafts that flew overhead for several miles down the I-70. Twelve days later, several members of the Fox and Sac Tribe sighted a V-formation of blue lights streaking over the tribal lands of the Meskwaki Nation. Yet nobody had reported a spinning wheel like the one over her house—confirmation to Kaitlyn it had come specifically for her father.

She had already promised her mother not to tell anyone about it. While her mother feared scorn and ridicule, Kaitlyn had no desire to share her experience with anyone else. It was as private as losing her virginity, only this was even more personal, a spiritual moment between her and her father before his departure from Earth.

She hadn't even told her best friend Jenna, whose blaring text alert was Taylor Swift singing, "I don't want to live forever." It was the last thing Kaitlyn wanted to hear right now. But she still opened her messages, and the latest one read: *Are you okay?*

Couldn't be better, Kaitlyn sarcastically texted back. She was still mad at her friend for how she'd dressed for the funeral—short black skirt and spiked heels, which were far more appropriate for a nightclub. More than once, Kaitlyn had seen her sneak off texts to whichever boy of the week she was supposedly in love with.

Jenna: When are you coming back to school?
Kaitlyn: *Idk*

Jenna: I miss you.

Kaitlyn: Thanks.

Jenna: Garrett Haggerty was asking about you.

Kaitlyn: Gross, he always stares at my chest.

Jenna: I'm jealous lol.

Kaitlyn: You can have him.

Jenna: Jsuk ily *(Just so you know, I love you).*

Kaitlyn hesitated before responding. Maybe her mother was right; perhaps she was being too hard on her friend. Not a day had passed when Jenna hadn't texted at least several times to check on her. With her ADHD, Jenna could never stay focused on one thing for more than a minute, including a funeral sermon. But was it really asking too much to put the phone away for just one hour of her precious life? And not to look so damn sexy with Kaitlyn's father lying dead in a coffin just twenty feet away?

Ilyt she texted back, letting her know she loved her too. *Bfn (Bye for now).*

Returning to her UFO Sightings Map, she saw a breaking headline on her phone: *Teen Boy Abducted by UFO in Washington State.*

(LEMLEY, WA) Zachary Taylor, an 18-year-old senior at Lemley High School, reported to school authorities that he missed school Wednesday after being abducted by an alien spacecraft. According to school sources, the aliens conducted experiments on Taylor before safely returning him to his home. Taylor is currently unavailable for comment.

Kaitlyn curiously tapped his photo, which appeared to be from a school yearbook. He was the most adorable boy she'd ever seen. Big brown eyes and floppy dark hair. The reluctant smile of someone who was inherently kind but didn't want to expose himself to a world he didn't trust. Just by looking at his photo, she felt as if she understood him. He was unlike the boys at school who were trying so hard to be the exact opposite of their true selves.

She quickly Googled Zachary Taylor, and saw the twelfth U.S. President in black and white photos taken before the Civil War. Kaitlyn vaguely remembered him from eighth-grade history as the president who kept the Union together before dying in office from a mysterious stomach ailment. Far more interesting was the conspiracy theory that followed. If he wasn't assassinated, he might have been poisoned by his wife, and likely for good reason, thought Kaitlyn.

Now on Instagram, she encountered dozens more Zachary Taylors. None of them presidents but all sharing common first and last names. None of them was *her* Zachary, if she could call him that already without sounding too creepy, even to herself. A search on Facebook, Twitter, and Snapchat produced similar results—meaning none. That was impossible. Nobody their age ghosted themselves like this, at least nobody she knew of. He obviously didn't want to be found, which made him even more mysterious.

After some more Googling, she discovered a Taylor Automotive Group in Lemley, Washington. Their website featured photos of last year's Fourth of July Blow-Out Sale Event. Pictured with his family, Zachary was the only one not in costume. Both parents donned silly Uncle Sam hats and red, white, and blue suits. A girl who was obviously his sister wore sparkly glitter on her face, her designer tank top displaying the Stars and Stripes in summer fashion. Judging by the same brown eyes, she and Zachary appeared to be twins, but something in her facial expression lacked his sincerity. The longer Kaitlyn looked at his photo, the more she saw how vulnerable he was, until she finally pried her eyes away to continue her search.

She next found Taylor Automotive Group on Facebook, which led to personal profiles of Mom (Delores), Dad (Russ), and sister (Hailey), the latter of whom hadn't posted anything in ages. A moment later, Kaitlyn located her on Instagram. Several videos showed Hailey with a cool crowd of cheerleaders and jocks. Even if they weren't 1,762 miles apart (she Google-Mapped it), Kaitlyn suspected they would never be friends, but she had nothing to lose by reaching out with a DM (direct message in Boomer speak):

Hey Hailey,

I saw your brother on the news and would really like to connect with him. Would you please give him my number? 563-187-2400

Thanks,

Kaitlyn.

PS — You're very pretty.

Hitting send, she instantly regretted the pretty comment. Intended as a compliment to break the ice, it might come across as stalkerish and weird, even if people in the Pacific Northwest *were* far more liberated than her farming community in Iowa. If she wasn't mistaken, Washington was one of the first states to legalize both same-sex marriage and cannabis, which made her wonder if Zachary ever used drugs. Hopefully not, if it meant his UFO experience was nothing more than a chemically altered hallucination. Zooming in on his yearbook portrait, she suddenly realized she had stopped thinking of her father for the first time all week. A twinge of wholesome Midwestern shame quickly followed.

The Taylors' home was now surrounded by TV reporters, production crews, and news vans. Most were from local stations, but a few were also from big markets like Seattle, which, ninety miles away and on the other side of the mountains, was the nearest metropolitan area. The only media giant there was CNA, Cable News America, its mounted satellite ready to project to anywhere in the world from its tank-sized vehicle.

"You are going out there right now," said Zachary's father, "and telling them that you made this all up to get out of school."

"It was a silly prank," said his mother, "but you meant nothing by it."

"Oh my God, you are such an embarrassment," said Hailey, daring to peek out their living room curtains at the media circus stationed on their front lawn.

Zachary stood facing all the members of his immediate family, wondering how he shared the same DNA with any of them. "How do you know I wasn't really abducted?"

"You don't really expect us to believe that, do you?" said his father with a tightened jaw.

"No," said Zachary," but that doesn't mean it couldn't have happened."

"You're not making any sense!" said Hailey.

"I don't have to make sense," said Zachary. "Not if I invoke my Fifth Amendment rights."

"You're not under arrest," said Hailey in annoyance.

"No, but I still have the right to remain silent," said Zachary, as in not telling her that her blonde highlights clashed with the dark roots growing out.

"You never talk to anyone as it is," said Hailey. "Which is why everyone thinks you're such a freak."

"What everyone thinks is all you care about," said Zachary. "You've never had an original thought in your life."

"At least I have friends."

"Friends who would disown you if something tragic ever happened."

"You're so dark and depressing all the time," said Hailey. "No wonder nobody wants to be around—"

"Stop it!" said their mother. "We're a family, for God's sake!"

"And right now," said their father, "we have to think about our family business."

"'Our name is our reputation,'" said their mother, quoting the company slogan used in all their radio and TV ads.

"So that's what this is about?" said Zachary. "Selling SUVs?"

"Damn right!" said his father. "Those same SUVs that bought this house and put the food on the table that you ate tonight."

Truth be told, Zachary was tired of meals filled with beef dishes and GMOs, but now wasn't the time to recommend a vegetarian diet that they could produce with their own sustainable garden.

"It's more than that," said his mother. "We don't want you to become a— well, you know. A social outcast."

"Oh, my God," said Hailey. "It's a little late for that, don't you think?"

Clearing his throat, Zachary said, "You're right, Mom and Dad. We're a family, with a family business to think about." He went to the front door and flung it open, the bright lights of media cameras hitting his face as dozens of reporters shouted over one another:

"Zachary! Were you really abducted by alien life forces?"

"How big was the UFO?

"What did the aliens look like?"

"Were they friendly?"

"How long were you with them?"

"Did they say what they wanted?"

"What kind of experiments did they run on you?"

Through the blinding glare, Zachary squinted at the reporters, their expressions like dogs begging for table scraps. "I'm not really sure," he said, thinking of how he'd dozed off reading his novel. "It's all kind of hazy, like waking from a dream."

"Did they erase your memory?" a reporter called out.

"Most of it, I think," said Zachary uncertainly, which made him all the more convincing.

"What *do* you remember?" asked a familiar face from CNA—Greta Grogan, a sassy brunette who'd chased hurricanes, dirty politicians, and crocodiles, all to get a good story.

"Well," said Zachary, "they had comfortable seating in their spaceship, even though it was designed for their little bodies. Their heads and eyes were very large."

"Did they speak to you?" inquired Susan Wong, a familiar face on KING TV News, Seattle.

"Sort of," said Zachary, fully enjoying himself now. "They communicated through telepathy to deliver a message."

"What did they say!?" shouted several voices. "What was the message?"

Zachary stared into their cameras, his eyes finally adjusting to the harsh lights. With the poise of a US president he wasn't quite named after, he announced, "They say it's not too late to save our planet by reducing carbon emissions and eating less meat. They said it can start right here, at Taylor Automotive Group in Lemley, Washington."

"Is this a cheap publicity stunt?" questioned another reporter. "To help your family sell cars?"

"You're the ones who came to my house uninvited," responded Zachary. "But while you're here, you're invited to our Big Electric Vehicle Sale Event this weekend. Come test drive a new EV and get a free vegan hot dog!"

As the reporters bombarded him with more questions, he quickly interjected, "Well, I think I hear my mom calling me, so I'll see you there!" He closed the door on the mayhem outside. Turning to face his family, he saw the shocked horror on their faces.

"I hate you," said a teary Hailey, running off to her room upstairs.

His mother looked at him in shame. "I hope you're proud of yourself," she said, "for ruining our family name."

His father was so angry he could barely speak. "Well, hotshot," he whispered through clenched teeth, "what do you have to say for yourself now?"

"You're welcome," said Zachary.

"You're welcome for ruining our business?" his mother asked incredulously.

A door slammed upstairs and his sister screamed, "I hope you die, freak!"

"Yes, Mom," said Zachary with impressive calm. "It's called free advertising, with a few million viewers watching just now."

"We don't sell electric vehicles," said his father, as if speaking to a two-year-old.

"Not yet," said Zachary, "but you can order a new fleet tomorrow."

"You don't understand, son," his father said. "We don't make our money on sales. We make it on service and repairs."

"And electric vehicles don't need as much maintenance," said his mother.

"You mean they're better cars," said Zachary.

"Better cars perhaps," admitted his father. "But not better for us."

"If it's money you're after," said Zachary, "put some charging stations on the lot. Solar-powered, with a small fee. It's still much cheaper than gas, only you'll be making the profits instead of the oil companies. Better yet, while people are waiting to charge their vehicles, sell them coffee and snacks. And car washes with recycled water."

His parents exchanged a look.

"But first things first," said Zachary. "Let's get some showroom models ASAP, along with hundreds of vegan hot dogs." Heading off for the basement, he left his parents to quietly ponder their new business model.

Kaitlyn had lost track of how many times she'd watched the YouTube clip of Zachary speaking to reporters outside his house (now up to 1,203,490 views, with 71K thumbs up, 45.3K thumbs down, and hundreds of girls commenting on how cute he was). He obviously didn't care what people thought of him. Kaitlyn wondered if he'd always been so courageous, or if the aliens had used their powers to influence him. Whatever the case, he had cut the interview short, with so many questions left unanswered. Like what did the spacecraft look like? Was it anything like the spinning wheel of lights that took her father away?

Watching the YouTube clip again, she chuckled on hearing him say, "Well, I think I hear my mom calling me, so I'll see you there!" Live on camera, he was even cuter than his glossy yearbook photo. More importantly, Zachary must have a good soul, or the aliens wouldn't have chosen him to deliver such an important message.

Kaitlyn had never before been so mystified by a boy. Checking her phone, she saw five new text messages from Jenna, but nothing from Zachary. Hailey had yet to respond on Instagram, making her wonder if she would ever pass her number to him. Or maybe Zachary had gotten it but had no interest in talking to her.

Taking a breath, she knew what a waste of energy it was to worry about things she couldn't control. She'd learned that from watching her father die.

In the refuge of the basement, Zachary felt sorry for his family, yet he wanted to believe he'd done the right thing. His parents and sister had been living a lie for as long as he could remember, so surely he was entitled to one little falsehood, especially if the end justified the means for achieving a higher good. Surfing channels on their massive flat screen TV, he saw a replay of his interview on Cable News America.

It was strangely surreal to see himself on television. He looked different somehow, and he truly hated the sound of his own voice. Hard to believe he'd become a national media story, even if it was a thirty-second puff piece. There had to be bigger issues to focus on—issues affecting the world in ways far more *newsworthy*.

Zachary wondered how the media even got his number when his family's wireless plan had each of them unlisted. Never wanting a phone in the first place, Zachary feared his data was being collected by corporations and by the government so they could control him. Unfortunately, his parents insisted that he carry one in case of an emergency (alien abduction was never on their minds).

Daring to turn his phone on, Zachary saw 175 missed calls, 43 voicemails, and 326 text messages. He opened one to read: *It's Heather Parker from KIRO News in Seattle. Would love to interview you.* Several messages that followed said pretty much the same thing from reporters across the nation. There was even one from Berlin, and another from Tokyo. Seeing enough, he turned off his phone. He couldn't believe what he had started, or more precisely, gotten himself into.

A bundle of nervous energy, he went out to the garage to wash and detail his parents' Land Rovers, a white one belonging to Mom, and a black one to his father. During the weekends, he did this type of work at their auto center, spending hours on customer vehicles and keeping the showroom models shiny and clean. Unlike his sister, he preferred to earn his weekly allowance, even if he secretly hoped the SUVs were the equivalent of high-priced artworks that never actually sold.

As he vacuumed his mother's interior, the tedious labor helped distract him from the sudden whirlwind of events. It was also the only way he knew how to say he was sorry.

003

Kaitlyn had a hard time staying asleep. Every time she dozed off, she envisioned her father lying dead in his coffin. It was the last image she'd had of him. He looked like a man she wouldn't have recognized before he'd fallen ill. After several months of chemo and radiation, he looked like a skeleton wrapped in baggy skin. Worse yet, his suit was three sizes too big for his body, and an awful yellow tie was chosen by the mortician because neither Kaitlyn nor her mother was ready to part with his favorite blue silk one.

Had he been alive, he would have joked, "I wouldn't be caught dead in that thing" or "I wouldn't wear that to my own funeral." Gone was his wavy mess of black hair. His head was swollen from the toxic poisons the doctors had prescribed. Lex Luther, the evil antagonist from Superman, unwittingly came to mind, with his fat, bald head concocting his next diabolical plot.

Turning over in bed, Kaitlyn closed her eyes and tried to think of her father before he was sick, and before he could no longer form a sentence. Before he no longer recognized her or her mother. She pictured him dragging a Christmas tree into the house, whistling as he stomped snow off his boots near the fireplace. "Doodles," he used to call her, short for snickerdoodles—she'd had a sweet tooth for them in her younger years.

With a smile, she held onto that memory, a pleasant snapshot from her father's time on Earth. Drifting off, it wasn't long before her father's corpse floated back into her consciousness. She awakened in a cold sweat, the darkness around her terrifying. It was after midnight. She would not be returning to sleep anytime soon.

Crawling out of her blankets, she headed downstairs to watch for a sign.

It was a perfectly clear night, giving Kaitlyn a view of a sky spanning miles over the plains, a magnificent blacktop covered in brightly burning stars. Watching them from her porch swing, she thought of Ezekiel's wheel over Babylon thousands of years ago. Long ago, before the internet and cell phones, Ezekiel wouldn't have known that in ancient India, their holy Sanskrit described gods flying around in golden sky ships known as *vimanas*. In other civilizations across South America and Asia, many early cultures told of creatures coming down from the sky in cosmic eggs, and giving rise to numerous creation theories. Way too freaky, Kaitlyn decided. She had even read an article theorizing that the Garden of Eden was a reptilian alien experiment, with the snake tempting Adam and Eve as the first human guinea pigs.

She might have thought that completely insane if not for a NASA scientist (Dr. Rich Terrile) claiming that human reality is actually a hologram created by aliens. Because particles don't have a definitive state unless they're being observed, someone must be observing us. Otherwise, we would remain inanimate. With God as the cosmic computer programmer, we're living in a matrix brought into our consciousness, just as that famous sci-fi movie suggested.

In the brisk evening air, the idea of God as a reptilian programmer gave Kaitlyn chills (she pictured a fat spotted lizard wearing mad scientist glasses and munching from a bag of M&Ms at his computer). If she dared to discuss these theories with Reverend Jacob at their Sacred Trinity Church, he would quickly dismiss them as "New Age garbage." But he couldn't deny Ezekiel from the Old Testament, even if he wanted to interpret the text as Kaitlyn's mother did—with a stubbornly closed mind.

Nor could he deny the Book of Genesis accounting for the Nephilim, the sons and daughters of fallen angels who mated with humans. Appearing on *Ancient Aliens*, her favorite TV show, were scholars who said the angels were really aliens—the giants who existed before the Flood. Noah himself was described in the Dead Sea Scrolls as having alien features—a strange complexion and glowing eyes that could light up a room. His own father even questioned if Noah was truly his son or offspring of the Watchers, those fallen angels of God above.

Despite what Reverend Jacob or her mother might say, it wasn't so crazy to entertain these ideas. Thousands of others watched the same type of programs on the History Channel and on National Geographic, seeking answers to this big mystery called life. If the ancient astronaut theory was correct, we descended from an alien race, which might also explain the missing link to human evolution.

Even more mind-boggling, aliens could be our future selves, coming to visit in spacecrafts designed for time travel. Our heads and eyes would grow larger through future advancement, our bodies smaller and our skin paler from less exposure to sunlight—the same way extraterrestrials have often been described by those who encountered them. She thought of Zachary while secretly hoping for a text message.

Kaitlyn also knew of scientists applying quantum physics to the subconscious and how it must live forever because energy never dies. In immortality, we live as Light Beings, bright and radiant forms of atoms and electrons outside of our skin.

"What are you thinking about?" asked her mother, the screen door banging shut behind her.

"Nothing, really," said Kaitlyn, each knowing her father was on her mind.

"It's awfully cold out here for this time of the year," said her mother, bundling her jacket over flannel pajamas. "You must be freezing."

"Climate change," Kaitlyn wanted to tell her, as she enjoyed the crisp autumn air in her Iowa State sweats and fuzzy pink slippers. However, that would lead to an argument about climate versus weather, her mother arguing that the cooler temperatures were proof against global warming.

"I can't sleep either," said her mother, taking a seat beside her on the porch swing, her breath smelling faintly of alcohol. Before Kaitlyn's father was diagnosed with cancer, she would, only on occasion, order a glass of wine at dinner, and never drank in the late evening. As she looked more closely, Kaitlyn saw deepened wrinkles on her mother's face. In the past year, she'd aged a decade, though she was still beautiful in her early forties. "My fair scarlet queen of the Midwest," her father used to call her.

"He loved you so much," said Kaitlyn.

Her mother smiled sadly. "I know," she said. "And he loved you just as much. We were lucky to have him in our lives, which are much too short on Earth already."

Tears misting her eyes, Kaitlyn rested her head on her mother's shoulder, feeling the safety and comfort of her younger childhood. As she watched the sky, she focused on a shimmering star and imagined her father as a distant Light Being. Traversing the planes of spiritual and physical existence, he would make his way home in the same spinning time machine that had taken him away.

004

"**M**y boy is a marketing genius," Zachary's father announced to his family at the dinner table. Wearing a proud smile, he passed a tray of vegan hot dogs, the few remaining from their Big Electric Vehicle Sale Event that weekend. "We sold over a hundred EVs, and that's just the beginning."

Zachary was glad to hear the news. It made his recent notoriety a little more bearable. All weekend long, he had posed for pictures and signed autographs at his family's auto center.

"Today's my sixteenth birthday," a cute brunette with braces had told him. "My parents are buying me a new EV, but I really wanted to meet you."

"I drove all the way from Portland," said a college girl with nose and lip piercings. "I already have an EV, but I just wanted to feel the vibe here."

"My husband was abducted by aliens," said a middle-aged woman. "He left in the middle of the night and never came back."

"I'm sorry to hear that," said Zachary, picturing whoever he was with another woman halfway across the country.

"Stay away from my girlfriend," warned a hulking guy in a Seattle Seahawks jersey. "Or you really will go missing."

"No problem," said Zachary, having no idea who or where his girlfriend even was.

A teenage girl from Idaho gave him her lacy pink underwear on which her phone number was written. He couldn't read her handwriting, or he might have called. Too bad they didn't teach penmanship in public schools any more.

After hundreds of exchanges with total strangers who pretended to have known him all their lives, he was finally approached by their small-town radio station KLEM ("You're listening to the Lemon on 99.8 FM!"), along with some local TV news affiliates.

"Thanks to all your media coverage," said his mother at the table, "we're getting calls from every major automaker, begging to send us their latest models, with all the newest gadgets and technology."

"Pretty soon," said his father, forking a vegan hot dog to put in a bun, "we'll have those solar charging stations and a car wash using recycled water."

"No more wasting water or electricity," said his mother, "which will save us a lot of money."

"And while people wait," said his father," they'll be spending money on snacks and beverages."

"Just as you suggested," praised his mother.

"Great," said Zachary. "But if we can avoid plastic bottles and—"

"Sunglasses, air fresheners, even little stuffed alien dolls," his mother continued. "And racks of greeting cards and paperback novels."

"Recycled paper, of course," said Zachary. "With bins for—"

"I gotta admit it, son," his father interrupted, "those electric cars have some serious power. I drove the Mustang Mach-E home today, and it's like a race car on testosterone."

Zachary wasn't used to his father bragging about him. That was usually saved for Hailey, who was now sulking at the end of the table. "Everyone at school thinks he's a weirdo-path," she said, cutting her vegan dog as if dissecting her twin into small pieces. "My brother, the most famous weirdo-path in America."

"Sounds like someone might be a little jealous," teased their mother with a smile.

"Is weirdo-path even a word?" asked their father, taking a bite of his vegan

24

dog after smothering it with various condiments. "Mmm, this isn't so bad. Kind of rubbery, but with the relish and mustard, I can barely tell it's not real meat."

"It's not real meat because it *isn't* meat," said Hailey. "And if it's made of soy, I'm not eating it. Too much estrogen isn't healthy."

"This stuff has estrogen?" said their father in alarm. "I'm not gonna grow man boobs from this thing, am I?"

Zachary quietly chuckled, picturing his father in his mother's bra. "One time isn't going to hurt you," he promised. "If we served them to our customers, we should eat them ourselves, you know."

"That's true," said their father, daring to take another bite. "We don't want to be hypocrites."

"You're deceiving the public!" said Hailey. "Which has got to be a felony, and you'll end up in prison!"

"Oh, Hailey," said their mother. "Don't you think you're being overly dramatic?"

"Overly dramatic?" said Hailey. "In case you didn't notice, there are still reporters outside our house. Some kooky lady from the *Alien Chronicle* asked if she could come inside and hypnotize my goofball brother so he could recall his experience for some article she's writing."

"They're just doing their job," said Zachary, having dodged the media gathering on his way home from school all week by cutting through Mr. Jones' yard next door and entering his house through the back. The heels of his Converse bore tiny nip marks from their neighbor's pesky Chihuahua.

"We're having a fence installed tomorrow," said their mother. "With a security gate in the driveway."

"Twelve feet high with barbed wire," said their father, "and ten-thousand volts of electricity—the max allowed."

"Building a wall," said Hailey, "won't stop people from messaging me on Instagram. Hundreds, if not thousands, of psycho girls and UFO enthusiasts want me to put them in touch with this weirdo-path."

"Sounds like my boy is quite the lady killer now," their father said proudly, making Zachary wince at the barbaric expression.

"More like a future serial killer," said Hailey. "He's so antisocial, he's not even on Instagram, which is why I'm getting bugged to death."

"You should really start using social media," said their mother to Zachary. "To help publicize our dealership."

"And get more girls," said their father with a wink at his son. Zachary couldn't help but smile back, enjoying the approval for a change.

"Does no one even care that he's lying?" asked Hailey in disgust. "After all, you're the ones who ordered him to tell the media it was all a hoax."

Their parents exchanged a look. "Well," said their father, shifting uncomfortably in his chair, "we don't know for sure if Zachary was making it up or not."

"That's right," said their mother. "Only Zachary knows if he was abducted by aliens or not. Isn't that right, honey?" Barely nodding, Zachary felt his face growing hot with shame. All week long, he had stuck to his original story. The public and media kept asking him questions, but his memory was still "hazy" from the alien encounter, though he added just enough details to make him credibly entertaining.

Glaring at him, Hailey said, "Well, I can tell you he most definitely wasn't abducted. He's turning this family into the butt of his little joke."

"It's no joke we're selling lots of electric vehicles," said their father. "If they didn't believe in your brother, they wouldn't believe in our family name."

Their mother smiled at Hailey. "So, let's not go bad-mouthing him outside this house, okay?"

Zachary nodded at his sister, which made her even angrier. "Fine! Just fine!" she said, standing up to leave the table. "I hope those aliens come back and take him away forever!"

"You don't really mean that!" said their mother.

"Yes, I do!" she said, storming off toward her room. "It's like he's from another planet anyway!"

Left alone with his parents, Zachary broke into a gloating smile. Without even trying, he had dethroned his perfect sister as their favorite child.

"Say, Dad, would you pass the mustard?"

005

The school seemed smaller somehow. After just two weeks away, Kaitlyn wondered if she had outgrown East Plains High or if it was never that big and intimidating in the first place. As she passed down a noisy hallway packed with students, she noticed several pitiful glances from people she barely knew.

"Sorry for your loss," said a purple-haired girl from last year's trigonometry class. Briana was her name. Or was it Brenda? Back then, her hair was green.

"Thanks," said Kaitlyn, suddenly remembering it was Brittany.

On his way to Iowa history class, her favorite teacher, Mr. Jankowski, appeared in his usual bow-tie and round-framed glasses. "Hey, Kaitlyn," he said with a sympathetic look. "Sorry for your loss."

"Thanks," said Kaitlyn, which came out more cheerful than intended.

"Sorry for your loss," echoed several more students and teachers while passing.

"Sorry for your loss," said Grayson Jones, a towering offensive lineman who stopped to block a path for her.

"Thanks," said Kaitlyn, slipping by with a nervous smile. All this attention was so new to her, she didn't know how to react.

"If you need anything," said the gray-haired Mrs. Crenshaw, "just let us know." She quickly escaped to her biology classroom before Kaitlyn might actually ask for something. *Money!* she wanted to yell out. *To help with the funeral costs!*

"Hey, Kaitlyn!" said Garrett Haggerty, hovering near the wall as if waiting for her. In his wrestling team sweatshirt, he was short and muscular and wore his hair in a buzz cut. Lots of girls liked him for his pretty blue eyes, which happened to be staring at Kaitlyn's chest.

"Hey," said Kaitlyn, self-consciously crossing her arms in front of her. In ninth grade, she'd matured from an A-cup to a C-cup, which is when he finally took notice of her.

"I'm sorry for your loss," he said, presenting her a red rose bouquet from behind his back. "You can read the card later," he pointed out. Shoving the flowers at her, he finally made eye contact before darting off.

"It's not Valentine's Day!" she called after him, but he was already out of earshot. With two dozen roses, she really drew attention now. Tempted to throw them in the trash, she debated whether that was the right thing to do. At the very least, she could give them away rather than waste something so beautiful. She would read his card later, out of curiosity if nothing else. It ought to contain a written apology for always staring at her breasts.

Approaching a row of lockers, Kaitlyn overheard some drill team girls huddled in conversation. "Oh my God," said their squad captain Nora Paisley. "I think I gained like five pounds over the weekend."

"Me too," said a redhead named Wendy. "No more pizza parties, okay, Heidi?"

The team gave accusatory stares at Heidi, a tall slim brunette who probably couldn't gain an ounce if she tried. "I don't think it was the pizza," said Heidi, "so much as the five cases of wine coolers you crazy hoes sucked down."

Highly amused with themselves, the girls laughed in unison.

"Oh my God," said Wendy. "I got so turn't, I made out with Jason Hughes."

The girls howled even louder, one of them making a "man-slut" crack which Kaitlyn didn't find funny at all, yet they all laughed harder.

"Well," said Nora, taking charge of her squad, "now we have like three weeks to shed the pounds. Or we're not going to fit into our Halloween costumes."

"Oh my God!" said another girl. "I'm like freaking out, my ass is so big!"

Sneaking past them with the roses, Kaitlyn had a harder time than ever relating to their so-called problems. Not that life was easy before her father's illness, but now it was pissing her off, and she never used to be an angry person. Maybe her mother was right—she needed to talk to someone. But she had no desire to meet again with Dr. Spalding, with his standardized questions about how she was feeling and who she was protecting, blah-blah-blah. It would feel better to punch him, or at least a punching bag, and it might be more effective, too.

"Hey, girl!" said Jenna, waiting for Kaitlyn to finally arrive at her locker. "Didn't know if you were going to show today." As Jenna went to hug her, a thorny stem snagged her sleeve. "Ouch! What's with the roses?" she asked as if just noticing them.

"Garrett Haggerty," said Kaitlyn, stuffing the bouquet in her locker and grabbing her lab assignment for chemistry.

"Oh my God!" said Jenna. "He's like the hottest guy in school!"

"Not my type," said Kaitlyn. "And besides, you said that about Gavin Utley, and before that, Gavin Myers. Remember?"

"The Gavins were so last semester," said Jenna. "Garrett is super swol and sweet, with those amazing blue eyes."

"I think he has X-ray vision, which can see through my bra," said Kaitlyn. Closing her locker with a thud, she headed off for class with her friend.

"Maybe he's just afraid of making contact with those piercing green cat eyes of yours," said Jenna. "Oh my God, the two of you would have such gorgeous babies together, with the most amazing eyes ever!"

"Teen pregnancy with a perv," said Kaitlyn. "Just what I need after my dad dying."

"I didn't mean like right now," said Jenna. "But his family is super rich, you know. It'd be like marrying into royalty, and you'd have a super extravagant wedding."

"Didn't he ask you out once?" said Kaitlyn, changing the subject from a fairy tale wedding that would never happen.

"Freshman year," said Jenna. "He asked me to the prom, but I said no. I was waiting for Truman Heinz to ask me."

"I can't see you with a theater guy," said Kaitlyn. "You have way too much drama in your life already."

"He was totally boring and a horrible kisser," said Jenna, "and now I've apparently missed my chance with Garrett. He's totally into you now, and I'm like invisible."

"Please," said Kaitlyn. Jenna was voluptuous, with big hazel eyes, naturally pouty lips, and a springy bounce in her curly blonde hair. "You're way hotter than me."

"Yeah, whatever," said Jenna, eager to catch her up on the recent gossip. "Oh my God, you should see Emily Ravenscroft's new haircut! I'd almost feel sorry for her if she wasn't such a bitch, and Kevin Parks and Susan Ashby broke up. *Again*. This time it was her, but I think she's just getting revenge for the time he…"

Kaitlyn had already tuned out. As they headed into their first-period chemistry class, she took out her phone to check her text messages—nothing from Zachary Taylor. Oh, well. It was becoming ever more likely that she'd never hear from him, she realized, and now felt incredibly stupid for having messaged his sister on Instagram in the first place.

Since becoming a fixture in mass media, Zachary could no longer walk the school hallways unnoticed. On his way to his locker between classes, he passed a group of girls huddled together, whispering as they watched him go by. Coming out of the teachers' lounge, a group of tax-paid educators stopped to gawk at him, one of them spilling his coffee as he bumped into the band conductor, Ms. Horn. Ignoring them, Zachary continued past a cluster of freshmen who stared at him in awe.

Just last week, he was nothing more than the genetic freak twin of Hailey Taylor, senior class president and homecoming queen. As she walked toward him now, Hailey was still the one person at school to completely ignore him. Her friends snuck little smiles at Zachary as they passed by. He nervously smiled back, enjoying the attention from pretty girls but struggling to adapt to his sudden popularity—it was so much easier to be invisible.

At his locker, he put away his notebook computer and grabbed his bag of clothes for gym, his least favorite class, and up next on his schedule. A few lockers down, he sensed someone lingering. That someone was Camila Corte, one of the prettiest girls in his senior class. She normally paid him little attention, even at his sister's pool party last summer. "Hey, Zach," she said with a flirtatious smile. "How's it goin'?"

"Um, good," said Zachary, his face turning red as he used his backpack to cover the swelling in his pants. Since seeing her in a bikini, he'd lost track of how many times he'd had erotic dreams about her. That wet black hair running down her naked back...

"Say," she almost whispered, ducked behind her open locker door, "if you're not doing anything after school, come by my house. You know where it is, right?"

Zachary nodded in disbelief. "Did you want to study for our biology test?"

Camila glanced amusingly at the backpack shielding his crotch. "Something to do with biology, perhaps," she said. She saw her friends approaching with lattés, their backpacks slung coolly over their shoulders. "My mom leaves at four, but let's keep it private, okay?"

"Okay," he said, almost asking if she was still going out with the tatted drummer whose band played at weddings and parties. Closing her locker door, she headed off to greet her friends as if they'd never spoken.

Dazed by raging hormones, Zachary wasn't sure if he should be offended or not. Heading off for the gymnasium, he was fairly certain she was planning on having sex with him. If so, it would be his first experience, something he was embarrassed to admit. He was nervous about disappointing her (though effort would definitely compensate for his lack of expertise.)

As he entered the locker room, a row of jocks began singing the soundtrack from a recent movie about alien invaders, sending a wave of laughter down the aisle of boys changing into sweatpants and sneakers. "Martian Boy!" several voices called out.

With a sinking feeling in his chest, Zachary continued toward his locker. Though he may have been a celebrity, which carried its own aphrodisiacal powers, he was far from being a star like a famous actor, musician, or athlete. Unbuttoning his shirt, he accepted the fact that Camila wanted to satisfy her curious infatuation with a sideshow freak. Too bad for her, he'd already lost the desire to be her dirty little secret.

Kaitlyn decided to put the roses on the mantel in hopes of cheering up the house a little. While searching the cupboards for a vase, she discovered several bottles of wine which her mother had stowed away. Snooping further, she checked the garbage and recycling bins. The latter contained two recently discarded bottles. At least her mother was recycling, even if it was to hide her new drinking habit.

"Are you okay, Mom?" she asked when they sat down for dinner. It was a cheesy pasta dish which they had made together. "Comfort food," her dad would have called it. Before chemotherapy, he truly loved to eat.

"Meaning what?" asked her mother, raising her glass of Chardonnay as if she had nothing to hide.

"Well," said Kaitlyn, "it's just that you were never a drinker, and now you constantly have a glass of wine in hand."

"It's only half-filled," said her mother, swirling her glass like a connoisseur.

"It's always half-filled," said Kaitlyn. She remembered her father telling a joke about a bartender with a bottomless mug, but she couldn't remember how it went.

"It helps me relax," said her mother. "Without it, I can't sleep a wink. The doctor wanted to give me a sleeping pill, but those are far more dangerous than something made from the grapes of God's green earth."

"I'm just worried about you, Mom," said Kaitlyn, taking a bite of pasta.

"Well, thanks," said her mother, "but even Reverend Jacob will tell you what the first miracle of Jesus was."

"Turning water into wine," said Kaitlyn, pouring a glass for herself, to make a point more than anything.

"That's enough," said her mother, stopping her with a raised palm before she could even fill a quarter of a glass.

"Helps me relax, Mom. I'm not sleeping so well myself."

Her mother looked at her in concern. "We just have to take it one day at a time. That's what Dr. Spalding said."

"Until when?" asked Kaitlyn. "Things will never be normal again, you know."

"No," said her mother, moving her food around her plate with her fork. "That will be the challenge—learning to accept the new *normal* while being grateful to have each other."

Kaitlyn silently chewed her food, not wanting to accept the thought that life could be normal without her father in the house. His laughter still echoed off its walls like that of a ghost. "I don't ever want to forget him," she said, a rise of anger in her voice.

"Oh, sweetie," said her mother, brushing a strand of shiny black hair from Kaitlyn's eyes. "He'll always be with us, no matter what."

Kaitlyn nodded, choking back tears that made it difficult to swallow her food. "You didn't even notice the roses," she mumbled, wanting to blame her mother for everything she could.

"They're beautiful," she said. "But you took out the card, so I thought you were keeping it private."

"Um, I thought you would ask."

"I'm asking now," said her mother. "Who is he?"

"Garrett Haggerty. He gives me the creeps."

"He was nice enough to give you roses, which are very expensive, by the way."

"Who cares?" said Kaitlyn. "His daddy's rich, from owning a savings and loan."

"But still," said her mother, taking a small bite of pasta. "He thought of you and wanted to show he was sorry for your loss."

"If one more person says that, I think I'll scream," said Kaitlyn. "And what kind of person gives someone roses after their father dies? I tried telling him it wasn't Valentine's Day, but he ran off before I could reject his stupid flowers."

"Must be shy," said her mother.

"That's what Jenna thinks," said Kaitlyn, "which is why he never makes eye contact." She neglected to tell her mother where his attention usually focused.

"Shy is not such a bad trait," said her mother. "Your father was just the opposite—when we first met, a little too full of himself."

Kaitlyn smiled, thinking of her father so full of gusto and life. "But you liked it when he serenaded you outside your dorm room window."

Her mother laughed for the first time in months. "That's the story he always told, but you never heard the full version."

Kaitlyn looked at her in surprise, afraid to ask, "What's that?" All her life, she'd heard that her father showed up outside her mother's dorm room window at Iowa State University, singing "Meet Me Under the Mistletoe" with a quartet of boys all wearing Santa Claus hats on a snowy December night. It was the night he swept her off her feet, or so she'd been told until now.

"It was two in the morning, and your dad and his friends were so drunk, my dorm mate called the police when they decided to show up unannounced after a party on campus. Your dad was hoping to see me there, but I'd stayed in to study for a final exam."

"So what happened then?" asked Kaitlyn. Though she was curious, she wasn't sure she wanted to know.

"After the campus police arrested your father and his friends for public intoxication, he quickly sobered up, and guess who he called to come bail him out?"

"You're kidding?" said Kaitlyn, looking at her mother in disbelief.

Her mother smiled and shook her head. "Second time he woke me up that night—my dorm mate too. She wanted to strangle him."

"Don't tell me you bailed him out?"

"Let's just say that I went to the police station. I let him know that if he ever pulled that kind of stunt again, I'd file a restraining order."

Kaitlyn was stunned. She was hearing all this for the first time. "Did he say he was sorry?"

"Yes, he did," said her mother. "Many times, throughout the semester. As you know, we had a class together, so we ran into each other a few times a week. But I made him suffer for a month or two before I finally agreed to go out with him. By then, he'd proven he was a gentleman and not some drunken frat boy."

Kaitlyn could picture her father as a little wild in his younger days— someone with a big heart who needed taming. A smile spread over her face. She wanted to know: "How come you never told me this until now?"

"Well," said her mother, "it's not something you share with a child, so we gave you the Disney version. But you're old enough to vote now, so I think you can handle the fact that your parents aren't perfect."

"It's still a nice story," said Kaitlyn, who appreciated that her mother was treating her as an adult, even though she'd just turned eighteen last month. "In fact, I like it even better."

"Your dad was no saint, but he was genuine," said her mother. "Sometimes you have to give people a chance to know who they really are, you know?"

Kaitlyn nodded, rejecting any comparison between her father and Garrett Haggerty.

006

Though the sun was shining through the scattered clouds, Zachary was still in a funk, his mind replaying the day at school with Camila and everyone else making him feel like a circus freak. In hopes of cheering himself up, he stopped by his parents' auto center to see the progress underway. Filling the lots were hundreds of electric vehicles, sectioned off in endless rows of VW Buzzes (buses turned electric), Audi e-Trons, BMW i4s, Mercedes EQCs, Toyota RAV4s, Nissan Leafs, Jaguar I-Paces, and endless more EVs beyond his view.

The biggest seller was no longer a gas-guzzling SUV, but the Ford Mustang Mach-E, a sleek and beautiful piece of machinery that could go zero to sixty in just 3.5 seconds. It also had a sticker price that equaled the average yearly income in India multiplied by two hundred. Despite the economic disparities, Zachary loved the sporty vehicle and figured he could fight only one battle at a time. In a perfect world, everyone would be able to afford a new Mustang, though carpooling or public transportation were far better options.

For now, Zachary was proud to see the family car wash under renovation, a group of technicians installing a closed-loop recycling system. Zachary had done his research before recommending this outfitter to his parents.

"What's that awful smell?!" shouted his father, watching a Chevy Bolt come through the dark tunnel of spinning brushes and monster-like top curtains, which had terrified Zachary as a small child.

Catching a whiff of something foul, Zachary approached his father to say, "Don't worry," but his voice was drowned out by the final rinse and air-blown dryer. The Bolt finally emerged with its black paint covered in dirty spots.

"Damn it!" screamed his father, taking notice of his son as the closest target. "You told me this company was the best!"

"Calm down, Dad," said Zachary, catching another whiff of something that reeked like rotten eggs. "This is just a test run. They still haven't put in the RO filtration system."

"R-O? What is that?"

"Reverse osmosis to ensure a spot-free rinse."

"What about this God-awful smell?!"

"Once the water's aerated, it won't stink anymore."

"Then get it aerated!" said his father. "ASAP!"

"They're putting in the filters now," said Zachary, watching the technicians across the way. "That will also keep the TDS levels down—total dissolved solids," he explained before his father could ask. "Like chemicals, waxes, or clay particles, which you won't see at all after the final rinse."

"Better hope not," said his father, disgusted by the sight of the spotted Bolt circling back around. "Or it's coming out of your allowance."

"Considering the money you'll save on water," said Zachary, "plus the tax rebates for going green, we should really consider renegotiating my salary. In fact, I'm thinking of starting a labor union to increase the salaries of our support staff here."

"Real funny, hotshot," said his father, clamping a hand on Zachary's shoulder to lead him inside the car wash lobby. "Come see what your mother's done to the place."

Zachary followed his father past the new solar charging stations to enter the massive lobby, its racks filled with endless snacks, sunglasses, greeting cards, car fresheners, and floor mats. "Geez, Mom," he said, passing a shelf lined with stuffed alien dolls, whose enormous eyes peered out towards the aisle.

"Hi, Zach," she said, cutting open a box as they approached. "We got those reusable cups you asked for."

"No plastic bottles or paper cups," said his father, pointing out the sprawling beverage counter. Its several coffee pots and fountain drink machines were ready to go.

"Awesome," said Zachary with a growing smile.

"What do you think?" said his mother, propping up a life-sized cardboard display of Zachary looking up toward the sky as if watching a spaceship descend from the clouds.

"No effing way!" he protested.

"Watch your language," said his father, sounding like the Air Force drill instructor he once was.

"I didn't swear, Dad."

"You just used the 'F' word."

"Effing is not the 'F' word."

"It starts with an 'F' and doesn't sound nice."

"If you spell it out, it actually starts with an 'E' as in 'Effort.'"

"Then please make an 'Effort' not to 'Effing' use it because we all know what it really stands for."

"Well, I'm sorry," said Zachary, "but this has to go." Picking up his cardboard twin, he headed outside and tossed it in the recycling dumpster.

"There he is!" shouted someone as Zachary retreated for the car wash lobby. Before he could reach the door, he was mobbed by tourists or potential customers. He wasn't sure which. Phones held high, they crowded next to him snapping selfies.

"Uh, where you from?" he asked the couple sandwiching him for a photo.

"Yakima," said the wife, smiling at her phone to snap the shot.

"I love Yakima!" said Zachary's father, coming outside with a stack of business cards. "And if you're looking for a new EV to drive back in, my boy here would be happy to take y'all out for a little test drive."

"Actually, I have some homework to do," said Zachary, his father giving him a scolding frown. "But I'd be happy to show you all the new Mustang."

For the past few hours, Kaitlyn had forced herself to focus on homework, on which she was still way behind. When her father was undergoing cancer treatment, she would solve calculus problems in the hospital's waiting room. Math was her favorite subject, so it was much easier to concentrate on numbers than try to read and comprehend assignments in other classes.

As she tried studying for an Iowa history exam the next day, her mind drifted to questions about how her father got sick in the first place. Was it his diet? Genetics? Too much time on his cell phone making sales calls? If so, why did the tumor appear on the left side of his brain when he held his phone on the right? More puzzling than that, she questioned why it had to be her father, a decent human being, when evil dictators and corrupted CEOs lived well into their nineties. It made her question God as the ruling light of the universe, and why her prayers to God had been ignored.

"Don't question God," her father had told her right after his prognosis. "We can ask for direction, but it's the path He's chosen for us." Kaitlyn still had a very hard time accepting that. What, she wondered, was the purpose of life here on Earth?

If her father had been here right now, he would tell her to get back to her homework. "Okay, Dad," she said, turning her attention to the Ioway people, the Native American tribe her state was named after.

After dinner that evening, Zachary was alone in his room, trying to write an essay on *Romeo and Juliet*, but all he could think about was Camila. He wondered if someday, when he was forty and bald like his father, he'd look back with regret for not showing up at her house as invited. He considered texting her with an excuse that a family emergency had come up, which was partially true, at least at his parents' auto center. There was nothing to lose, and once his fifteen minutes of fame was over, she would lose all interest in him forever, if she hadn't already.

Powering his phone on, he still had her number in his call log. She'd misplaced her phone at his sister's pool party and asked him to call it. The thought of her in that white bikini drove him wild with lust, so much so that his rise in testosterone wiped out his logic and self-respect once again.

Hey Camila, he typed. *I got super busy after school—*

A text alert startled him—as nobody ever contacted him. Checking the message, he didn't recognize the area code.

256-724-23XX: Hey Zachary, I go to school in Alabama. Text me back.

He opened her photo to see a cute redhead wearing an Auburn Tigers T-shirt tied in a knot at her belly button, her cheeks reddened from the sun. Zooming in, he saw she was cute and quickly forgot about Camila. Curious how she got his number, he started to text her back when he got several more blaring alerts in rapid succession.

818-340-23XX: Sheila in LA. Let's talk ;)

228-551-05XX: I was abducted by aliens 2.

340-228-29XX: Hi gorgeous. Let's meet irl. XXO Eden.

957-843-87XX: Let's have sex

714-539-00XX: I'm Winter. Text me back.

629-622-72XX: Hey Zach! Nice to meet you!

503-677-21XX: I want 2 get your pants off.

484-188-64XX: Saw you on tv. You have a gf?

760-271-55XX: Ashley here. Want to trade pics?

402-777-01XX: I have a bf but we can still get naked on camera.

Overwhelmed, Zachary couldn't open them fast enough—his message box quickly exceeded a hundred, while the alerts continued to sound like an alarm until he finally figured out how to mute them. Most just wanted to chat or inquire of his girlfriend status, while several others were obsessed with UFOs, including men and women of all ages. A woman in the 718 area code wrote:

I'm pregnant with an alien baby and looking for the father.

Hitting delete to that one, Zachary scrolled through several more photos, the girls ranging from pretty to not so attractive. A woman his mother's age wore nothing but a boa constrictor wrapped around her body. She might have been sexy if she hadn't freaked him out so much. Blocking her from future contact, he dared to open a video attachment from a 637 area code, in hopes it was a college co-ed surprising him with something X-rated. Instead, it was an old gray-haired couple sitting side by side on the couch.

"Hi Zachary," said Granny. "We saw you on the TV and were hoping you could help us find our dog Snookers."

Grandpa nodded, uncertain where to find the phone's camera. "We let him out to pee, and the next thing you know, he vanished into thin air."

"But the police are no use," said Granny. "They told us a coyote probably took him."

"When we know it was the aliens!" said Grandpa. "So, if you're able to contact them, please ask them where our little Snookers is!"

"You're very handsome, by the way," said Granny with a smile.

"Stop flirting, you old hussy," said Grandpa.

Zachary chuckled. He missed his own grandparents, who were deceased on his mother's side, while his father's parents were now living their retirement years in Palm Springs. Feeling sorry for the couple, he texted back:

I'm sorry you lost your dog, but unfortunately, I am not able to make contact.

Hitting send, he quickly received a response.

(205) 762-94XX: Okay☹Hopefully Snookers is happy on his new planet.

Zachary: Yes, I'm sure it has fewer carbon emissions and better puppy chow ☺

(205) 762-94XX: He left his favorite toy behind ☹

Zachary: I'm sure he still thinks of you every day and wags his little tail.

(205) 762-94XX: Thanks. You're a nice boy.

Zachary: Wish I could help you more. By the way, how did you get my number?

(205) 762-94XX: We found your sister on Instagram.

Zachary: She gave it to you???

(205) 762-94XX: She posted it for everyone to see.

In a sudden panic, Zachary went to check her Instagram page but couldn't log in without an account. He tried doing so through Facebook but then remembered deactivating it a couple of years back. After signing up on Instagram, he found his sister's profile, and the first thing that came to view was an image of himself with a Photoshopped UFO hovering overhead. Over the cloudy background was her typed message:

Thanks to everyone wanting to connect with my brother Zachary. I'm not his press agent, so if you want to contact him, please do so directly at his cell number: 509-146-3200.

Anger coursed through him, but Zachary reminded himself he couldn't blame Hailey for the mess he'd created. After all, she was the one being harassed by endless strangers, like the guy whose bald head was covered in symbolic tattoos to signal the mothership. Thankfully, he was in an 805 area code, more than 2,500 miles away in Pensacola, Florida (according to Zachary's Google search). Nevertheless, Hailey didn't *have* to give out his number, even if he rarely had his phone on. Giving out his email address would have been far less intrusive. Hailey was clearly acting out of spite.

In Zachary's defense, he never meant to steal her spotlight, which she had tirelessly worked for her entire life. He wanted to say he was sorry, that he never intended to upset her, but the steady bombardment of text messages made him quickly forget.

He had adoring followers to tend to.

007

After ignoring several text alerts from Jenna, Kaitlyn was finally finished with her schoolwork. Most likely, Jenna wanted to know what Garrett had written in the card, which remained unopened in front of her. Kaitlyn did not want to be manipulated by someone taking advantage of her grief to get down her pants or to feel her up. If only her mother knew that, she might not make excuses for him, but all she had to go by were the beautiful roses.

Had the roses been white to symbolize friendship, Kaitlyn might have felt differently. Red was the color for passion and romance, even violence. Red was also the color of blood, which reminded her of her father's death. No, she realized, that was overanalyzing. Most likely, Garrett hadn't put that much thought into it. Yet she couldn't call him thoughtless since he had obviously showed enough consideration to bring her a card with roses in the first place. He clearly meant well, even if he could have shown better tact.

Looking at the envelope on which he'd carefully handwritten her name, she finally surrendered to curiosity and tore it open. *Sorry for Your Loss* appeared in mournful calligraphy on the cover, its photo of a bright sun shining glorious rays over *Psalms 62:1—My soul finds rest in God alone; my salvation comes from him.* Kaitlyn felt a flash of rage. He knew nothing about her grief, yet he thought he could lay her father's soul to rest with a one-line quote from Psalms. He barely knew her, much less her father. Ready to lash out against him, she opened the card to read his handwritten message:

Kaitlyn,

I'm truly sorry that you lost your dad. I barely knew him, but I wanted to share the one memory I will always have of him. When I was in the third or fourth grade, I was selling candy bars for my little league team in front of Wal-Mart. On his way in, he was nice enough to buy one and ask me how my team was doing. On his way out, he saw I was already getting ready to leave because I wasn't selling very many. It was cold out and everyone kept rushing past.

I told him it was okay because my parents would buy what I had left—several boxes. Your dad told me that was cheating. He said I should tough it out because even if I didn't sell any more, at least I would not be a quitter. I didn't feel like staying, but I didn't want to feel like a quitter either. So, I stayed four more hours and sold two more boxes of candy bars.

It may sound cheesy, but it was a "defining moment" in my life (I heard a sportscaster say that once but it's true). After that, I started trying harder in sports and in school. I don't mean to brag, but I'm a good wrestler because I never give up on the mat.

I doubt your father remembered me much after that day, but I will always remember him. Sometimes I wish my own dad was more like him, instead of just writing me a check like that will solve all my problems. Anyway, I'm sorry for such a long letter and more sorry for you and your mom.

Sincerely,

Garrett

Done reading, Kaitlyn wiped the tears streaming down her cheeks, her chest tight from sobbing. She had no idea that her father had made such an impact on Garrett's life after a routine trip to Wal-Mart. While her father's actions didn't surprise her, she *was* surprised that Garrett was able to express himself with so much depth and emotion. Up until now, she'd always seen him as the muscle-headed jock who cared about nothing beyond the physical arena of sports and girls, all of which proved her mother right. It was impossible to judge someone without looking beyond the surface.

Even so, she could never see them as a couple. While many girls, including Jenna, thought Garrett was "swol," he was too big and bulky for Kaitlyn's tastes. She couldn't picture getting her arms around him, and the thought of him being on top of her was truly frightening. She imagined her ribs breaking, her cry for help muffled beneath his crushing weight. If men were supposed to be their protectors, it was never in her DNA to be attracted to someone like Garrett, though she had to admit he had gorgeous eyes (if only they could make contact with her own for once). Maybe she'd feel differently if he grew his hair out, but even then, he simply wasn't her type.

That didn't mean they couldn't be friends. Had she known he thought so highly of her father, they could have started hanging out long ago. In fact, he could have been the big brother she never had (in that case, the bigger and stronger, the better).

Rereading the card, she thought of thanking him but did not have his number. Most likely, Jenna did, or could readily track down someone who did. Taking her phone from the drawer, she unlocked it to see an Instagram notification: Hailey had sent her a DM. Taken aback, Kaitlyn held her breath in excitement while opening it:

Thanks for the compliment. You're pretty too and can do way better than my brother. I won't give him your number bc I'm not talking to the freak. But you can have his which I just posted. Btw, if you're a serial killer, that's fine. Just leave the rest of my family alone.

Ignoring another text alert from Jenna, Kaitlyn quickly opened Hailey's post to see Zachary with a Photoshopped UFO above him. Her message clearly stated she was not his press agent, which meant thousands of other girls must have been trying to reach him. That might explain why Hailey was calling her brother a freak. The attention from his alien abduction likely caused her both embarrassment and jealousy. Though Kaitlyn had no experience with sibling rivalries, she definitely could understand the competition among his growing fan club of female admirers.

Highly discouraged, she didn't even know if she wanted to contact him now. Most likely, he would never respond when thousands of girls out there were far prettier and sexier, and living in more exciting places like Miami, New York, or Los Angeles. She was doubtful he would have any interest in a Midwest girl from a little farming community unless he was thrilled by the occasional tornado that tore through their region. Against her better judgment, though, she began typing him a message:

Hi Zachary, I'm Kaitlyn, a senior at East Plains High in Iowa. I witnessed a UFO over my house the night my father died of cancer a few weeks ago. I'm not crazy, I swear. I am just seeking answers and was hoping you might be able to help. Thanks.

She ended with a smiley face but quickly deleted it. Hitting send, she felt she had nothing to lose by reaching out. If he wanted to respond, fine. If not, then he wasn't worth her time in the first place.

The phone vibrated in her hand. It was Jenna calling on Facetime after Kaitlyn failed to respond to her string of texts. Taking the call, Kaitlyn looked at her friend on the screen. "S'up, girl?"

"Oh my God!" said Jenna, wearing designer glasses for fashion more than vision—her eyesight was nearly perfect. "I've texted you like a hundred times!

Are you okay?"

Kaitlyn was tired of people asking her that. "I was catching up on homework and put my phone away."

"Whatever!" said Jenna. "You've gotta tell me what Garrett wrote in the card!"

Just what Kaitlyn had suspected. "Oh, not much," she said. "Just that he joined some commune in Oregon last summer and now has nine wives and several kids. He wants to make me his tenth, just to put him into double digits."

"You dork," said Jenna. "Garrett was at wrestling camp last summer. University of Iowa."

"So I guess he was lying then," said Kaitlyn. "There goes my chance for that super extravagant wedding you were hoping for."

"Come on!" said Jenna. "Was there a love poem? Something cheesy that rhymed? Or was he playing the strong male role, offering his shoulder to cry on?"

"Come to think of it," said Kaitlyn, "maybe you *should* date a drama club guy. Is Truman Heinz still available?"

"He has a boyfriend now," said Jenna, making a face. "And you're being a total A-wipe."

Kaitlyn chuckled, still not ready to share what Garrett had written. "It was no big deal," she said. "Just another sympathy card, with a quote from Psalms. All he did was sign it, saying he was sorry for my mom and me." She hated lying to her friend, despite its being partly true. On Facetime, she had the extra challenge of looking her in the eye without flinching.

Jenna stared back in disappointment, either because the note *was* truly unexciting or because she suspected Kaitlyn of withholding information. "How did he sign it?" she asked. "Was it 'Love Garrett' or just 'Garrett?'"

"Just Garrett. He didn't even write 'Sincerely,'" Kaitlyn fibbed.

"Nobody says that anymore," said Jenna. "Do they?"

"Probably not," said Kaitlyn, checking her text messages to see that Zachary had yet to respond. "Say," she said, bringing her friend back into view, "did you happen to see that guy in the Pacific Northwest? The one abducted by a UFO?"

"Yeah, he's super cute," said Jenna. "But he must be doing shrooms with all that rain up there. Next thing ya know, he'll be claiming to have seen Bigfoot tromping around in their woods."

"Yeah," said Kaitlyn, unsurprised by her friend's response.

"So, like, what's the deal with you and Garrett anyway?" said Jenna. "Are you going to go out with him or what?"

"No," said Kaitlyn, "but I've got the perfect excuse to keep from hurting him."

"What's that?" said Jenna.

Kaitlyn looked at her on the phone screen. "My best friend is totally crushing on him."

After reading hundreds of messages from people claiming to have witnessed a UFO and/or been abducted by aliens, Zachary could no longer believe that every one of them was crazy or fabricating an outlandish story. Even the Pentagon had recognized "unidentified aerial objects" after several US Navy pilots reported multiple encounters in recent years.

Regardless of scientific proof, he felt sorry for whoever this Kaitlyn was, though his eyes were burning by the time he got to her text—well beyond midnight. She must not be very attractive, he figured, or she would have attached a photo like the vast majority of other girls. He pictured a sad, lonely farm girl, in the middle of the countryside, whose only friends were the livestock she cared for. Most likely her hands were strong and callused from milking cows, if they even had dairy farms in Iowa (he pictured lots of corn).

Unlike so many of those other girls, this Kaitlyn wasn't asking for a boyfriend, hookup, or exchange of naked pictures—his phone was now filled with trashy poses. She was simply a girl in pain who was seeking comfort. Unsure how to respond, Zachary typed out:

Hi, Kaitlyn. I'm sorry your father died. That is very sad. About the UFO that came to your house that night, I'm sure it was more than a coincidence...a sign from the heavens above that your father was going to a better place. I hope that helps give you some peace of mind. Take care, Zachary. ☺

Before hitting send, he deleted the smiley face, which looked sarcastic. He wanted to cheer her up. Finally done for the night, he went to pee and brush his teeth before crashing out in his bed.

008

Kaitlyn hated the sound of her phone's alarm clock perhaps more than anything in the entire world. The night before, her father's corpse had haunted her dreams once again and disrupted her sleep. After waking up several times in a feverish sweat, she finally submerged herself in deep REM sleep when it was almost time to get up for school. Reaching for her phone, she blindly hit the snooze feature to give her ten more minutes in her warm and cozy bed. The biting chill of morning awaited her.

Those ten minutes felt more like ten seconds when the alarm went off again. Horribly cranky, she forced herself to sit up, an effort that made her feel as if she weighed a thousand pounds. One eye half-open, she turned off the alarm to see a message from a 509 area code, which she instantly recognized as Zachary's. Quickly waking up, she opened it to read:

509-146-3200: Hi, Kaitlyn. I'm sorry your father died. That is very sad. About the UFO that came to your house that night, I'm sure it was more than a coincidence...a sign from the heavens above that your father was going to a better place. I hope that helps give you some peace of mind. Take care, Zachary.

She read it twice more, excited he'd written back but searching for some deeper, hidden meaning. It seemed he was writing out of intuition more than fact, unless he was "sure it was more than a coincidence" based on something he'd learned from the aliens. Whatever the case, he obviously cared enough to respond, which suggested what kind of person he was.

She had a million questions regarding his abduction but didn't want to scare him away by coming on too hard, too fast. In fact, she wasn't even sure if she should text him back right away or wait a day or two. Normally, it was the guy who had to consider such strategic moves, but then again, she *was* the one who initiated contact, and it wasn't as if they were dating (though by no means was she opposed to the idea). She texted:

Hi, Zachary, Thanks for getting back to me. I would love to chat some more whenever you are ready. Kaitlyn ☺

She was about to hit send when she thought it made her sound desperate. Deleting her previous message, she typed out:

Thanks. Text me back if u want to talk some more.

No. That sounded too cold and casual. Seeing the time on her phone, she needed to get ready for school.

Thanks for responding. If you want to talk some more, lemme know. ☺

Deciding on the smiley face, she hit send.

Out of bed, she grabbed her clothes from the dresser and hustled for the bathroom to shower.

Zachary awakened well before his alarm, thinking of that girl in Iowa—Kaitlyn, though he had no idea why. He checked his phone to see if she had texted him back. Her number appeared among a long list of messages from random strangers. She wanted to chat some more, but he still wanted a better idea of the person with whom he could be chatting.

Unaware of her last name, he searched for her on Instagram, finding five people named Kaitlyn in East Plains, Iowa, but four of them spelled their first names with a "C" or other variation. By process of elimination, he had his girl, one Kaitlyn Stokes. Tapping open her profile, he was limited to a small round photo of a snowman donning a scarf, because her account was set to private. In hopes of gaining access to her photos and videos, he sent a request to follow her. Not expecting her to be attractive, he still wanted to see the face of this small-town girl who'd witnessed a UFO the night her father died.

Hopefully, she was telling the truth that she wasn't crazy.

Kaitlyn got out of the shower and quickly wrapped herself in a towel. Shivering in the brisk morning air, she grabbed her phone from the counter to see a notification. Zachary Taylor had sent an Instagram request to follow her. Heart racing, she wiped the steam from her screen to select "approve" or "ignore." She couldn't just ignore him, but she didn't like the feeling of being tested—that if he didn't like her photos, he wouldn't respond to her last text message, which he had obviously gotten.

She pictured him with a tall, skinny blonde model, not a raven-haired Midwest girl with thicker shoulders and thighs passed down by her mother's Scandinavian ancestors, straight black hair from her paternal great grand-mother, a Dakota Sioux, and green eyes from her grandfather, a Scotch-Irishman from whom she'd inherited her last name of Stokes, along with the family trademark—a bump on the nose.

Removing the towel, she looked at her steamy reflection in the mirror. The human body was an art form, and she was grateful for the face and body the Creator had blessed her with. She would never get a nose job or liposuction to conform to someone else's idea of beauty. When the right man came along, he would see the true light of her being and want her the way she was.

Overcome by a sudden dare, she wiped the glass clear. Standing naked before it, she snapped a photo on her phone—her nipples were erect from the cold air colliding with hot mist. Impulsively, she felt like sending it to Zachary. After a fleeting fantasy of how he would react, she deleted the photo, knowing she never really intended to press send. Instead, she accepted his request and quickly dried off and got dressed.

Still in bed with his phone, Zachary took one glance at her Instagram photo and felt the breath knocked out of him. This Kaitlyn had striking green eyes, which stood out even more because of the shiny black hair that fell past her shoulders. Yet, even with bold high cheekbones, her face was far from perfect, and her nose a little too big or oddly shaped. Zooming in, he saw a sprinkle of freckles on her cheeks. To him, her imperfections made her more naturally beautiful.

Tapping open a video she'd posted, he watched her and a curly blonde friend as they showed off a steaming pan of lasagna in someone's kitchen. "Tah-dah!" said the friend, taking center stage. "We did it—homemade lasagna!"

"It was my grandma's recipe," said Kaitlyn, with a hint of sadness in her voice. Zachary liked the sound of it, yet it was somehow different than he might have expected. Maybe it was the flattened vowels of her Midwest accent.

"It's *Italiano* night!" said the friend, imitating an Italian chef with exaggerated gusto. "With gelato to follow! Oh, my God, I'm a poet and didn't know it!" She laughed a little too loudly at her own joke, and seemed like a bit of a showoff.

"No gelato for me," said Kaitlyn. "I'm not blessed with Jenna's metabolism." Standing there in jeans and a T-shirt, she looked perfectly fine to Zachary. He liked many female body types, and Kaitlyn was somewhere in the middle. Her thick curves were a definite turn-on, but it was her feline green eyes that really captivated him.

"Whatever," said Jenna, putting her arm around her friend. "We're just gonna binge on some Netflix and grub and take our mind off things tonight."

Kaitlyn sadly nodded, making Zachary wonder how recently her father had died and what had caused his passing. The video's date was more than six months ago, suggesting he might have been sick or suffered an accident that ultimately took his life.

He opened several more pictures and videos which she had posted. The more he watched her, the more he felt something strange, scary and wonderful that he'd never felt before. Nothing could explain this sudden pain in his chest. Love at first sight—that's what it was. It made him realize why the ancient Greeks believed in a Cupid who shot invisible arrows through people's hearts.

But she was more than 1,700 miles away on Google Maps. If the distance between them wasn't enough of an obstacle, there was an even bigger problem to face. Their relationship had begun with his outlandish hoax.

Kaitlyn and her mother were eating breakfast at the kitchen table. Dressed for work at the country feed store, her mother wore jeans, blouse, and cowboy boots. Her clothes were too baggy because she'd lost her appetite months ago. Hair wet from a shower, she should have looked more refreshed, but her eyes were still puffy from lack of sleep the night before, or too much wine. Watching her, Kaitlyn was glad to see her halfway through her scrambled eggs on a slice of toast. Some crumbs were falling on some unpaid bills, and her mother was anxiously pressing numbers on the calculator set in front of her.

"I can get my job back at Daisy's," said Kaitlyn, referring to the local family diner. She'd quit her job as a waitress there to spend more time with her father in his final months, and to help her mother out around the house.

"It's okay," said her mother, looking up from her accounting. "You've already sacrificed enough this past year."

"I need to start saving for college," said Kaitlyn. "I can start at a JC while living at home the first two years."

"You're always welcome here," said her mother, "but it's not the same as living on campus at a four-year university."

"Even if I wanted to live in the dorms," said Kaitlyn, not liking the idea of leaving her mother all alone, "we can't afford it."

"You won't know that until after you apply," said her mother.

"I've looked at ISU," said Kaitlyn, meaning Iowa State University. "But I don't have the grades or SATs to earn a full scholarship." During the past year, her grade point average had dipped substantially, and she couldn't focus on studying for the SAT, so her score was disappointing, to say the least.

"You can retake the SAT," said her mother. "And we'll figure out a way to get you through. Your father didn't leave us totally destitute, you know."

Kaitlyn looked at the stack of bills causing the worry on her mother's face. "You said it yourself, Mom. I'm an adult now. I need to manage on my own."

"I said you're old enough to vote," said her mother. "Not that I couldn't help you out anymore, so don't put words in my mouth."

Kaitlyn shrugged, checked her phone, and immediately saw that Jenna had texted her three times already this morning, but nothing from Zachary.

"Lemme guess," said her mother, stirring cream into her coffee. "It's that boy who gave you the roses. Garrett, right?"

"No," said Kaitlyn, not even close to telling her about a complete stranger she'd connected with on Instagram—a UFO abductee living in another part of the country. "It's nobody."

Her mother smiled. "For being a nobody," she said, "you sure look disappointed."

"He's probably getting ready for school," said Kaitlyn, "and didn't have time to text me back. No biggie."

"Who is he?" asked her mother, curiously watching her.

"Oh, it doesn't matter," said Kaitlyn. "He lives too far away, and I don't really want a boyfriend right now anyway."

"This past year, you've barely even dated anyone," said her mother.

Kaitlyn nodded, scooping wobbly eggs onto her toast. "With Dad dying, the spring prom and Tolo just seemed so trivial. Besides, there was nobody I wanted to ask," she said, speaking of the latter event, where the girl had to ask a boy to be her date.

"Surely you've had a crush on somebody," said her mother.

Kaitlyn took a crunchy bite of eggs on toast. "There was a boy in my calculus class," she said of Bryce Collins, a bright, witty hunk and captain of their Mathletes team. "But he was only talking to me so he could get to know Jenna, who, it turned out, had zero interest in him."

"If it's that Bryce fellow," said her mother, "I always thought he seemed arrogant. He thinks he's a lot better looking than he really is."

Kaitlyn nodded, scooping more eggs onto a wedge of toast. "I'm so done with high school. It doesn't matter."

"But it's your senior year," said her mother, "and you deserve to enjoy the experience. It's what your dad would have wanted, you know."

"I know," said Kaitlyn, "but Dad won't be here to watch me graduate, so what's the point?"

Short of answers, her mother looked at her in concern. "We can still make an appointment to talk to somebody."

"That's okay," said Kaitlyn, rising from the table. "I'll take care of the dishes when I get home." She kissed her mother on the forehead, grabbed her plate, and took it to the sink on her way out.

Kaitlyn had been driving her dad's old pickup truck to school, a Dodge Ram wasting far more fossil fuel than she wanted to think about. Prior to his illness, she'd been trying to convince him to get a more environmentally friendly vehicle. If not electric, at least something smaller, because it was rare that they needed to haul a piece of furniture or larger appliance. With only three in their family, he could have easily gotten by in something like what her mom drove, a red Ford Focus, which he called her "little ladybug." Her mother would argue the only bug on the road was a VW Bug, another vehicle he would never consider driving. But her father sold to farmers and insisted on a big truck, even if he wasn't responsible for delivering what they bought. Kaitlyn knew he wasn't perfect, and now she insisted on keeping the truck because it was the only part of him still running.

On the seat beside her was his Iowa State sweatshirt, something he used to wear all the time. Its Cyclones logo was faded from too many washings, as if it had barely weathered the tornadoes after which it was named. With their biggest football game of the season coming up, she changed the radio station to KCYL. Broadcast from Des Moines, KCYL would be talking Cyclones all week. In fact, the radio hosts were currently arguing about who should start at quarterback this coming Saturday.

Passing through the countryside, Kaitlyn imagined her father sitting where she did right now, saying it wouldn't matter who started because they would likely get blown out by Michigan anyway. Even so, he would cheer them on till the end. "Anyone can follow a winner," he used to say, "but a team named the Cyclones deserves far better than fair-weather fans, whose loyalty has been tested by many disappointing seasons."

"I miss you, Dad," she said, still hearing his voice in her head, and a whiff of his lingering aftershave making it feel as if he were there in the cab with her. As soon as the words left her lips, a pop of static came over the radio, followed by loud crackling and a strange, high-pitched frequency in wavering tones.

That's weird, she thought, tuning the station to make sure it was on 101.2 FM. Des Moines was more than twenty miles away, but that didn't explain this crazy static. Some clouds had pushed in from the north, but nothing to interfere with the broadcast—the only things present for miles all around were cornfields and rolling farmlands. Baffled, she turned the dial to other stations, most of them from Des Moines or even farther away, and all of which came in crystal clear. She turned past Big Country 104.5, her father's favorite music station, to land on 107.1, which was playing a new pop hit from Doja Cat. It was the kind of music her father would quietly tolerate before escaping the room.

As she continued driving, a cold chill passed through her, despite the warm air blowing inside the truck. She had the strange sensation of having left her father behind on the highway. In the rearview mirror, she glimpsed her hair settling down, only to realize it'd been standing straight up from static electricity. "Dad!" she cried out, quickly changing the station back to 101.2. Now the airwaves were perfectly clear as the radio hosts debated if the play-calling would improve this season.

"Dad!" she nearly shouted, whipping the truck to the side of the road and skidding over gravel to a stop. Flinging her door open, she scrambled outside to watch the sky above. "Dad!" she screamed, hoping to see the spinning wheel emerge from the clouds—to see again those bright, mysterious lights which had taken him away. A car whizzed by, and she could feel the gawking stares of its occupants.

Clambering back into the truck, she slammed the door and jimmied the radio dial back and forth, hoping to retrieve whatever frequency had been lost. The radio hosts were now blabbering about defensive schemes. "Damn it! Damn it! Damn it!" she screamed, pounding her fists on the steering wheel. Her father was trying to make contact, and she'd turned the dial like a complete idiot. Breaking into an angry sob, she leaned her head against the steering wheel until she could pull herself together. "Sorry, Dad," she said, wiping her eyes and combing her fingers through her hair, where she still felt the shock of remaining electrons. It was like touching the shadow of his ghost.

009

In the Pacific Northwest, it was two hours earlier than Central Time, and Zachary could not go back to sleep. Propped up against his pillow, he still had forty-five minutes before his alarm would go off. He used the extra time to study for a pop quiz in biology, which was never really a pop quiz because Mr. Mullin regularly conducted them on days their assignments were due, which happened to be today.

Unable to concentrate on bird classifications, Zachary had yet to respond to Kaitlyn's last text. If they were going to start chatting, he should tell her right now that he'd never been abducted by a UFO and how the story was never intended to go beyond the walls of the school principal's office. If that was her main reason for messaging him in the first place, though, she might instantly lose interest in talking to him.

She probably had a boyfriend anyway, which would explain why, unlike the other girls, she didn't send a photo, thereby forcing him to find a picture of her on Instagram. If that were the case, he had nothing to lose by telling her the truth. But if the truth upset her, she could expose him on social media as a total fraud. Then his parents would be angry and disappointed, blaming him for the negative publicity and loss of business. Right now, their electric vehicles were selling faster than their inventory could keep up with, which he hoped was giving a slight delay to the end of human life on Planet Earth.

Plus, there was Hailey with whom to contend. After throwing a tantrum, she would continue her passive-aggressive silent treatment while secretly gloating about reclaiming her throne as the favorite child.

With so much at stake, Zachary had no idea what to do. He flipped through Kaitlyn's photos on his phone, fearing whatever message he responded with would backfire. In hopes of taking his mind off the situation, he returned to bird classifications. As he read about pigeons mating for life, he couldn't help but envy how much easier they had it. They could simply peck each other out and live happily ever after in a city park.

Kaitlyn barely remembered the rest of the drive to school, her mind replaying the strange occurrence with the radio and trying to make sense of it. Eager to check her UFO sightings map, she kept her phone locked in the glovebox so she wouldn't be tempted to look while driving. It was a practice she'd followed since watching a film at school on the dangers of texting and driving—the gory images of fatal teen crashes had stayed in her mind. After being so close to death at home, Kaitlyn took the film more seriously than some of her peers. Her biggest fear now was leaving her mother all alone—an added pressure of being the only child of a suddenly and prematurely widowed parent.

Arriving at the school's parking lot, she quickly retrieved her phone, powered it on, and checked her UFO Sightings Map for any recent activity in the area. Early this morning, a farmer in Topeka, Kansas reported crop circles in his fields about 250 miles away. Late last night, a pilot flying over Grand Rapids, Michigan observed a streak of lights that he feared might collide with his Cessna. The nearest air traffic controller assured him there were no other aircraft in the area, yet the pilot's radar showed otherwise.

Looking at the map, Kaitlyn saw a direct line of travel between Topeka, Grand Rapids, and her hometown in Iowa. She pictured her father in direct orbit overhead, sending signals from high above the clouds. That might be one explanation. However, if the aliens had truly come for him, as they did for

Ezekiel, then he should have been transported to God—unless he had unfinished business to do on Earth, such as a proper farewell with some fatherly advice on her future life ahead. Then she could let him go. Any crop marks left behind would be a permanent reminder they'd all be together soon enough.

The blaring voice of Taylor Swift singing, "I don't want to live forever," signaled an incoming text from Jenna, her fifth that morning. Kaitlyn finally checked it.

Jenna: Are you here yet?

Kaitlyn: Yes, omw.

On my way, as in after she checked her other messages, that is. Seeing nothing from Zachary, she felt disappointed, and wondered if he was getting ready for school himself, or maybe he didn't like her Instagram pictures and had already ghosted her.

Out of the truck, she headed for East Plains High's entrance—its mural painting, in red and black school colors, of a bison charging with lowered horns. "GO BUFFALOES!" While it sucked to be rejected, she would still want to chat with Zachary as a friend. She hoped Garrett would feel the same way, and wondered if it was harder to reject someone else, or to be rejected. Instead of dodging Garrett or giving him false hope with friendly hellos in the hallways, she decided to seek him out right away.

Slight delay, she texted Jenna, ignoring her immediate response asking why.

A few minutes later, she found him by his locker talking to a wolfpack of fellow wrestlers. "Hey, Garrett," she said, awkwardly waiting for a moment of privacy. Garrett nodded at his friends, and they took the hint to leave. As they headed off for class, they all turned to look back at the much rumored-about new couple.

"Thanks for the flowers," she said, self-consciously crossing her arms over her chest. "They're really beautiful. My mom liked them, too."

Garrett blushed a little. "You get a chance to read the card?"

"Yes," said Kaitlyn. "I was just coming by to say what you wrote was beautiful. I had no idea that you and my father had ever crossed paths and that he had made such an impact."

Garrett nodded shyly, his bright blue eyes meeting hers before he flinched and looked away, making her realize he might not be a perv, but someone too nervous to maintain eye contact—just as Jenna and her mother had suggested. "But it's not just that," he said. "I think having a dad like that must've rubbed off on you, and it makes me feel like we've had this distant connection, even though we've never really hung out together."

Taken aback, Kaitlyn said, "That's really sweet, Garrett. My dad would be happy to know I have a new friend looking out for me, like a big brother."

"Yeah," he said, looking as if she'd just sucker-punched him below the waist. "Only I don't really see you as a sister, but more as the hottest girl I know."

Kaitlyn was stunned, feeling the intensity of his eyes and almost wishing they would deflect to her chest. "I…I had no idea," she said, "but I don't really think—"

"It's more than being hot," he interrupted. "Hell, I've dated most of the girls in this school, but there's something deeper about you, more mysterious, like you're keeping something secret when everyone else is trying so hard to get attention."

"I wish I had a secret," said Kaitlyn with a nervous chuckle. "But I'm really just shy, I think."

"You're not shy," he said, "or you wouldn't have walked right up to me in front of a pack of guys like you just did. Most girls would've dodged me, but you had the guts to come tell me you're not interested." Eyes misting, he cleared a lump in his throat to say, "I respect that."

Kaitlyn wanted to hug him, to let him know it was going to be okay. She wasn't what Garrett described, and he deserved someone who was totally into him. "You know Jenna's got this thing for you, right?"

He looked at her in surprise. "I asked her out freshman year. She blew me off, and she's too much of a drama queen."

"She's a little high-strung, but she has a real heart of gold," said Kaitlyn, truly meaning that about her best friend. "And what does anyone really know their freshman year? She's grown up a lot since then and thinks you're the hottest guy she's ever seen. Her words, not mine." As Garrett frowned, she instantly regretted the slight. "What I meant was—"

"It's okay," he said, grabbing a notebook from his locker and stuffing it in his backpack. "I don't need a consolation prize, but thanks anyway."

Kaitlyn nodded, feeling foolish for trying to pawn her friend off.

"I truly am sorry for your loss," he said, tapping his locker door shut. As Kaitlyn watched him go, she didn't remember feeling this bad, even after discovering that Bryce Collins was talking to her solely to get to Jenna.

Rejecting someone else had to be worse than being rejected.

010

Zachary's school day began badly. He found his locker graffitied with the drawing of a cross-eyed alien stepping out of a flying saucer. "You failed our experiment, LOSER!" Zachary might have been amused by the artist's work if it wasn't so humiliating, as amplified by the sarcastic laughter of students passing by.

Grabbing a notebook and a couple of pens for his "pop quiz" in biology, he reminded himself of his thousands of loyal followers on Instagram—something he never expected to care about. In fact, he was instantly ashamed for even letting that cross his mind. As he traipsed off for class, he suddenly experienced a horrible feeling of loneliness in a crowded hallway filled with noise and gawking passersby.

While it was safe to hide in the shadows, he realized he would have to take a chance if he ever wanted someone special in his life. Right or wrong, he made up his mind to text Kaitlyn back. Adding her name to his short list of phone contacts, he made certain to spell it correctly. If she had a boyfriend, so be it. He would soon find out.

By now, she obviously knew he'd seen her photos on Instagram, so he wasn't sure if he should pay her a compliment or not. He didn't want to seem overly aggressive, especially if she had no interest in him beyond his so-called alien experience. On the other hand, if he said nothing about her appearance, it might suggest he wasn't attracted to her. He knew he was overthinking this, but he was inexperienced when it came to texting, sexting, and girls.

If Hailey was still talking to him, he might have asked her for some sisterly advice, but she blew right past him in the hallway. Her face was flushed from embarrassment after seeing the locker graffiti. Surprised to see her alone, he hoped it was by choice, and not because her usual crowd of cool people was suddenly excluding her. "Hailey!" he called.

"Leave me alone, freak!" she called back, dashing away.

"Fine," he muttered under his breath. He didn't want her help anyway.

The first to finish his "pop quiz" in biology class, Zachary had typed and deleted several text messages to Kaitlyn before sending them, making little effort to hide the phone beneath his desk.

"Mr. Taylor," said his teacher, Mr. Mullin, who, as usual, was wearing the same gray sweater he seemed to have on every day. "Is your life in danger?"

"Yeah," said Ridley Cooper, the class clown, who fittingly had curly red hair. "The aliens are coming for him!" The class burst into laughter as Ridley sang the notes from that stupid alien horror movie.

"I was asking Mr. Taylor," said an irritated Mr. Mullin, waiting for the laughter to die down.

"No, sir," said Zachary, feeling his face turning red.

Mr. Mullin took a step toward him. "Then why don't you tell me what my policy on phones in class is?"

"Is this a pop quiz?" asked Zachary, unintentionally drawing another burst of laughter from the class, which annoyed Mr. Mullin even more.

"If it was," he said, coming down the aisle toward Zachary, "you would have failed since I made it clear at the beginning of the year that using your phone in class meant confiscation until the end of the school day."

"I probably forgot," said Zachary, "since I don't normally use a phone."

"LOSE-ERRR!" said a voice behind him, drawing a few more snickers.

Approaching Zachary's desk, Mr. Mullin held out his hand to collect the phone. "You can pick it up after the final bell," he said. Zachary nodded, turning off the device to hand it over. From across the room, he sensed the intense stare of Camila and glanced her way. If she could read his expression, it was painfully obvious he was upset over another girl. Turning away, he knew it would be nearly five p.m. in Iowa before he could finally respond to her.

That seemed like an eternity to him.

Nose in her phone, Kaitlyn had barely touched the slice of cafeteria pizza she'd grabbed on the way out to her truck at lunchtime. With no current updates on her UFO Sightings Map, she was now reading about radio signals and how they worked. She'd also tuned in to 101.2 FM, where a show caller was saying, "I think our D-line is going to come up big this Saturday."

"Since when do you care *this* much about a football game?" asked Jenna, eating a tuna salad sandwich in the passenger seat.

"I want to keep the streak alive," said Kaitlyn, focused on her radio signal article. As she suspected, radio signals were nothing more than electronic currents which traveled very quickly between transmitter and receiver, which didn't quite explain why her hair had stood straight up earlier that morning. A major body change like that would require an electromagnetic charge far more powerful than something in the FM frequency range.

"What streak is that?" asked Jenna, her sandwich stinking up the cab.

"Since I was born, I've watched every game with my dad," said Kaitlyn, buzzing the window down to let some fresh air in. "Even when I was a baby, I was on his lap, wearing my little Cyclones shirt." She flipped to a photo on her phone to show her.

"Oh my God!" said Jenna. "That is too cute! And your dad was a total hottie back then." She suddenly looked embarrassed. "Sorry, I didn't mean it like that. Just that he was, you know, handsome, and you totally have his eyes and hair."

Kaitlyn nodded. "It's going to be weird, watching games without him," she said, her voice filled with sadness.

"I'm so sorry," said Jenna, showing genuine love for her best friend.

"If Rollins has another losing year," said the radio show host, "I think he and his entire coaching staff need to go."

"I agree," said Jenna, "but don't they have an app for this station?" On her iPhone, she quickly found one.

"It's not the same," said Kaitlyn, knowing her friend could never understand. If her father were to make contact again, it would be in this truck—*his* truck. The DMV registration was still in his name, and right beside her in the middle console.

"Whatever," said Jenna, buzzing up her window. "It's freezing in here, and we're like the only two people in school not eating in the cafeteria."

"You just want to see Garrett," said Kaitlyn, having already told her about their conversation this morning.

"I'm not going to be his rebound chick," said Jenna, "when he's really into you."

"That's a first," said Kaitlyn, flipping through more family photos that included her father—birthdays, Easter egg hunts, sledding at Christmas. She still couldn't imagine the coming holidays without him. A feeling of dread came over her.

"What's that supposed to mean?" said Jenna.

"Guys always want you more," said Kaitlyn, still flipping through photos to avoid her stare.

"That's not true!"

"Yes, it is."

"No, it's not! Name one guy who wanted me instead of you."

"Bryce Collins," said Kaitlyn, glancing up from her phone to finally make eye contact.

"That Mathletes' nerd?" said Jenna, wrinkling her nose in dismay. "Who cares?

"I did," said Kaitlyn. "But you acted like it was nothing—that he was talking to me to get to you."

"What was I supposed to do?" said Jenna, her cheeks turning pink. "I never brought it on. I think he's a total dork!"

"You could have told him what a pretentious slimebag he was."

"I never say slimebag. It's not in my vocab."

"Sleazebag, scumbag? Whatever! You could've shown some loyalty!"

"I never went out with him!"

"But you were still nice to him!"

"I politely let him down," said Jenna with a theatrical sigh. "Had I known better, I would've kicked him in the family jewels. I'm sorry."

Kaitlyn chuckled, a cathartic release of pent-up energy.

"You're just super-sensitive right now," said Jenna, "with everything going on."

Kaitlyn nodded, her eyes turning moist.

"Come here," said Jenna, reaching over to give her a hug while inadvertently smashing the piece of pizza in its little cardboard box. "No stupid guy will ever come between us, even though I'm totally jealous that Garrett wants you now, and I missed my chance. What was I thinking, anyway?"

"To hell with them all," said Kaitlyn, returning her friend's hug. She was really talking about Zachary, who still hadn't texted her back.

In third-period English class, all Zachary could think about was getting his phone back so he could finish writing his text message to Kaitlyn. He used to make fun of his teenage peers for being so dependent on their handheld devices. That was before he felt this desperate need to connect with someone.

"There are many themes at work in *Romeo and Juliet*," said his teacher, Miss Tisdale, a middle-aged woman with curly hair piled atop her head. "Love and fate are the obvious ones. But there's also time. From the very beginning of the story, the young lovers are at odds against time, having only a short period together before Juliet's death."

Watching the clock on the wall, the seconds creeping past, Zachary also felt at odds against time, and this class period couldn't end soon enough.

Kaitlyn had dropped third-year French for study hall after her grades started to drop. The school counselor, Miss Wetzel, had suggested she do so, not only to protect her GPA, but for the obvious reason of giving her more time to focus on her core classes while caring for her father at home. Kaitlyn regretted not learning the language of love, even if Ms. Dubois, her former French teacher, used to joke that "love needs no language." Her class of beginners had no idea what she was saying in her native *Francais* tongue. Now, at least, Kaitlyn had a free hour to read about humans contacting aliens via radio communications.

"Is that homework, Miss Stokes?" said Mr. Fogerty, looking up from his laptop. A second-year English teacher, he'd volunteered to monitor study hall so he could write his novel—something having to do with a dysfunctional family, which he claimed was a "dark comedy."

"It's for science," said Kaitlyn, holding up her phone to show an article picturing the "Big Ear" Telescope at Ohio State University's Radio Observatory.

"Okay," said Mr. Fogerty, returning to his slow, methodical typing and pensive expression.

Back to her article, Kaitlyn learned that in 1977 the "Big Ear" Telescope recorded a 72-second pulse from the direction of Sagittarius. Named the "Wow! signal" by Dr. Jerry R. Ehman, the astronomer in charge, it may have been nothing more than a black hole event. Since then, several well-funded programs had extended the search for extraterrestrials, but with no response. Most likely, we had yet to discover the right frequency through which to make contact. But that was no excuse. According to one scientist, Seth Shostak, "Columbus didn't wait for a 747 to get him across the Atlantic."

To hell with Columbus, thought Kaitlyn. She felt like reaching out to the scientific community, letting them know she had made contact through the antenna of an old pickup truck. The connection between a father and daughter was more powerful than a well-to-do radio observatory. The question now was when would he send another signal? And how would she be able to decode it when he did?

At least next time, she would be ready, assuming there was a next time.

Taking notes in Pacific Northwest history class, Zachary learned of the Great Seattle Fire in 1898, which burned so much of the city they decided to rebuild over top it. That left the Seattle Underground, which can still be visited today with guided tours. Far more intriguing was how the wrong person was initially blamed for the fire. The *Seattle Post-Intelligencer* reported it began in James McGough's paint shop, where a pot of boiling glue was knocked over. Two weeks later, the newspaper published a correction that the blaze began in the cabinet shop just below McGough's. Yet poor Mr. McGough would continue to be blamed for generations to come. Truth be told, he was nowhere near his shop when the fire broke out. In fact, he was rushing to put out the flames as a volunteer firefighter.

"So, let me ask you," said their teacher, Mrs. Daniels, best known around school for wearing silver-framed glasses to match her hair. "Has the media changed in over a hundred and fifty years?"

"Not really," said Zachary, as everyone turned to look his way. "Technology has changed. The internet and television have largely replaced newspapers, but the people reading or watching the news haven't changed at all."

"Is that because of the media and what they feed the people?" asked Mrs. Daniels. "Or are the people to blame for not caring about the truth?"

Zachary had to think about that one. "I think it's a little of both. But the media should be more responsible."

"You should know," said a boy's voice from the back of the room. "Nobody really believes you were abducted by aliens."

"I do!" said a nerdy girl in the front row.

"So do I!" said her chubby, freckled friend, looking back at Zachary with a smile.

"You just want to have his alien baby," said another boy, triggering a big laugh from the class.

"We're not here to discuss Zachary," said Mrs. Daniels, giving him a warm smile, "though I have to admit, your story has been the most exciting thing to happen in this town since I moved here thirty-five years ago."

Zachary nodded in embarrassment, feeling the stares of his classmates as he glanced away at the clock. Three more hours, and he'd finally get his phone back.

11

After school, Kaitlyn stopped off at Daisy's Diner to see if they had some part-time hours available. Coming out of the kitchen was Daisy herself, her hair having turned grayer since the last time Kaitlyn had seen her. "Sorry to hear about your dad," she said, a spot of fresh gravy on her lacy pink apron. "But I've got too many waitresses right now. 'Less you don't mind bussing tables and working in the back."

"I'll take whatever you have," said Kaitlyn, preferring to scrub pots and pans in the steamy hot kitchen over people giving her that sad, pathetic look and repeating, "Sorry for your loss."

"Okay then," said Daisy, heading over to answer a ringing phone. "I'll be in touch with you soon. Give your mom my best."

"Will do," said Kaitlyn, heading out the door, which jingled shut behind her.

Kaitlyn drove the scenic route home from Daisy's. Passing the cornfields at sunset, she looked out at the golden landscape of harvest season. With the windows buzzed down, she breathed in the cool autumn air, which had always filled her with a sense of beauty and sadness. Her favorite season of the year involved something magical and mysterious, which could not be explained.

Tired of sports talk on the radio, she kept the volume low while secretly hoping for another signal from her father. As she passed Thompson's farm, she recognized a combine harvester that her father had sold him a few years back, a John Deere X-Series, which Kaitlyn could proudly name by model as a Class

11. At the time, most of the corn farmers were replacing their hired labor with machinery, and sparking debate between her parents.

"What about the H-2A workers?" her mother had asked, referring to the migrant workers in need of jobs to retain their right to stay in the U.S., not to mention feeding their families and keeping shoes on their children's feet.

"I'm not the idiot in Washington D.C. who passed those stupid laws," her father responded, his voice replaying in Kaitlyn's head. "They're the ones who created a labor shortage, which raised the demand for machinery in the first place."

"So where are they supposed to go?" asked her mother.

"If they go to Washington State, they can still pick apples and cherries. Or peppers in California. Or pumpkins right here in Iowa," said her father. When her mother wasn't around, he'd once told Kaitlyn that robots would replace both farm workers and machinery in the not-too-distant future. "If John Deere doesn't start producing A.I. instead of tractors, I may soon be out of a job myself," he half-jokingly predicted. That was before he'd been diagnosed with cancer.

Gazing out at the fields, Kaitlyn was spooked by the idea of seeing robots, their metal backs reflecting the sun as they pulled and twisted the cobs off the vines. If that was the future, she wondered how anyone outside the tech industry would have a job and be able to buy food.

Up ahead, she saw Barton's Pumpkin Orchard, a beautiful spectacle of bright orange balls scattered across the fields. She remembered her father taking her here every year as a little girl, letting her pick out a pumpkin after a hayride, and allowing her a wild romp through the corn maze with the other kids, just about all of them in Halloween costumes.

A sad smile crossed her face. She was grateful for the memory. She knew that millions of other children in the world had never been given what she had. But it also made her miss him all that much more. She couldn't help but wonder if it was easier for people who never had someone to love. They wouldn't have to experience the pain of loss. With that in mind, she should be glad that Zachary hadn't texted her back. Why start something with someone who wasn't really interested in her? It would only lead to much greater heartache down the road.

Gazing out at the pumpkin patch, she decided that being rejected was actually far worse than rejecting someone else.

Time was dragging again. Following lunch and PE, Zachary was taking notes in Mr. Whitehead's advanced science class, his teacher's monotone the perfect delivery for Einstein's theory of relativity. It stated that time goes fast when one is enjoying oneself, and not so fast when one is bored, as when waiting for a bus or train, or hoping class would soon end. If Zachary had Einstein's I.Q., he'd be working on bending time right now to finally end this interminable school day.

When Kaitlyn got home, which was much later than usual, she found her mother's red Focus in their gravel driveway. Parking her truck in reverse, she watched the final rays of sunset touch down on the fields across the way, the endless sports chatter still playing on low volume.

"Come on, Dad," she said, trying to will him down from the sky. Just recently, she'd watched a documentary about the "Phoenix Lights" over Arizona, in which several extraterrestrial vehicles arrived on a night when thousands of people were already watching the sky for the Hale-Bopp comet. Captured on video by several witnesses, the spectacle became a major media story at the time, and the public demanded answers.

Responding at a press conference, Governor Fife Symington downplayed the incident by introducing a man in an alien costume. The stunt drew a laugh from his audience of reporters. It wasn't until Symington was out of office years later that he admitted he had no other answers. Most likely, the extraterrestrials had paid a visit. The incident occurred a short time before Kaitlyn was born.

As dusk settled in, she continued watching the sky for a sign. Catching another faint whiff of her father's aftershave, she wanted to stay in the cab and feel a part of him. But inside the house was a living, breathing soul. Right now, her mother was likely starting dinner and looking forward to her company.

Retrieving her phone from the glovebox, Kaitlyn got out of the truck and headed into the house. The smell of corn chowder on the stove greeted her like a warm hello.

"Hey, Mom, I'm home."

Zachary always liked having shop as his final class of the day. For him, it was the perfect way to burn off some energy without having to think too much. Good with tools, he'd learned to use them at his parents' auto center and was getting better at fixing other things. At the moment, he was repairing a lawnmower with his shop partner Sven, a shy, lanky junior who never said a word. They got along perfectly. Their workspace reminded Zachary of a prison shop class he'd once seen on the Learning Channel.

As the bell finally rang to end the school day, his classmates robotically put all tools away at their various stations. "See ya, Sven!" said Zachary, handing him a wrench as he darted out of the workshop. Normally, he wouldn't leave his partner stuck cleaning up, but he was nearly running down the hallway to Mr. Mullin's office, where he soon discovered the door was locked. *Damn it!* Frantically banging, he heard a sour voice behind him. "He always finishes his coffee in the teacher's lounge before coming back here to finish grading papers." It was Camila, giving him an icy stare.

"What are you doing here?" said Zachary, sounding somewhat accusatory. "I mean, you didn't get *your* phone confiscated?"

"I came to get my after-school spanking," she said. "After all, how do you think I'm getting an A in this class?"

Zachary looked at her in disbelief. "You're kidding, right?"

"Of course, I'm kidding, you moron," said Camila. "I'm getting an A without anyone's help but my own. But if you really need to know, which you don't, I'm asking for a letter of recommendation for college."

"Where do you plan on going?"

"None of your business," she said, clearly done talking to him.

"Look," said Zachary apologetically, "I meant to come by that day, but something came up and—"

"I don't know what you're talking about."

"You—invited me over to—"

"You must have me confused with whoever you were texting in class," she said, looking at her phone and sighing with irritation. "When Mr. Mullin finally gets here, tell him I'll be back later, as in *after* you're gone." She huffed off down the hallway.

Watching her, Zachary could see she was obviously jealous of a girl in Iowa he'd never even met. More surprising was how obvious his texting must have been to her.

"Mr. Taylor," said Mr. Mullin, approaching with a stack of half-graded papers. "I'm assuming you're here for your phone and not to debate Darwin's theory of evolution, which the school district no longer allows me to teach."

"No debate from me, sir," said Zachary, "though I happen to think the human-ape was better off before we came down from the trees."

Unlocking the door, Mr. Mullin gave him an amused smile. "You're a natural cynic like myself, Zachary, but falling in love will change you." At his desk, he dug through a messy drawer for the phone and handed it over. "You can finish texting her now."

Zachary looked at him in surprise.

"Yeah," said Mr. Mullin. "It's that obvious."

Waiting for Mom's corn chowder at the kitchen table, Kaitlyn was on her father's iPad, filling out her online application for Iowa State University. Her 3.2 GPA had fallen well below the 3.65 average of incoming freshmen, but she was surprised to see that her SAT score was above the median, along with her RAI (Regent Admission Index), which included her high school core courses. Clicking bubbles and drop-down tabs, she was proud to type in both parents' names as family members who'd graduated from the university. Undecided on a major, she could defer making that decision for now, though she was leaning toward mathematics or physics.

Suddenly, a text alert beeped on her phone. It couldn't be Jenna, or Taylor Swift would be singing how she didn't want to live forever (Kaitlyn really needed to change that message tone). She thought of turning her text alerts off altogether, but curiosity got the better of her. Seeing a 509 number, she instantly knew it was Zachary. She held her breath in suspense as she opened the text to read:

509-146-3200: I would love to talk some more ☺ Lemme know when is a good time.

Kaitlyn smiled. She was tempted to respond but figured she should keep him waiting after his long delay in getting back to her. He followed with another pinging text.

509-146-3200: Btw, sorry for the late response. I don't normally text in school and my phone was confiscated in class this morning.

Kaitlyn suddenly felt foolish for getting so upset. She was about to text him back when he beat her to it with another message:

509-146-3200. I hope you don't mind me saying, but I think you're the most beautiful girl I have ever seen.

Kaitlyn's smile grew wider. That was hard to believe, especially with all the girls who must have been texting him, but she still appreciated the compliment. She typed:

That is very sweet, but I think you're just being nice.

509-146-3200: I'm glad you think so. But I mean it. I have never told anyone that before. Unless you count my mom when I was in kindergarten.

Kaitlyn laughed, as her own mother appeared over her shoulder with two bowls of steaming hot chowder. "How's the application going?" she asked, in a tone suggesting that's what Kaitlyn should be working on.

"Good," said Kaitlyn, shielding her phone with her body as she typed:

My mom's behind me. Talk to you soon.

509-146-3200: Sounds good. I'll be around tonight hint hint ;)

Kaitlyn signed off with a smiley face in return. Her mother asked, "Who's that?"

"Just a boy I'm talking to," she said, saving Zachary's number to her phone contact list.

"How do you know him?" asked her mother, taking a seat at the table.

"Oh, this really nice girl put us in touch," said Kaitlyn, referring to Zachary's sister as if they were old friends.

"It wasn't Jenna?" said her mother.

Kaitlyn dipped her spoon in the chowder and blew off the steam. "No, she likes Garrett," she said, hoping to change the subject.

"The boy who gave you roses?"

"Yeah," said Kaitlyn, slurping the creamy, delicious chowder. "This is really good, Mom."

"Thanks," said her mother, waiting for hers to cool down. "We should really say grace before eating."

Kaitlyn put her spoon down with a weary nod. For several months, she and her mother had begged the Almighty to cure her father, but the higher power wasn't listening, so what was the point? As her mother reached out to take her hand, she bowed her head to join her.

"Dear Lord," prayed her mother, "thank you for this nourishment and this home that keeps us safe and warm. And more than anything, thank you for this time with my beautiful daughter, Kaitlyn, and for her knowing how much I love her."

"Amen," said Kaitlyn, giving her mom's hand a little squeeze.

"Well," said her mother, digging her spoon into her bowl, "sounds like musical chairs in the high school dating scene."

"I guess," said Kaitlyn, peeking at her phone to reread Zachary's message, the one telling her she was the most beautiful girl he'd ever seen.

"Well, I'm just glad to see you looking so happy," said her mother. "It's been too long."

"Thanks, Mom," she said, suddenly noticing their glasses were filled with water. "No wine tonight?"

"Not tonight," said her mother, slurping a spoonful of soup with a slight frown. "Could probably use another pinch of salt." It was her turn to change the subject, so Kaitlyn didn't push the issue. Most likely, she had been hung over this morning and didn't feel like poisoning herself with any more alcohol tonight. At least that's what Kaitlyn hoped.

Easy for her to say. She was *intoxicated* by Zachary's messages.

012

Zachary normally walked home from school. It was just a short hike through the city park and vacant lot between the high school and his house. Long before the ongoing cold war with his sister, he used to carpool with her, but they spent far more time driving around in search of a parking space at school than the time it took to simply hoof it. "It's good exercise and better for the environment," he'd tried telling her, to which Hailey responded, "Only dorks walk to school." She cared far more about looking cool in the Jeep their parents had given her on her sixteenth birthday. Shiny and red, it had been traded in for a new SUV at their auto center.

Stumbling over a depression in the field, Zachary read Kaitlyn's messages for the umpteenth time. She obviously liked his compliment, or she wouldn't have given him the smiley face and suggested talking sometime soon. But she'd also ended the conversation fairly abruptly, making him wonder if she was just being polite. No, he decided, she *was* interested in him as more than a friend.

In fact, it made him wonder if *she* was telling the truth about seeing a UFO the night her father died. How ironic would it be if she had made up some wild story to get his attention? He almost wished that were true; it would make things a lot easier for him. But something in his gut told him otherwise. This girl seemed real. Judging by her videos on Instagram, there was something pure about her.

As his neighborhood came into view, he stopped behind some fir trees to peer at his house down the street. Some workers were nearly done installing the security fence, and his driveway was now accessible only through a security gate with sensor lights all around.

Out on the sidewalk, the crowd of gawkers, ranging from New Age hippies to older, more conservative-looking people, had dwindled. Taking the long way around, Zachary cut through the yards of his neighbors once again, hopping the fence of Mr. Jones into his backyard so he could sneak in through his home's rear entry, despite that pesky chihuahua nipping at his heels.

The price of fame was well worth it if it brought one Kaitlyn Stokes into his life.

Propped up in bed with her father's iPad, Kaitlyn had promised her mother to finish her college application before any more texting tonight. Finally done with the tedious online forms, she clicked the bubble promising that everything was true, and then submitted her fate to the admissions officers at Iowa State University.

Picking up her phone, she saw it was a little after nine, meaning it was seven o'clock in Zachary's time zone. *Hey*, she texted, *u there*? Most likely, he was eating dinner, or finishing a hike in an area without cell phone reception. Her image of the Pacific Northwest included Bigfoot and UFOs in those woodsy mountains where Zachary was abducted.

A pinging text suddenly arrived.

Zachary: Hey, what you up to?

Kaitlyn: Not much. Just applied to Iowa State U.

Zachary: Wow! Good luck.

Kaitlyn: Thanks.

Zachary: What do you plan on studying?

Kaitlyn: Math, physics, maybe theology.

Zachary: I thought most physicists were atheists.

Kaitlyn: Yes, but not all. Some are studying things like subconscious life beyond death.

Zachary: Interesting. When did your dad pass away?

Kaitlyn: A few weeks ago.

Zachary: I'm very sorry to hear that.

Kaitlyn. Thanks. You planning on college?

Zachary: Maybe. I'm considering Wazzu.

Kaitlyn: Where's that?

Zachary: Oh. Sorry. Washington State U.

Kaitlyn: In Seattle?

Zachary: Eastern Washington. Farmland.

Kaitlyn: Sounds good to this country girl ☺

Zachary: Lol. My parents went there. It's their idea.

Kaitlyn: Do you want to go?

Zachary: I was thinking of working for GreenPeace, but they think that's stupid.

Kaitlyn: No it's not!

Zachary: Thanks. I'm glad you agree.

Kaitlyn: Is that why the aliens chose you? bc you care so much about the environment?

Zachary: I don't know...

Kaitlyn: We don't have to talk about it.

Zachary: It's okay. Do you mind if I ask what your dad died from?

Kaitlyn: Cancer. Brain tumor.

Zachary: That's horrible. I really am sorry.

Kaitlyn: Thanks. It has been a hard time for me and my mom.

Zachary: I can only imagine. No brothers or sisters?

Kaitlyn: No. What about you?

Zachary: Just me and my twin sister. But we are nothing alike. So much for genes...or horoscopes.

Kaitlyn: What is your sign?

Zachary: Libra. You?

Kaitlyn: I'm a Libra too. When is your bday?

Zachary: September 24.

Kaitlyn: Me too!

Zachary: No way!

Kaitlyn: Yes, I swear!

Zachary: Crazy that we were born on the same day.

Kaitlyn: What are the odds?

Zachary: 1 out of 365. lol.

Kaitlyn: Lol. True.

Zachary: But still pretty bizarre.

Kaitlyn: Yes. Like how I saw a UFO just before you were taken by one.

Zachary: Are you sure it wasn't a government drone or military craft?

Kaitlyn: Definitely not. Big flying saucer with flashing lights around its edges. Green, red, yellow, blue. Lit up at night like a big Ferris wheel in the sky.

Zachary: Wow. Sounds really beautiful.

Kaitlyn: Yes. Did yours look like that?

Zachary: It was daytime and foggy. So I can't really say.

Kaitlyn: Was it big and round though?

Zachary: Don't remember too much. Not sure I want to.

Kaitlyn: It's okay. No pressure.

Zachary: Sorry. I know you just want answers because of your dad.

Kaitlyn: Yes. If you remember anything pls lemme know.

Zachary: Okay.

Kaitlyn: I appreciate it.

Zachary: No problem.

Kaitlyn: Something weird happened today. Do you want to hear?

Zachary: Sure.

Kaitlyn: I think my dad interfered with the FM station in his truck, the one he always listened to.

Zachary: His spirit? Or ghost you mean?

Kaitlyn: Sort of. If the subconscious lives beyond death, we become Light Beings, our spirits a form of energy. I believe that.

Zachary: And you think the aliens came to get him the night he died?

Kaitlyn: Yes.

Zachary: Sounds very New Age.

Kaitlyn: Old Testament actually. Ezekiel was taken by a flying saucer to visit with God in the mountains…i.e. heaven.

Zachary: Ezekiel's wheel?

Kaitlyn: Yes! You know it!

Zachary: I've heard of it. But I'm not very religious.

Kaitlyn: It's okay. I'm a Christian but I think God is the master scientist. The better we understand science and math, the closer we get to the higher power.

Zachary. You're far more interesting than the girls at my school.

Kaitlyn: Lol, thanks, but they must be all over you. Especially now that you're super famous.

Zachary: Serial killers are famous. It's not always a good thing.

Kaitlyn: Lol, well, I bet they all want to go out with you.

Zachary: They gawk at me like I'm some kind of circus freak.

Kaitlyn: Do you juggle swords and swallow fire?

Zachary: Still working on it. Need a better clown costume.

Kaitlyn: Lol, well, it's getting late and I still have homework to finish.

Zachary: Okay, my mom is about to serve dinner to her perfect family.

Kaitlyn: Lol. Chat tomorrow?

Zachary: Sounds good ☺

Kaitlyn: Ttyl, have a good night ☺

Zachary: You too. Good night ☺

Kaitlyn: ☺

Zachary: ☺

On his way downstairs after texting with Kaitlyn, a girl who was beautifully magical and unlike any of the girls he knew at school, Zachary felt as if he were floating on air. Yet a part of him felt weighted down by the burden of that little white lie, which kept growing heavier. He wanted to tell her the truth but just didn't know how.

If they ever ended up in a relationship, he would have to tell her sometime. For now, the nearly 1,800 miles between them were like a safety buffer. With time and distance, it might not matter so much. By the time they finally met in person, his "UFO encounter" would simply be what had initially brought them together. It would be no different than running into someone in a dog park, grocery aisle, or fender bender. So long as nobody was injured, it didn't matter how they first connected. At least that's what he tried to convince himself as he came down into the dining room.

"We're taking a break from beef tonight," his father announced, carrying a tray of barbecue pork ribs to the table. His chef's apron was covered in tangy red sauce.

"Thanks to you, Zach, we're becoming more eco-friendly," said his mother, bringing a salad bowl from the kitchen.

Zachary smiled at his parents, knowing their effort would require baby steps. "Pork definitely produces a lot less methane than beef," he said, "but we should still aim for going vegetarian, to save our forests from becoming grazing lands, and to keep all those pesticides and waste from polluting our streams and—"

"Try telling that to your sister," his mother interrupted. "You know how much she loves your dad's pork ribs."

"I'm not hungry," said Hailey, sulking at the end of the table.

"What's wrong, honey?" asked their mother.

"I stepped down as senior class president today," she answered.

"Why?" said their parents in alarm.

"Billy Carter," she said, her family looking at her in confusion. "He was the drunken, redneck brother of President Jimmy Carter and a constant embarrassment during his four years in the White House. They even came out with Billy Beer at the time, with his picture on the front of the can."

"And what does this have to do with you?" asked their father.

"Zachary's locker was graffitied at school today, and everyone was talking about it. Mr. Klausen asked me to speak about bullying at the assembly this Friday, but I just can't do it. Not when I'm going to get laughed at by the entire school body, and not when I feel like I'm the one getting bullied by my evil twin."

"I never bullied you!" said Zachary. "And unlike Billy Carter, I'm promoting clean energy, which is far more important than anything you've done as class president."

"The year just began!" said Hailey. "And I was planning a fundraiser to buy new uniforms for the girls' basketball team! Plus free Wi-Fi across campus, and a fresh paint job on the gymnasium mural!"

"Rah-rah!" said Zachary. "It'll look good on your college applications."

"It would have," said Hailey. "But not now."

"Your grades are still good," said their mother. "Along with your SATs."

"Good enough to get in, maybe," said Hailey. "But I'm really going to need the scholarship money now."

"Why's that?" said their father. "You know we can help you."

"NYU is expensive, Dad, especially living in Manhattan, and I don't expect you and Mom to have to pick up the tab."

"Why New York?" said their mother in dismay. "That's all the way across the country."

"Exactly," said Hailey. "If I change my last name, too, then hopefully nobody will know I'm this weirdo's twin sister."

"You're just upset right now," said their mother. "Give it some time."

"Someone called me Hailey's Comet today. I really need to get away."

"Hailey's Comet," repeated their father. "That's pretty clever."

"Genius," Hailey said sarcastically.

"It's your decision," said their mother, passing the tray of ribs. "But starving yourself isn't going to help."

Hailey looked at the glistening spareribs, so tender they were falling off the bone. "What the hell?" she said, piling her plate with ribs, a big slab of butter on her mashed potatoes. "I dropped out of Homecoming court too, so I don't have to worry about fitting into that stupid prom queen dress anymore."

Zachary smiled at his sister, whose face was now smeared with greasy red sauce. If only she could be like this more often—and even better if she finished with a loud belch to show the world she no longer cared what anyone thought.

Out in her father's truck, Kaitlyn reclined the seat to gaze up at a bright harvest moon. She turned the radio on at low volume—a sports show broadcast earlier that day. It was a typically quiet evening in the country, and her mother had gone to bed after watching the local news. Tornado season was over, but she still wanted to hear it from the weatherman on Channel Four himself so they could sleep peacefully tonight. Not that either of them could sleep very well just weeks after the funeral. Thinking of Zachary, Kaitlyn wondered if he believed her story of witnessing the UFO over her house. He'd probably heard some pretty wacky stories from the thousands of girls wanting to get to know him or simply to get his pants off.

But she, along with the thousands of haters on social media, had reason to doubt him. If Kaitlyn was being honest with herself, she'd privately wondered if he'd made the story up to get attention for his environmental cause, or simply to rebel against his parents' business. If it was all a hoax, she might feel differently about him, no matter how cute and charming he might have been. She wanted to believe a cosmic force had brought them together. Then again, as her mother always warned her: If someone seems too good to be true, that's usually the case.

Most suspicious was his hazy memory, which could be an easy excuse to avoid providing a lot of details about his abduction. But it was also consistent with multiple accounts she'd read about close encounters of the fifth kind, when humans made direct contact with aliens. Upon their return, it was common for these subjects to feel as if they'd awakened from a dream in which they could remember only bits and pieces. Oftentimes, their memories resurfaced after several weeks or even months. Their subconscious would bring their experiences to light during REM sleep or hypnotherapy.

If Zachary *were* to remember, it would have to come naturally, of his own accord. She couldn't pressure him, or it would only repress him even more while driving him away from her. Through patience and kindness, she hoped to nurture him into recalling his experience. With any luck, he might know something to help connect her to her father. And if not, it might at least help Zachary come to terms with his own supernatural occurrence.

With the window half down, she drew in a deep breath of autumn air, her lungs filled with the cold, painful splendor of ever-changing seasons. Strange how, just days after her father departed the Earth, Zachary had entered her life. If he were here right now, she would rest her head on his shoulder and feel the warmth of his arm across her shoulders. Right now, the 1,762 miles between them felt as far away as her father, wherever he was in that starry expanse of the universe.

Zachary woke up in the middle of the night, thinking he should come clean with the truth right now. The longer he waited, the more difficult it would become, and the greater the consequences. He was fooling himself to think otherwise. Grabbing his phone from the bedside stand, he began texting Kaitlyn: *I was never abducted by a UFO, but I could still be a good friend and don't want to lie to you.* He was about to hit send when he saw it was 2:40—or rather 4:40 a.m. in Kaitlyn time (he'd already named a time zone after her). Afraid it might wake her up if she had her phone on, he decided against sending it, and hit delete.

Lying awake in the dark, he wondered why, in the first place, he ever said he'd been abducted by a UFO. While he believed in life on other planets, he was never obsessed with the topic. The only time he gave the subject any thought was during the occasional news piece or advertisements for that stupid alien horror movie which he had no desire to see: *ETI (Extraterrestrial Invasion)*. The images might have lingered in his mind without his even realizing it, and may have been the reason he blurted out what he did in the school principal's office.

Whatever his motivation, his deceit had brought Kaitlyn into his life, and the truth was, he shouldn't regret that. After several minutes of thinking and rethinking ways to justify his situation, he finally drifted into sleep, the lights outside his window flashing green, red, yellow, and blue. *Must be the sensors on the new security fence* was his final conscious thought.

He then dreamt of a flying saucer passing over his house, its pulsating colors transmitting a message he would not remember when he woke up the next morning. But it was planted in his mind, a seed of thought to nurture and grow.

All it needed was a little TLC from a girl in Iowa.

013

The following morning, Zachary was summoned to the school principal's
office, where he anxiously waited for Mr. Klausen to call him in. Having
no idea what he was in trouble for, he could foresee himself being caught on
CCTV, spending the day by the river with his novel when he claimed to have
been abducted by a UFO. He could already see Mr. Klausen holding a press
conference to apologize for his student's behavior and how it didn't reflect
on the rest of the proud student body of the Lemley High School Lions.

Expelled from school, Zachary would return home to face his parents,
their business would verge onto bankruptcy, and the Justice Department would
investigate his family's business for fraudulent practices designed to deceive
the public. Adding insult to injury, Hailey would post about it on Instagram,
telling thousands of followers that her brother's mental illness had caused
much suffering in her family, but if she could forgive him, so should they,
while everyone should pray he received the right treatment.

His knees shaking, Zachary figured he should confess to Kaitlyn before
she saw it in the news. Taking his phone out, he sent her a text:

Hey, I have something to tell you.

He waited for a response, but she was probably in the middle of class.

"Mr. Taylor," said Mr. Klausen, suddenly materializing in an all-black suit
that made him look like a vampire mortician. "Come with me."

Putting the phone away, Zachary nervously followed him into his back-
office chambers. The door closed behind them with a heavy thud, and they sat
down in chairs facing each other on opposite sides of his desk.

"As you may likely know, your sister has resigned as senior class president," said Mr. Klausen, "so I want you to run in her place."

Zachary was stunned. It was the last thing he expected to hear. "But sir," he said, his mouth still dry from nerves, "I'm the least popular person in this school. Well, I was, before the—you know. But what I'm saying is, I'm not a politician."

"Which is why I think you'd make a good senior class president," said Mr. Klausen.

"But I generally resent power and authority. No offense, sir," said Zachary.

"None taken," said the principal, his pointy eyebrows raised in amusement. "In fact, it's all the more reason to run."

"I don't understand, sir," said Zachary, confused.

"Did you see *Game of Thrones*?" asked Mr. Klausen, referring to the HBO series which everyone at the school had watched, including even Zachary, before it finally ended its run. The airing of the final episode seemed like eons ago.

"I was rooting for the dwarf," Zachary said, referring to the character played by Peter Dinklage in the seven-kingdom battle that pitted families and family members against one another for the rule of the Iron Throne.

"And why was that?" asked Mr. Klausen.

"Because the rest of his royal family looked down on him, both literally and figuratively. Plus, he had a good heart, and I guess I just generally root for the underdog."

Mr. Klausen gave him a thoughtful nod. "But after the war finally ended, who did the court finally decide on as their ultimate ruler?"

Zachary had already forgotten the character's name. "The blind kid who could foresee the future through visions."

"Bran Stark," said Mr. Klausen. "But did he even want the Iron Throne?"

"No," said Zachary, "which is why they picked him."

"Exactly," said Mr. Klausen. "Because people who want power often abuse it."

"Then why did you become a school principal?" said Zachary, immediately regretting his question.

"I never wanted to," said Mr. Klausen. "I only wanted to teach, but years ago, the principal put me in the same chair where you sit now, asking me to be his replacement after he retired."

Zachary had never felt so honored. "But sir, I don't think I deserve it. I mean, I was only half-joking that day when I told you—"

"As you already mentioned," Mr. Klausen interrupted. "The boy with vision took the throne. It's what the seven kingdoms needed more than anything else."

"But I'm not telepathic," said Zachary.

"You have a vision for renewable energy, and that's exactly what I've been trying to get for this school for the past two decades," said Mr. Klausen. "But the school board doesn't want to hear from an old fart like me. Young people like you have to make some noise. And you've already become their spokesperson."

Zachary felt his chair becoming the big iron throne he'd never asked for. "But even if I run, nobody's going to vote for me. They all think I'm a weirdo-path."

"The girls think you're cute," said Mr. Klausen, "and a lot of boys are secretly envious of your recent fame."

Zachary shrugged, a little embarrassed. "Maybe so, but that's not enough to beat Camila," who'd recently announced her candidacy. "She's super popular, and has already promised to get Nine Feet Tall to play here at the spring prom." They were an indie rock band but sounded more like hip-hop to Zachary.

"Nine Feet Tall just posted their world tour calendar," said Mr. Klausen. "They'll be in New Zealand at that time. You can point that out in your speech this Friday." A school assembly was planned for that day, with voting to take place immediately afterward.

"That's still not enough to beat her," said Zachary.

"You're probably right," said Mr. Klausen. "But you *could* promise them a vaping lounge."

"But you would never allow that," said Zachary.

"Of course not," said Mr. Klausen. "Nor would Washington State law. But sometimes you have to lure the sheep to a better path, even if they don't know what they're truly after."

"If the end justifies the means," said Zachary uncertainly.

"Yes," said Mr. Klausen. "But it's your campaign, so you decide."

Zachary considered how he'd already lied to the media and public to turn his parents' business electric, so what was the difference now if it helped the movement?

"Okay," he said, "let's hear your plan."

"Come on!" said Jenna, resplendent in gym shorts and an East Plains High sweatshirt emblazoned with its buffalo mascot. "We're going to be late!"

Standing in front of her PE locker, Kaitlyn was quickly texting Zachary back after just seeing his message. *What's that?* she wrote in response to his having something to tell her.

"Okay," she said, putting her phone in her locker and banging it shut. They headed out into the hallway that led to the gym, when a group of wrestlers came toward them. A few feet behind the pack, Garrett was wearing a glum expression, which seemed to worsen at the sight of Kaitlyn.

"Hey, Garrett," she said with an awkward smile.

"Hey, Kaitlyn," he said in a hollow voice, giving a nod to her friend. "Hey, Jenna."

"Hey, Garrett!" she replied, sounding a little too happy to see him. As they continued towards the gym, she excitedly whispered, "Did you hear what happened to him?"

"No," said Kaitlyn.

"He lost to a freshman yesterday," said Jenna.

"Official meets haven't even started yet," said Kaitlyn, well aware that wrestling season actually started in winter. The sport was very popular in their state. In fact, the University of Iowa had won several national championships.

"They started 'unofficial' scrimmages after school," said Jenna, "to get a jump on the season."

"Oh, well, it's not like he lost in an actual meet," said Kaitlyn.

"Doesn't matter," said Jenna, "He gave up on the mat. That's what has people talking." She looked at Kaitlyn as if she were to blame.

"Well, don't look at me!" she said.

"I think you broke his heart," said Jenna.

Kaitlyn felt bad for him but still had to say, "So I'm supposed to go out with someone just to support our wrestling team?"

"I never said that," said Jenna.

"You sort of just did," said Kaitlyn.

"I'm just saying, you might reconsider," said Jenna, "especially when every other girl in the school would love to be in your gym shoes right now."

"Yeah, lucky me," said Kaitlyn, wearing shorts and a sweatshirt that matched her friend's. "I get to break the heart of a really sweet guy, then I'm given a bonus for ruining his wrestling scholarship chances."

"Oh my God," said Jenna, "you sound like the victim now."

"If this is about winning and losing," said Kaitlyn, "he needs to use that broken heart as motivation."

"How's that?" said Jenna, as they hurried into the gym to join the rest of their class, already lined up for roll call.

"Depression is inverted anger," said Kaitlyn. "So he needs to let that anger surface when he's competing."

"You sound like my mom's therapist," said Jenna.

"Dr. Spalding once told me that," said Kaitlyn. Their teacher, Miss Prisbo, was calling out names. "Adams!"

"Here!"

"Baker!"

"Here!

"Beasley!"

"Here!" said Jenna, falling into line. "We'll talk about this later," she whispered to Kaitlyn.

"That's okay," she whispered back. "We really don't need to."

Jenna saw her expression and knew she meant it.

Zachary finally left the principal's office after a lengthy discussion about his plans to run for senior class president and what he could do if elected. Checking his phone, he saw that Kaitlyn had responded to his text message, asking: *What's that?*

I'm running for senior class president, he texted back. He'd decided against a confession after all. If he could show her the good things he was doing, maybe that would be enough to prove he was a decent guy. *To turn our campus solar*, he added, with a smiley face. The phone vibrated in his hand:

Kaitlyn: Wow, that's great! I hope you win!

Zachary: Thanks. But I feel bad for my sister.

Kaitlyn: Why's that???

Zachary: She stepped down as class prez bc of me.

Kaitlyn: How is that your fault?

Zachary: My UFO story embarrasses her.

Kaitlyn: She should be proud you're promoting clean energy.

Zachary: We live in a former coal mining town. So hard to convince people. I hope it's not too late already...

Kaitlyn: I hear you. With so much climate change, I'm afraid of having kids someday. ☹

Zachary: Sad but true ☹ Doesn't seem fair to bring them into this world.

Kaitlyn: But I'd like to have a family someday.

Zachary: Me too. If only we could see the future, right?

Kaitlyn: Or talk to our future selves for advice...

Zachary: Future selves?

Kaitlyn: What people call aliens might actually be our future selves after years of evolution. They travel thru time to visit us.

Zachary: Like archaeologists today studying ancient Egyptian ruins?

Kaitlyn: May sound crazy, but it's a theory of other scientists.

Zachary: Wow. Mind blowing.

Kaitlyn: Makes sense, though. Our eyes and heads grow bigger, our bodies smaller. Like the ones you described on the spaceship.

Zachary: Hmm, could be they're just coming here for cheap amusement. To watch us kill each other like dinosaurs in Jurassic Park.

Kaitlyn: I sure hope not!

Zachary: Sorry, didn't mean to be so grim.

Kaitlyn: It's okay. If we lived in that future, I'd be a time travel agent.

Zachary: Wow. Now that would be a cool job!

Kaitlyn: You'd have to really know your history. Knowing where to send people.

Zachary: True. Where would you go first?

Kaitlyn: Back to the 1700s to visit the Native Americans on the plains. My great grandma was Dakota Sioux, but I know little of her culture.

Zachary: Too bad. But that explains your beautiful black hair.

Kaitlyn: Thanks ;) Where would your first trip be?

Zachary: Ancient Rome. Or third grade to get even with a bully.

Kaitlyn: Lol. Rome first. Take a gladiator with you back to third grade.

Zachary: Haha! That would scare him.

Kaitlyn: Probably against school regulations.

Zachary: The sword for sure. Talk later? I'm heading to class.

Kaitlyn: Sounds good. My friend is waiting to eat lunch.

Zachary: Ok. Bye, beautiful.

Kaitlyn: Bye, handsome.

Zachary: ☺

Kaitlyn: ☺

On his way down the hall, Zachary nearly bumped into a crowd of students while reading her texts again. He truly felt high, only this was a natural rush of endorphins. Everything was starting out perfectly, so why ruin it? Whether or not a UFO had abducted him, he'd been lifted by some invisible force to feel what he was feeling now. If that wasn't a supernatural occurrence, then what else could explain it?

In a noisy hallway crammed with students, Jenna waited for Kaitlyn by her locker. "I can't do lunch in your truck again," she said with a little sniffle. "I think I'm catching a cold."

"I'm sorry," said Kaitlyn, spinning the combo on her locker to retrieve her sweater. "It's supposed to get warmer again this weekend."

"Speaking of," said Jenna, "would you like to help us out this Saturday?" She'd recently begun to lead a troupe of Blossoms, a boys-and-girls organization with lots of attractive college guys as fellow counselors. "We're going to Barton's Pumpkin Orchard, just like we did as kids. And there's a counselor I want you to meet. Math major at ICCC. You guys would totally hit it off, I think."

"If I don't have to work," said Kaitlyn. Earlier that day, Daisy had left her a voicemail, letting her know that a dishwasher hadn't shown up, and there could be some hours available this weekend. "Plus, the game's on in the morning."

"Okay," said Jenna, looking disappointed. "Maybe we can go on a double-date sometime. His best friend was asking about me, and—" She had to sneeze.

"Damn it, I *am* catching a cold."

"You should probably rest this weekend," said Kaitlyn, putting on her sweater in the chilly hallway.

"I'll be fine," said Jenna, blowing her nose with a crumpled Subway napkin taken from her purse. "But I really want you to meet Craig, the counselor."

"Craig, the counselor—has a real ring to it," said Kaitlyn, who had zero interest in meeting him. Closing her locker, she started down the hallway with her friend.

"Are you being sarcastic?" said Jenna, sounding congested.

"Blind dating has never been my thing," said Kaitlyn. "You know that." On her phone, she was searching through photos to send to Zachary.

"Who are you sending pics to anyway?" asked Jenna.

"Oh, just some guy I'm chatting with," said Kaitlyn.

"Does he go here?" said Jenna, watching her in curiosity.

"No, he lives a ways away," said Kaitlyn, still not ready to tell her about Zachary or how they'd connected.

"Where's he from?" said Jenna. "How'd you meet him?"

"We just started talking," said Kaitlyn, still flipping through photos. "If I tell you too much now, I'm afraid I'll jinx it."

"Now I really want to know," said Jenna.

"If I tell you now, it will spoil the surprise," said Kaitlyn, glancing up with a smile.

Jenna frowned and blew her nose. "You're acting really strange," she said in a stuffy voice.

Kaitlyn found a photo showing her in a green top that matched her eyes. Taken just before her father's diagnosis, it made her appear carefree and innocent. Hitting send, she hoped he liked it, and that he would think of her as much as she was thinking of him. "Come on," she said, leading her friend toward the cafeteria. "Let's get you some hot soup."

Zachary did not see her photo until the end of second period, after he turned on his phone to check his messages. Set against her long black hair, her sparkling green eyes came vividly to life, and she was even more beautiful than he'd originally thought possible. He felt an ache in his chest.

Arriving at his locker, he finally glanced up from his phone. Traces of graffiti remained, though the custodian had done his best to remove it all. The paint was scrubbed down to shiny bare metal in places.

"She's pretty," said Camila, standing at her locker a few feet away.

Zachary looked her way in surprise. "Thanks," he said, lowering his phone from view. "I mean, yeah, she is."

"I hear you're running for class prez," said Camila, a little bitterly.

"Yeah," said Zachary, opening his locker to grab a notebook. "Looks like it's just you and me."

"There is no you and me," she said with a hostile stare. "You had your chance, Martian Boy, and now I'm going to destroy you." Slamming her locker, she headed off to greet a large gathering of friends, many of them wearing little campaign stickers: "Camila for Prez."

As Zachary watched her, he didn't believe he had the slightest chance of beating her, but he was all the more inspired to try his hardest.

014

It was Thursday night, and Kaitlyn was getting ready for her first FaceTime date with Zachary. At least it felt like a date as she put on some light makeup and combed her hair in the mirror. She'd chosen a black top that was casual, dressy, and revealed just the right amount of cleavage. Applying some lipstick, she pouted her lips and dabbed them with a Kleenex.

"Going out tonight?" said her mother, appearing without warning in the bathroom doorway.

"Geez, Mom, ever hear of knocking?"

"You're the one who left the door open," said her mother, hanging up a freshly laundered hand towel and placing some folded washrags near the sink. "You're beautiful, by the way."

Screwing the lipstick closed, Kaitlyn smiled at her mother in the mirror. "Thanks, Mom. So are you."

"Well, thanks," said her mother, returning her smile. "Be careful on the roads tonight. It might rain."

"I'm not going out," said Kaitlyn, brushing her hair from nervous energy more than anything else. She had ten more minutes before their scheduled call. "We're going to FaceTime."

"That boy who lives far away?"

"Yeah," said Kaitlyn. Just an hour ago, Zachary had given her his new number. He'd changed it to avoid the endless texts and calls from girls across the country. If he was telling the truth, he'd given it only to his parents and to Kaitlyn, not even trusting his sister after she'd posted his digits on Instagram.

"Can you at least tell me his name?" asked her mother.

"Zachary," said Kaitlyn. "He's very smart and funny and super cute."

"And hopefully trustworthy," said her mother.

"Hopefully," said Kaitlyn, deciding on a pair of studded earrings, which she clasped on.

"Guess I should be relieved by all this technology," said her mother. "Keeps you safe indoors."

"Yeah," said Kaitlyn, knowing she was really talking about her getting pregnant. "I'll be safe, all right."

"Have fun," said her mother, closing the door behind her a little awkwardly.

Left alone, Kaitlyn faced herself in the mirror. She felt ready.

"You'll miss having that hair someday," his father often reminded him, but right now, Zachary hated his floppy mess, which had a stubborn personality of its own. He'd changed into a blue Oxford shirt, which, he hoped, didn't make him look too conservative. He just wanted to show he was making an effort to dress up for her. In Iowa, they were probably more old-fashioned, so he figured to play it safe in their first face-to-face call. It felt like a first date, and his stomach was full of butterflies.

Checking the time on his phone, he was already a minute late. Quick to find the FaceTime app, he made the call and anxiously waited a few rings. After each one, his heart beat a little faster until Kaitlyn appeared on his screen. She was so beautiful, he stared at her, seemingly in a daze. Her raven hair flowed past her bare shoulders. She wore a sexy black top, which exposed a hint of cleavage, and her mouth seemed lusciously full.

"Is your sound on, Zach?" she asked, her Midwest accent bringing her to life just inches away.

"Oh, yeah, hi!" he said, seeing his own nervous expression, which he tried to correct. "You look really nice, by the way."

"Thanks," she said, glowing with happiness. "So do you."

Alone in his room, Zachary was glad she couldn't see his lower-half or he'd be quite embarrassed. His teenage erection was far more stubborn than his floppy hair.

"Zachary, did you mute your sound again?"

"Yeah," he said, "I mean no. Yes, I'm here."

She gave him an amused smile. "So, what've you been up to?"

"Oh, I've been working on my campaign speech for tomorrow."

"How's that coming?"

"Uh, not so well. I mean, I know everything I want to say, but I'm not sure how to get started without sounding cheesy."

"Do you want to read me what you have so far?" she said, peering at him on the screen with eyes so brilliant and entrancing.

"How 'bout later? After it doesn't sound so lame."

"No problem," she said. "Whenever you're ready."

"Thanks," said Zachary, his anxiety settling down. "So, what's it like in Iowa? Do you live on a farm?"

"No," she said with a growing smile. "But I live in the country, with lots of farmers for neighbors. Mostly corn and soybeans, but also livestock."

"I've always wanted a pet pig," said Zachary. "But my parents said no."

"They're actually smarter than dogs," said Kaitlyn, "but I don't think I'd want one as a house pet."

"We can't have a dog either," said Zachary. "Or a cat. My sister's allergic to animals—unless she's eating them, that is."

"So, it's probably best you can't have a pig," teased Kaitlyn, "or it might end up in a ham sandwich."

"She does love my dad's pork ribs," said Zachary, the two of them chuckling. "How 'bout you? Any pets?"

"We had a dog," said Kaitlyn, her expression sobering. "A golden retriever named Checkers. We had to give him to my aunt in Nebraska after my dad started chemo."

"Why's that?" asked Zachary, thinking pets were therapeutic.

"He was used to my dad taking him out in the mornings. So, when my dad got sick, Checkers kept trying to get him out of bed and left scratches on his arms, which got badly infected because the chemo weakened his immune system."

"That's really too bad. I'm sorry to hear that."

"My life sounds like a country music song, so I hope I'm not depressing you."

"Not at all," he assured her. "But now that your father is gone," he started to ask. "Sorry, I didn't mean to—"

"It's okay," she said. "My mom and I talked about bringing Checkers back home, but he was really my dad's dog, and we don't know if he'd adjust to my dad not being here. Plus, by now, he's gotten used to my aunt and her family. They've sent us videos, and he looks really happy."

"That's good to hear," he said, trying to sound upbeat.

Kaitlyn nodded, but she seemed troubled by something. "I haven't told this to anyone," she said, "but a part of me is relieved."

"That your dog has a new home?"

"Well, that too," she said, her face filled with grief. "But really that my father finally died after suffering for so long. It was so hard to watch, especially what those final weeks did to someone I loved so much—" Clearing a lump in her throat, she continued, "I don't know why I just told you that. I didn't even share that with this stupid therapist my mom made me go see."

"It's okay," he said, wanting to reach through the phone to comfort her. "I'm glad you told me, and there's reason to be sorry."

"It sounds so horrible," she said, "but it was also taking a major toll on my mom. She was so exhausted, fighting a losing battle while praying for a miracle that wasn't coming."

"How's she doing now?"

"She lost a lot of weight, but is starting to eat again."

"That's a good sign."

"Yeah, but she was also drinking too much, though I think she stopped after a nasty workday hangover."

"That could do it, I guess," said Zachary.

"Do you drink much?" she asked, looking somewhat concerned.

"Not really. I'm not exactly hanging out with the party crowd."

"Have you ever been drunk?"

"Yeah, junior year, when my parents were out of town, my sister threw a pool party at our house. I drank too much of this punch they made. It was super tasty, and I got totally turn't out."

"Did you throw up?"

"Yeah, I puked in my dad's barbecue grill. Since then, I've only been buzzed a few times with this neighbor kid I used to play video games with. We'd steal his dad's beer from the basement cooler. Half the excitement was trying not to get caught."

Kaitlyn smiled, her face close on the screen. "That's what my dad always said. That making it illegal only made people our age want it even more."

"Unlike Europe, where kids younger than us have wine or beer with dinner."

"Exactly. We're the only western country since the Industrial Revolution to have Prohibition."

"So, do you drink with your parents?" asked Zachary, immediately catching his error. "Your mom, I mean?"

"Not really," said Kaitlyn. "When she was out of the house, my dad would give me a beer if we were watching a game together or out fishing, just the two of us."

"You go fishing?" said Zachary, liking the thought of her tomboy side.

"Well, I did," said Kaitlyn, "but only with my dad. We'd go camping at the state park. What about you?"

"I've gone salmon fishing," said Zachary. "But it's being out on the water that I really love, especially Puget Sound in the summer. It has views of the mountains all around."

"I bet it's beautiful. I've always wanted to see the Pacific Northwest."

"Well, I'd be happy to take you fishing here sometime."

Kaitlyn smiled, her eyes shining with adventure. "Summer's a ways away, but you never know…"

"Yeah," said Zachary, assuming she meant they could be in a relationship by then. "Sounds good."

"Do you have a lot of magic mushrooms up there? With all the rain?"

"Uh, yeah," he said in surprise. "Did you want me to get you some?"

"No," she said, laughing. "I'm just curious if you've ever done them."

"No, I'm afraid of getting a bad shroom and dying."

"After seeing your UFO story, my friend thought you were on shrooms."

"The curly blonde in your Instagram videos?"

"Jenna. She's really nice but kind of rigid in her thinking."

"Well, maybe we can get her some shrooms. I hear they really open the mind."

Kaitlyn laughed, her face radiating a joyful beauty. "She won't even try mushrooms on her pizza, so I highly doubt it."

"Maybe a pot brownie," he suggested. "It's legal here, you know."

"I know," she said with a playful smile. "That was my next question."

"Well, I haven't done any brownies," said Zachary. "But I might've tried a cookie."

"What kind of cookie?"

"Chocolate chip."

"With cannabis?"

"Yeah," he admitted.

She looked at him in surprise. "You can just walk into a store there and buy a chocolate chip cookie that gets you high? And I'm not talking sugar high."

"Yeah, if you're twenty-one or over," said Zachary. "It's no different than buying beer. My friend got them for us."

"Lemme guess," she teased. "That same friend you stole beers with?"

"Dylan Browning was his name. He moved to Seattle after his dad got a job at Boeing."

"And they took the beer cooler with them?" she said with a grin.

"And all the beer," he said in feigned sadness.

"Pity," she joked. "So, you're eating cookies now instead?"

"Just that one time," said Zachary. "It made me so super paranoid, I thought my parents were conspiring to send me off to military school, which I later found out was partly true. My father was in the Air Force."

"So, you weren't on drugs when taken by the UFO?" she asked, closely watching his reaction.

Zachary nervously shifted in his seat, hoping to dodge the subject by telling a kernel of the truth. "No, I swear I haven't eaten any cookies since, except the Girl Scout kind. Scout's honor," he said, raising his hand in an oath to not using drugs.

"Sorry," said Kaitlyn, her face relaxing. "I didn't mean to sound like I was interrogating you."

"You were," Zachary half-jokingly said, "but that's okay."

She conceded with a smile. "Your turn," she said. "Ask me anything."

He considered asking how many guys she'd been with, but thought better of it. "Have you ever been in love?"

She flinched a little before responding, "I thought I was once or twice, but really they were just heavy crushes."

"How do you think you know when you really are?"

She smiled, her eyes filled with mystery. "I think it's like magic," she said. "You can't explain it, but we just know it's happening."

Zachary liked the way she said "we" even if it was the plural form of "one." "Couldn't have said it any better myself," he responded.

Later in the evening, Kaitlyn was still on the phone with Zachary, her shoes kicked off as she reclined on her bed. "No way," she said, laughing at his theory that Adam and Eve were really tree monkeys who began human evolution.

"Think about it," he said. "They had everything they needed, swinging naked, free, and without shame until that one little ape decided it wasn't enough to feed off the bananas that nature blessed them with. So, he followed his temptation to try the forbidden fruit on the ground, even if it meant leaving the tree's safety, and led the other monkeys into danger. It's really the fundamental basis of capitalism—taking risks for individual gains, with little regard for the collective whole."

"Interesting," said Kaitlyn, their eyes locked together through digital technology. "But why do you think a 'he' was the first to come down? If you believe in the Scriptures, it was Eve who tempted Adam with the apple."

"You're right," he said with a smile. "I was trying to avoid being the typical misogynist and blaming the female."

"Thanks," said Kaitlyn, returning his smile. "But it's still very Marxist, isn't it?"

"True," said Zachary, "but even Darwin would have to agree—it's survival of the fittest that advances our species. Had we stayed in the trees, we wouldn't be having this conversation, would we?"

"But don't forget," said Kaitlyn, "Adam and Eve were seeking knowledge more than food. In fact, their first sin was eating from the tree of knowledge."

"Which supports Darwin's theory that we evolved through our wits."

"You do have a point," she agreed.

"I'm glad you're not offended, being a Christian and all."

"Not at all," said Kaitlyn. "The early Christians had some interesting theories of their own. Have you ever heard of the Gnostics?"

"No, tell me about them."

"Mysterious texts, which contain the gospels of Thomas and Phillip, were found in Egypt in the 1940s. They talk about the origins of the universe, and describe a race of creatures known as Archons, which were robot-like reptiles."

"Okay," said Zachary, "you're really freaking me out here, but now I'm curious…"

118

Kaitlyn chuckled. "I've been watching too many episodes of *Ancient Aliens*, but some scientists believe the Garden of Eden was really a laboratory run by alien reptiles to genetically alter us into modern man by forming a hybrid between our primate species and theirs."

"Now I'm definitely going to have nightmares," said Zachary. "But I think we found the missing link."

"It gets even deeper," she said with a grin. "A NASA scientist believes we're living in a computer simulation like *The Matrix*."

"Created by a super-intelligence," said Zachary, "and we're being observed as part of an alien experiment."

"You know about this?!" she said, unable to contain her excitement.

"Elon Musk agrees with that theory," said Zachary, "but he's pretty far out there on a lot of stuff."

"Should've known you followed Musk," she said, referring to the founder of Space-X and Tesla, "as much as you love electric cars."

Zachary nodded. "But let's say he's right. Then wouldn't God be the master computer programmer controlling our reality?"

"Wow," she said, looking at Zachary on her screen. "I can't believe I found someone to talk about this stuff with. The people at my school would think I'm crazy—even my best friend, Jenna."

Zachary's smile widened, his gorgeous brown eyes soaking her in. "Likewise. There's no one at school I can talk to like this."

"We shouldn't be surprised," said Kaitlyn. "After all, it was a UFO that brought us together—well, sort of."

"Yeah," said Zachary, "but since we're going to have nightmares anyway, I have a serious question for you."

"What's that?" she asked, her pulse rising in anticipation.

"Have you ever seen a tornado?"

Kaitlyn laughed, expecting something else entirely. "Yes, and they're horribly scary," she said. "We've had a few that came way too close to home. The sky turns black, and you can feel its charge of electrons in the air, like this dark force of nature coming to wipe you off the face of the Earth."

"And I thought earthquakes were terrifying," said Zachary. "But that's nothing compared to the Midwest—"

"Good night!" called Kaitlyn's mom through her bedroom door.

"Good night, Mom!" she called back. Peeking at the time on her phone, she saw it was past her mother's bedtime. "Holy cow," Kaitlyn said to Zachary. "It's after ten-thirty here."

Taken aback, Zachary said, "We've been talking for like three hours now, and it's felt more like fifteen minutes."

"I know," she said with a smile. "Well, I still have some homework to finish, and it's getting late here."

"And I'm starving," said Zachary. "So, I'm going to go eat some leftover dinner."

"Lemme guess," she said. "Something vegetarian."

He nodded with a smile. "My dad barbecued a vegan patty for me. You should see him at his grill. The man is possessed."

"The one you puked in?" Kaitlyn teased.

Zachary's cheeks flushed pink, making him so boyishly cute she wanted to squeeze him tightly. "I thoroughly cleaned it," he said, "not to mention it's self-cleaning. My father still has no idea, by the way."

She chuckled and said, "Well, now I know how to blackmail you."

"Perfect timing," he joked, "now that I'm running for class president."

She gave him a smile. "Good luck, Zachary, and lemme know if you need any help with your speech."

"Thanks," he said, looking at her as if he wanted to kiss her goodnight. "Okay, sweet dreams, Kaitlyn, or whatever you say in Iowa."

She laughed. She had an intense craving to devour his lips. "Sweet dreams," she said, "or whatever you say in the Pacific Northwest."

"Good night."

"Good night."

After finally ending the call, she struggled to finish writing a book report for her English class. She'd chosen Lauren Groff's *Fates and Furies*, a moving novel about marriage in today's world. While Kaitlyn enjoyed the story, she was also turned off by the fast-paced life of New York City, and hoped it wasn't the type of marriage she would someday experience. She wanted a simple life at home, with a husband who supported her crazy scientific theories and the need to explore them.

So far, Zachary fit that ideal perfectly, a boy with whom she could talk about anything. At two-thousand words, she had reached the required word count and could finish in tomorrow's study hall session with Mr. Fogerty. He was the perfect teacher to critique and proofread her essay, though she hated to interrupt a budding novelist at work.

Closing her notebook computer, she kept thinking of her FaceTime call with Zachary. For a moment there, she'd thought he was going to ask how many guys she had slept with and wondered whether or not she would tell him the truth. She had actually slept with none, but she wasn't a virgin. She'd lost her innocence at science camp the summer before junior year. The boy was Lance Donaldson from Topeka, Kansas. Shy and sweet, he didn't seem to know how good-looking he was.

Assigned to be partners, they chose to build a rocket for their science project. Until it was ready to be test-fired, they spent their days in conversation and laughter. Out in the fields on a sweltering August day, they failed to get the rocket off the ground, but did manage to find themselves in the grass with their clothes coming off, their sweaty bodies tangled together in the throes of teenage passion.

It all happened so fast that she didn't have time to decide if she might later regret it. Lance was super sweet to her afterward, walking her back to camp hand in hand until they came into view of the counselors in charge.

On their last night together, they snuck out after midnight to make love beneath the stars. This time, he was prepared with a condom and lasted much longer. Though she knew she wasn't in love, she felt there was nothing wrong with what she'd done. It felt like a summer adventure, to finally experience her body as part of nature with a sweet, handsome boy.

The next morning, they exchanged phone numbers, but after returning to their homes in different states, they discovered they had little to text each other about.

As school began her junior year, she was late on her period by a day or two. By day three, she began to panic, praying desperately not to be pregnant while knowing it was too late to ask for help from above. When she finally began her cycle on day four, she thanked the heavens above, vowing to never again have unprotected sex, especially with someone who wasn't even her boyfriend.

Later that day, her parents said they needed to have a "sit down" talk, meaning it was serious. At first, she was horrified that they had learned of her misadventure with Lance, only to discover her father had been diagnosed with a malignant brain tumor, and the cancer had already spread throughout his body. Kaitlyn immediately blamed herself—her loss of virginity was a sin, and her father's life was the punishment. It was the only explanation that made any sense at the time. Her father was a good man who didn't deserve his dreadful fate.

She later altered her thinking. Had she truly been pregnant, her father would have loved her no matter what. He would have been disappointed about her recklessness, not her failed morality. That said, he and her mother would have encouraged her to have the baby. Their Christian ideals led them to oppose abortion. Had she decided otherwise, they would've been horribly disappointed, but deep down, she knew they would still love and forgive her.

Since her scare with Lance, she'd kissed two boys but hadn't wanted to date anyone while her father was bedridden. But now, she wanted to enjoy her body with someone with whom she could fall in love. Zachary could definitely be that guy.

Restless because of hormones, she stripped off her clothes to lie naked on the bed. Eyes shut tight, she thought of Zachary and imagined they were his hands, not her own, caressing her neck, shoulders, and breasts. She imagined his finger tracing gently down her stomach until dipping into the wetness between her legs. She wondered if he was hard for her when they were talking. It turned her on even more to think of him doing the same thing right now, touching himself while thinking of touching her. The heat built between her legs until she buckled with orgasm, her soft cry of his name muffled in her pillow.

Catching her breath, she felt better after releasing so much pent-up tension. But as she lay there in her quiet house, she was suddenly overwhelmed with a horrible sense of emptiness. Clutching her warm blanket, she fantasized about Zachary holding her close, telling her she was beautiful and stroking her hair and shoulders. That's what she needed right now, but the silence around her was too much a reminder of her loneliness.

Out of bed, she got dressed and went downstairs to read or to watch TV. Unable to focus on either one, she put on her fuzzy pink slippers to head out to her dad's truck. At eleven-thirty, there would be a replay of Connor & Donnor's sports show. With the Michigan game just two days away, she hoped for a surprise guest appearance—her father on the airwaves to let her know she was going to make the right decisions in the near future.

015

Pacing the hallway, Zachary couldn't take his mind off Kaitlyn, even now, while waiting to go out on the gymnasium floor to give his campaign speech for senior class president. The entire student body had filled the bleachers to hear Camila finish her turn at the podium. "If you vote for me," she nearly shouted into the microphone, "I will use my influence to bring a top performer like Nine Feet Tall to this year's spring prom!"

Thunderous applause rocked the gymnasium. She never actually promised Nine Feet Tall, but a top performer *like* them, which could be any garage band, really. Zachary had to admire her politician's skill, or at least acknowledge it as truly disgusting.

"I'm Camila Corte, your next senior class president!" she concluded, waving to the crowd of cheering supporters.

As Zachary watched her, he still thought she was hot, but she lacked Kaitlyn's warmth and depth. "Okay, let's go do it," he told himself, marching out onto the gym floor to take the podium from his opponent.

"Good luck, Zachary," she said, wearing the arrogant smile of someone who knew she'd already won.

"Thanks," said Zachary. "But I believe in skill more than luck." He enjoyed watching her flinch as she returned to her seat in the bleachers. Adjusting the microphone stand, he looked over the packed audience and felt a sudden wave of nausea.

"LOSE-ERRR!" someone shouted. Then came hooting catcalls and jeering whistles.

"I'd just like to say," began Zachary, the microphone screeching over the amplified speakers, and drawing another round of shouted insults.

"MARTIAN BOY!"

"GO BACK TO PLANET STUPID!"

"THE MOTHER SHIP IS WAITING!"

"YOU SUCK!"

"WE WANT YOUR SISTER!"

"I ALREADY HAD HER!"

"YOU WISH!"

A wave of laughter, then a chant breaking out in a section of jocks: "LOSER TWIN! LOSER TWIN! LOSER TWIN!"

Zachary looked for Hailey in the stands. Unable to spot her, he began again, "You obviously know my sister, and—"

"YOU WERE THE AFTERBIRTH!"

"Well, it's true. I *was* born after Hailey," said Zachary, his voice projecting over the raucous laughter that followed. "And now I'd like to thank her for everything she's done for this school and hopefully carry the torch in her honor." He finally located her in the front row near the exit, as if ready to make a quick escape. She glared at him with a scathing intensity that far exceeded the norms of sibling rivalry. "As senior class president," he continued, "I would like to bring solar energy to our school, so we can stop our dependence on foreign oil, fossil fuels, and—"

"MY FAMILY WORKS FOR THE POWER COMPANY!" shouted an angry voice.

"MINE TOO! DON'T TAKE AWAY OUR FUTURE JOBS!"

"WE HAVE RENEWABLE ENERGY RIGHT HERE!"

A mob of students clapped and whistled.

"Yes," said Zachary. "The hydroelectric plant was a big stride forward from the coal mines that built this town, but soon those jobs will be replaced by robots, so let's work together to—"

"YOU'VE BEEN WATCHING TOO MANY SCI-FI MOVIES!"

A section of boys began singing the notes from the alien horror movie, followed by another chant: "MAR-TIAN BOY! MAR-TIAN BOY! MAR-TIAN BOY!" The noise was deafening.

Waiting for everybody to calm down, Zachary watched his sister darting out, her face hot with shame and anger. As she brushed past Mr. Klausen standing guard near the exit, Zachary gave his principal a helpless look. Mr. Klausen gave him the nod.

"Okay, listen up!" shouted Zachary into the mic, the amplifiers screeching so loudly that many covered their ears with painful grimaces. "With solar energy, we not only save money on electricity, but we get a return on our investment. With those funds, I'd like to build a vaping lounge!"

The crowd went quiet, several faces looking back at him in disbelief.

"NOW YOU'RE TALKING, MARTIAN BOY!" someone shouted, followed by a round of applause and whistles.

"Technically," said Zachary, watching Camila grow antsy in the first row, "you're supposed to be twenty-one to buy nicotine or cannabis products in Washington State, but I will apply for a permit, allowing for—"

He felt a sudden grab on the arm, the tight grip of Mr. Klausen pulling him away from the podium. "You're coming with me, Taylor!" he said, whisking Zachary toward the exit, as a stunned silence filled the gymnasium.

"But Mr. Klausen!" said Zachary, his voice gasping with terror. "You're the one who suggested—"

"I said no such thing!" the principal said through clenched teeth.

"You—you set me up!" pleaded Zachary. As he was dragged out of the gym like a prisoner, a thunderous chant broke out: "ZACH-AR-Y! ZACH-AR-Y!

ZACH-AR-Y!"

Zachary couldn't believe what he was hearing. His arms were covered in goosebumps.

Out in the hallway, the principal loosened his grip once they were alone and out of view. "Congratulations," he said, a big grin spreading over his face. "I think you'll win this election by a landslide."

Overwhelmed by the sudden turn of events, Zachary gathered himself and said, "Thanks, Mr. Klausen. I had no idea what you were up to."

"I would've warned you," said the principal, "but I didn't want it to look rehearsed. We can't have you working on the same side as authority."

"ZACH-AR-Y! ZACH-AR-Y! ZACH-AR-Y!"

Hearing the echoed chant of his name, Zachary broke into a smile. While he may not have been named after the twelfth president of the United States of America, Zachary Taylor was on his way to becoming the eighty-ninth senior class president of Walter S. Lemley High School.

"Earth to Kaitlyn!" said Jenna at the cafeteria table. Still recovering from her head cold, Jenna had refused to eat in the truck ever again, having threatened a future hunger strike despite her love of food. "Hel-looo! Did you hear what I said?"

"What's that?" said Kaitlyn, texting Zachary back after learning his speech had gone *really well,* meaning he'd probably slayed it but was staying modestly low-key.

"Not *what*," said Jenna, "but *who*? Who on Earth are you talking to so much?"

Kaitlyn finally looked up from her phone. She'd barely touched her mac and cheese. "You promise not to freak if I tell you?"

"I promise," said Jenna, "unless it's some guy on death row, wanting conjugal visits."

"Real funny," said Kaitlyn, "but they don't allow phones in prison. At least they don't in the movies."

"They snuck one in on *Stripes are in Fashion*," said Jenna, referring to a hit cable series about a supermodel going to prison. She'd driven her Mercedes into her husband's swimming pool while he and his mistress were enjoying their final skinny dip together.

"Must've missed that one," said Kaitlyn, reading Zachary's text message that his sister hated him more than ever, which he didn't think was possible. *Don't worry*, she texted back. *She will get over it. So proud of you!! Talk to you soon!*

"So, who is he?" Jenna pleaded. "Come on, this isn't fair, especially when I tell you everything!"

"Okay," said Kaitlyn, finally giving her friend her full attention after Zachary responded with a thumbs up and a winking smile. "Remember that guy who was abducted by the UFO?"

Jenna looked at her in astonishment. "No. Effing. Way."

"Way," said Kaitlyn, imitating her dad's old joke from his college days.

Jenna turned speechless—a rare occurrence for her. Normally, she even talked in her sleep, something Kaitlyn had witnessed during slumber parties when they were younger. "How did that happen?" she finally mustered.

"I found him on social media," said Kaitlyn. "And we started chatting."

Jenna shook her head in disbelief. "Please don't tell me this is why you turned down Garrett?"

"No," said Kaitlyn. "Well, maybe a little. He gave me the roses and sweet card, but I seriously wasn't interested in him in the first place."

"I don't get it," said Jenna, still shaking her head. "That UFO guy lives all the way across the country, and he's probably out of his mind from taking too many—"

"Shrooms," said Kaitlyn. "You said that once before, which is why I haven't told you. But he said he doesn't do drugs. And I believe him."

"Just like you believe he was abducted by aliens?" said Jenna. "Because he *said* so?"

"I can tell he's not yet that comfortable talking about the abduction," said Kaitlyn, "which I totally understand."

"Don't tell me," said Jenna. "You were abducted too?"

"No," said Kaitlyn, "but if I told you I saw a flying saucer over my house the night my father died, would you think *I* was crazy or doing shrooms?"

Jenna looked closely at her friend, making sure she wasn't just toying with her. "I'd say you were under a lot of stress and probably sleepwalking," she said matter-of-factly.

"You sound just like my mom," said Kaitlyn. "She made me promise not to tell anyone for this very reason."

"Well, I'm not just *anyone*," said Jenna. "I'm your best friend."

"Exactly," said Kaitlyn, "which is why I thought you might actually believe me."

"I don't think you're lying," said Jenna. "I just don't think you saw what you believe you saw."

"Of course not," said Kaitlyn. "If it's not from this little town, then you can't possibly see it happening, especially if it's from another dimension or galaxy."

"What's that supposed to mean?" said Jenna, taking offense.

"Nothing," said Kaitlyn, taking a bite of her now cold mac and cheese.

"Nothing, huh?" said Jenna. "You were basically calling me a hick from the sticks, as if you're somehow better than me."

"I never said I was better than anyone," said Kaitlyn.

"You didn't have to," said Jenna. "You think you're smarter than everyone else here 'cause you're so much better at science and math."

"Not at all," said Kaitlyn. "But I think you can be really closed-minded sometimes."

"Closed-minded how?" said Jenna. "'Cause I don't believe in Martians flying around in little saucers?"

"It's not just that," said Kaitlyn. "It's—forget I ever said it..."

"No," said Jenna. "Since you brought it up, I wanna know."

Seeing that her friend would never drop the subject, Kaitlyn sighed. "Fine," she said. "I think you have mapped out a very limited plan for your life. Not that there's anything wrong with that. But I think you're selling yourself short."

"And what's this plan of mine?" said Jenna, her eyes misting with anger.

"You know," said Kaitlyn. "Meet a nice local boy, get married, raise his kids, and never experience the world beyond our little town."

"Oh, and why do you think that?" said Jenna, her voice trembling a little.

Kaitlyn struggled to meet her fiery gaze. "'Cause you never talk about anything but boys, unless you're clowning on their girlfriends. I know you're smarter than that."

"You're right," said Jenna. "In fact, I just applied to several colleges, including the University of Chicago."

"Chicago?" said Kaitlyn. She had no idea her friend was even contemplating college, much less such a prestigious, out of state university.

"They have a great program in elementary education," said Jenna, a bit defiantly.

"When did you decide to become a teacher?" asked Kaitlyn, still trying to overcome her initial shock.

"After working with the kids in my Blossoms troupe," said Jenna.

"But why Chicago?" asked Kaitlyn, suddenly terrified of her friend going away. "There's gotta be something closer."

"In case you don't remember," said Jenna, "I went to visit my cousins there last spring break."

Kaitlyn tried to recall, but her mind went blank.

"Yeah, I didn't think so," said Jenna. "Explains why you didn't respond to my texts."

"Well, in case *you* don't remember," Kaitlyn said hotly, "I was tending to my father after his radiation treatments, so I didn't have time to party it up on a road trip."

Jenna's eyes were stung with tears. "I know you've been through a lot lately," she said, "but you've totally blocked me out for several months now. I miss my friend, and I can't believe you think so little of me, that I care only about finding a man and having his babies."

"I'm so sorry," said Kaitlyn, feeling horrible now. "I really am. And I'm glad you're applying to college, and I think you'll be a great teacher someday. I really do."

Jenna nodded, sniffling back her tears. "Well, I'm sorry, too, but I don't believe you're right about this UFO guy," she said. "Be careful with him."

"His name's Zachary," said Kaitlyn, "and you gotta admit, he's pretty darn cute."

"Yeah, I'll give him that," said Jenna, dabbing her eyes with a napkin. "But don't tell me you're not going to go out with anyone here now? I mean, it's senior year, and you can't waste it on some guy you can't even see in person."

"We're just chatting and getting to know one another," said Kaitlyn, a little defensively. "After we graduate, who knows?"

"What?" said Jenna, in a condescending tone. "You're going to go off to college in Oregon or wherever he is?"

"Washington State," said Kaitlyn. "But no, I couldn't be that far from my mom."

Jenna gave her a skeptical look. "You don't really think he's going to move all the way out *here,* do you?"

"It's too early to bring that up," said Kaitlyn. "But you never know. We have good colleges and universities here in Iowa."

"Don't count on it," said Jenna, still clearly upset with her. "And if anyone's obsessed with a boy, I'm looking at her."

Avoiding her friend's stare, Kaitlyn looked down at her mac and cheese and took the last few bites, which tasted as bitterly cold as the truth in her friend's words.

"It was closer than I expected," said Mr. Klausen, referring to the stack of ballots on his desk across from which Zachary sat. "But they've been counted and recounted, and you're the senior class president."

Zachary nodded, feeling an overwhelming combination of fear and elation that came with this sudden rise to power.

"I should be congratulating you," said Mr. Klausen, "but first I'm going to have to suspend you."

Zachary looked at him in surprise. "But if I'm class president, what kind of message does that send?"

"That I'm trying to stop your solar energy plan," said Mr. Klausen, "by punishing you for proposing the vaping lounge."

Zachary nodded, understanding the scheme. "So you can be the Boomer who doesn't care about our future planet and what happens to us, the younger generation."

Mr. Klausen gave him an impressed look. "You're a natural-born politician," he said, meaning it as a compliment.

"I hope not, sir," said Zachary, feeling a tinge of repulsion. "In fact, I'm not so sure about this whole suspension thing as a PR stunt."

"You'll return a hero," said Mr. Klausen, "and the students will rally 'round you when you lead a campus walk-off and picket the school district headquarters. That could draw enough media attention to force the school board to act, especially when you start raising questions about kickbacks and collusion between district officials and the power company, which has been suspect for years."

Zachary still felt doubtful, which must have been expressed on his face.

"If you're worried about the suspension," said Mr. Klausen, "it won't show on your record when you apply to colleges."

"It's not that," said Zachary. "I'm more worried about my soul and what's going to happen to it if I keep deceiving the public."

Mr. Klausen nodded sympathetically. "Which is how I knew you'd be the perfect person for this job." Standing up, he shouted at the top of his lungs, "Now get out of my office! I don't want to hear any more about your solar energy plan or how many tax dollars I'm stealing by charging my personal electronic devices on campus! How dare you? I'm suspending you for two weeks!"

Zachary cowered in his chair as his principal loomed over him like an enraged grizzly bear. "Why are you yelling?" he managed to ask.

Mr. Klausen dropped his voice down to a conspiratorial whisper. "So that Mrs. Wilmer tells her daughter, and by lunchtime today, every student in the school will know about it."

Feeling a bit numb, Zachary nodded. On his way out of the office suite, he passed Mrs. Wilmer. She was already frantically texting the latest news.

"Hey, Mrs. Wilmer," he said. "Guess I'll see you in a couple of weeks."

"Okay, Mr. Senior Class President," she said, looking up from her phone with a smile. "My daughter Layla voted for you and says to take good care of yourself."

"Thanks," he said, feeling little joy in becoming a politician.

016

After school, Kaitlyn parked her truck within view of her father's grave. Just beyond the cemetery grounds was Sacred Trinity Church, where Reverend Jacob lived with his wife in the rectory next door. Kaitlyn hadn't been to Sunday sermon since her father's funeral weeks ago. The radio was playing on low volume—she still had it tuned to 101.2 FM for Cyclones' sports coverage.

"We need to gamble with safety blitzes," said the host, whose co-host disagreed. "Not with the mobility of Collins at quarterback. All it'll do is give him a wide-open receiver."

"It's our best chance of putting some pressure on him," said the host.

"Maybe on third and long," said the co-host. "But it's still a gamble."

"Dad," said Kaitlyn, pleading to his gravestone, "I seriously can't take any more of this sports talk, so if there's something you need to say, I wish you'd do so now." She watched the autumn leaves scatter in a gentle breeze, their bright fronds rattling across the headstones of her father and grandparents before him. If the leaves on the trees did not die, they would not produce such a beautiful display of red, yellow, and orange. It made her think of the cycle of life, and how it pertained to her father's death.

Across the way, she saw Reverend Jacob stepping out of the rectory with his wife Faizah, a beautiful Ethiopian woman whose dark complexion contrasted sharply with his pale skin and fiery red hair. The reverend wasn't unattractive, but his wife, who resembled a supermodel, seemed like such a mismatch. When Kaitlyn was eight or nine-years-old, he'd left one summer for a missionary visit to Addis Ababa, returning a few weeks later as Faizah's husband. That raised immediate suspicions among the church gossips that she could only be using him to get a green card and would surely leave him once she did. The fact that she had an Arab name made some question her even more. Any true Christian woman would have changed it.

"I think we should be less judgmental and more supporting," Kaitlyn's mother had said at the time. Her father bet anyone five hundred dollars that the couple would remain together. The church do-gooders quickly reminded him that gambling was in fact a sin. By the time of the couple's fifth anniversary, the gossip shifted to why they weren't having children. Many blamed Faizah for being infertile, to which Kaitlyn's mother responded that it was a sin to pass judgment on others. Upping the ante, her father staked a thousand dollars on the couple's eventual conception.

Fortunately for him, nobody accepted his wager because the couple was still childless as they walked hand in hand across the grounds, their faces peacefully content. How different the reverend appeared in his jeans and Cyclones' sweatshirt as opposed to his Sunday black apparel with stiff white collar.

At a small storage shed, he and Faizah retrieved a pair of rakes and set to work on the leaves. As he turned in Kaitlyn's direction, he spotted her parked behind the distant trees. Immediately recognizing her father's Dodge Ram, he hesitated before leaning his rake against a tree and heading her way.

Kaitlyn didn't feel like talking to him but couldn't just drive away. Buzzing down her window, she waited for him to approach a few moments later.

"Kaitlyn," he said with a friendly smile. "I thought that was you."

"Hi, Reverend Jacob," she said, lowering the radio sports talk to half a bar.

"Michigan, this Saturday, huh?" Never one to miss a game, he used to talk football with her father after every Sunday sermon.

"Yeah," said Kaitlyn, gazing out at her father's tomb. "It's going to be weird watching the game without him..."

Reverend Jacob gave her a caring look. "Death is so much harder on the living, isn't it?"

Kaitlyn somberly agreed and offered a little nod. "I just found out today my best friend is going out of state for college. Despite knowing her most of my life, I took her for granted. I don't know what I'll do once she's gone."

"That's several months away, though, right?"

"Yeah, but still," said Kaitlyn. "I've been wrapped up in my own problems so much I haven't been there for her. Actually, I've often been annoyed by her constant neediness."

"That's not uncommon for those dealing with a terminal illness in their families," the reverend counseled. "So don't be too hard on yourself."

"She thinks I'm stupid for having this major crush on a guy out of state who I've never even met," said Kaitlyn, feeling a sudden need to pour her guts out to a fatherly figure. "She's probably right. I mean, we just met, and as crazy as it sounds, I feel like I'm falling in love."

"Doesn't sound crazy to me," said Reverend Jacob. "I married my wife three weeks after meeting her on another continent. If it's God's will, it will happen."

Kaitlyn wondered if her father would agree. "If the dead go on living, do you believe they can still communicate with us?"

"If you're asking, do I believe in ghosts," said the reverend, "I'd have to say I've seen a thing or two living next to a cemetery."

"Really?" said Kaitlyn in surprise, assuming that would have contradicted his preaching that our souls go straight to heaven, with angels leading the way.

"When loved ones visit their gravesites too often," said the reverend, "I think it keeps their spirits from leaving us completely."

"Have you witnessed this yourself?" asked Kaitlyn, who was highly curious to know.

Reverend Jacob gave a slight nod. "When I was seven years old, my younger sister died unexpectedly of the flu. She was only five. For years, I blamed myself for taking her out in the snow to play, which is how she got sick in the first place, or so I thought."

He gazed out into the distance, the memory still affecting him. "Afterwards," he continued, "I visited her grave almost every day on the way home from school, telling her I was sorry, and begging for her forgiveness. Then one day, around Christmas time, I heard a tinkling sound from the closet in her room. When I hurried to check, I saw it had come from the bells she'd tied to her shoelaces during the holidays."

"You think it was her?" said Kaitlyn, feeling a strange chill pass through her.

"There was nothing else that could explain it," said the reverend. "I looked for a mouse, or for a draft blowing through the closet, but the door was firmly closed, and there was nothing to shake the house or the bells. It was perfectly calm out."

"What do you think she was trying to tell you?" Kaitlyn asked eagerly.

The reverend peered out at the cemetery, where his wife was raking leaves into a large pile. "For many years, I thought she was letting me know she was okay so I could finally let her go to the other side in peace. But now I think it was me she was letting go of."

"What do you mean?" said Kaitlyn.

"I was so obsessively blaming myself for her death that I stopped living myself. If there was a ghost in the house, it was mine more than hers."

Kaitlyn thought it over, his words weighing heavily on her.

"You still have several months to be with your friend," said the reverend.

"Enjoy your days with her and your mom, and time will tell if this boy is right for you. In the meantime, pray for your father's spirit. If he wants to reach you, he will do so with the Good Lord's blessing, of course, but also when the time is right."

Given a lot to absorb, Kaitlyn exhaled the breath she'd been unconsciously holding. "Thanks, Reverend," she said, the radio quietly playing an ad for men's hair restoration.

The reverend gave her a smile. His own red hair was barely thinning, though he was in his early forties. "Anytime," he said, seeing his wife's pile of leaves growing taller. "Well, looks like I'd better get back to work before Faizah divorces me." Heading off, he reminded Kaitlyn, "Our doors are always open if you need to talk."

Kaitlyn nodded and watched him go before starting the ignition. This weekend, she would accompany Jenna to the pumpkin orchard, even if it meant missing the big game or losing some hours at Daisy's. Driving off, she heard the radio hosts returning to their banter. "Sorry, Dad," she said, "but if you want to reach me, it's at the end of the dial." She turned the station to 107.1 and cranked up the volume on Dua Lipa's new song about overcoming a broken heart.

WINTER

◻1▷

With winter just around the corner, Kaitlyn was stringing Christmas lights in the windows of Daisy's Diner. It's what she did during the slow hours between the end of lunch and the start of dinner. Because the dishwasher had quit in October, followed by a hostess and two waitresses, she'd steadily picked up hours after school and on the weekends. Staying busy with work and school, she was able to distract herself from the first holiday season without her father, though nothing could completely fill that massive void. Thankfully, she had Jenna and her mother close by, and she'd been chatting and texting with Zachary every day. Her phone was constantly blaring the notes of Katy Perry's "Smile." It was the message tone she'd assigned to the boy who put a grin on her face.

After framing one window with blinking festive colors, she continued to the next pane of glass with her string of lights. Seated at a nearby table, two middle-aged men in Iowa State baseball caps were talking quietly over their cheeseburgers. Their faces were familiar, and she suddenly remembered their names—Bob Paulson and Fred Simms. Best friends and farmers, they used to buy equipment from her father, whose funeral they'd attended to pay their respects. That day, they'd donned ill-fitting suits, which likely hadn't been worn since their double wedding two decades before.

"Kaitlyn Stokes," said Bob, wiping his ruggedly handsome face with a napkin. "I thought that was you."

Fred turned in his seat to say, "My, how quickly you grew up."

Kaitlyn smiled, standing up on a chair to reach above her. "I'll be graduating from high school this spring," she said, stringing lights along the top window ledge.

Fred shook his head in disbelief. "Seems like yesterday that your daddy brought you by to sell me a tractor. You couldn't've been more than five or six at the time."

"Can't say I remember that," said Kaitlyn, "but I do remember chasing your pigs around."

The men chuckled. "Your momma wasn't too happy," Fred recalled, "when you went home covered in mud and smelling like swine."

"How's she doing anyway?" asked Bob, having lost his wife to the flu virus a few years prior. "I know how hard it is this time of year."

Kaitlyn gave him a weary nod. "She's hanging in there, I guess, but you know…" she said, her words trailing off.

"Yeah," said Bob, his expression turning somber. "Your father was a good man."

"He sure loved his 'Clones," said Fred. The Cyclones team had gone undefeated since losing to Michigan in overtime weeks earlier.

"Sure did," said Bob. "He was a true fan, through and through."

Kaitlyn regretted that her father couldn't be here to watch their best season ever. "Looks like we're headed to the Sugar Bowl," she said, "and I'll be yelling at the TV for the both of us."

The men chuckled softly, a hint of sadness in their expressions. Reaching for a fry, Fred asked, "You thinkin' of going to school there like your parents?"

"I submitted my application," said Kaitlyn, stepping down from her chair to continue stringing lights along the bottom sill. "And now I'm waiting to hear back."

"Well, smart as you are," said Bob, "I'm sure you'll get in."

"I sure hope so," she said. Truth be told, she'd already been accepted, but she was still waiting to learn of her financial aid status after applying for several grants and loans.

"There'll be a ton of handsome young boys on campus," said Fred, giving her a playful wink.

"And you'll have your pick of the litter," said Bob, dunking his fry in ketchup but in no hurry to eat it.

Kaitlyn finally had the entire window strung with lights. "I might actually have a boyfriend there with me," she proudly announced. Just a few days before, Zachary had been accepted to the same university. "But he's coming from out of state and still needs to talk to his parents before committing."

"If his parents are smart," said Bob, "they'll be glad to see him with a girl like you."

"Thanks," said Kaitlyn, enjoying the attention from men her father's age. "Can I get you guys some dessert?"

"I'm already stuffed," said Bob.

"Me too," said Fred, patting his softening belly.

The door jingled behind her as someone entered the diner. "Okay," said Kaitlyn. "I'll be right back with your check." As she turned and headed for the door, she saw it was Jenna, her face red from the cold, yet smiling as brightly as her curly blonde hair. "S'up, girl?" she said.

"Hey!" said Kaitlyn, greeting her with a little hug. Since their blow-up in the cafeteria, she'd been trying much harder to be a good friend. "You here to eat or just say hi?"

"A little of both," said Jenna with a secretive little grin.

"Okay," said Kaitlyn, grabbing a menu. "I'll get you a table."

"Table for two," said Jenna, with a playful nod in the direction of the door.

As it jingled open, Garrett stepped in, wearing a blue knit sweater that matched his eyes. He'd grown his hair out, and he was far more handsome than Kaitlyn had ever remembered.

"Hey, Kaitlyn," he said with a shy, awkward smile.

Kaitlyn looked at the two of them together, and sized them up in disbelief. "You mean…?"

"Garrett asked me out a few weeks ago," Jenna blurted out. "I was going to tell you, but like you said before, I didn't want to jinx it."

"You were right," Garrett told Kaitlyn, putting his arm around Jenna. "She's a great girl, even though she turned me down freshman year."

"I was a silly frosh. Get over it," said Jenna, giving him a kiss.

Kaitlyn grabbed another menu, still fazed by the initial shock. "I'll seat you two lovebirds in the back," she said, leading them toward a corner table in the rear. To her own surprise, Kaitlyn felt a twinge of jealousy, even though she had suggested the match. As the couple took their seats, Kaitlyn realized Garrett had quickly recovered from her rejection of him, meaning that she wasn't so special after all.

While she should have been happy for them both, she couldn't help but feel envious. They were sitting squeezed together, holding hands, their faces inches apart. Meanwhile, the boy she thought she loved would be 1,763 miles away during the holidays.

Ever since his sister had compared him to Billy Carter, Zachary had been reading about his older brother, James Earl Carter, Jr. aka "Jimmy." Though Jimmy never had a beer named after him during his single term in the White

House, or after, he was the first US President to have solar panels installed on its West Wing roof. Nearly half a century later, Zachary was proud to walk in his footsteps. As senior class president of Lemley High School, he admired the solar panels on its rooftop.

Down the hallway, he passed the Solar Student Lounge, which had become so popular that nobody cared to remember his vaping lounge proposal. Gathered round, a mass of students enjoyed the free Wi-Fi—his sister's idea for which he'd credited her—and the cappuccino machine. Refills were free so long as students brought their own reusable cups. The costs were covered by the surplus of electricity sold back to the power company.

"Hey, Z!"

"Yo, Z!"

"S'up, Z!" That's how many students were greeting Zachary these days.

"Hey, everyone," he said, skirting by his crowd of admirers. Just two months after his election, he was still adapting to the spotlight of popularity, after living in his sister's shadow for so many years.

"Progressive rebel" was the term their school newspaper, *The Weekly Lion*, had coined for him following his return from suspension. It was then that he led a student walkout after the power had "mysteriously" gone out across campus. Left in the dark, he'd immediately suspected Mr. Klausen of pulling the breaker switch like the great Wizard of Oz maneuvering levers behind his curtain.

Seizing the moment, Zachary used the flashlight on his phone to lead a student march on school district headquarters. The mob chanted "Solar Power Now!" until the local news stations arrived. In front of their cameras and reporters, Zachary announced it was time to audit district officials to see how many tax dollars they were spending on electricity for public schools and what kind of kickbacks, if any, the officials were receiving. The question alone raised enough concern to finally examine the costs and long-term savings of switching to solar energy.

So here he was now, his phone connected to solar-powered Wi-Fi as he messaged Kaitlyn. *Hey, gorgeous, omw to class. SGA meeting after school* ☺. He dreaded student government meetings. They mostly consisted of long-winded debates over silly proposals. The one last Tuesday was still fresh on his mind.

"I propose a bill," their sophomore class president Chang Lee began, "which pays students to come to class, with additional bonuses for good grades."

"I second that," said freshman class president Winter Davidson.

"That devalues our education," said SGA treasurer Mercedes Jones, "when many third-world countries can't provide any to their children."

"Case in point," said junior class president Steven Herdsman. "There are kids in other places who have much bigger worries, like tigers coming into their village. So we should be grateful for having a safe environment to come to school in."

"On that note," said Winter, "I think we should change our school name from Lions to Pacifists, so we don't sound so aggressive and hostile."

"The Lemley Pacifists?!" said Steven in dismay. "How will our football team perform with a name like that?"

"He's right," said Mercedes. "Are we going to punt every time we have the ball?"

"How 'bout something strong and proud yet less carnivorous?" suggested Steven.

"We could be the Social Justice Warriors," said Chang, proudly smiling at his idea.

"Yeah!" said Winter, "with a logo of a peaceful protestor."

"It's a good idea," Zachary finally intervened. "But it's kind of long, and people will call us the Warriors anyway, which is still aggressive."

"It's a good name for a football team," said Steven, warming to the idea.

"But a warrior is a person," said Chang, "which is far more threatening than a lion who merely acts according to his predatory nature."

"Actually," said Winter, "it's mostly the lioness that hunts while the male lies around doing nothing all day."

"But Chang has a point," said Steven. "A human can choose to become a warrior, whereas a lion has to kill for food."

"It's true," said Mercedes. "I tried turning my cat vegan, and he nearly died. The vet told me he needs meat in his diet."

Zachary did his best not to laugh. Now, he could finally do so as a proud Lemley Lion on his way to class. A dinner bell rang on his phone. It was the message tone he'd given to his girl in the Iowa countryside.

Kaitlyn: Hey, Mr. Prez! Omw to lunch w/ Jenna. Working after school till 8 my time.

Zachary: OK, I'm having the talk with my parents tonight.

Kaitlyn: OMG! Fingers crossed. Lemme know how it goes.

Zachary: Will do! Call you after.

Kaitlyn: Good luck! Hugs and kisses ☺

Zachary: Thanks. ☺ Back at you.

As Zachary continued toward his locker, another flock of students enthusiastically greeted him by name. The girls on the drill team even shook their pom-poms at him and smiled glowingly.

Deep down, he knew he could have almost any girl in the school, but none of them were Kaitlyn, the girl constantly in his thoughts, the one who made it hard to breathe because he felt so much for her. In six months, he'd be graduating and could then move to Iowa and spend their summer together, before starting in the fall at Iowa State University.

But first, he would need his parents' blessing.

"If he really wants to come to Iowa," said Jenna, talking over the crowded hallway noise as they headed for their fourth-period classes, "then why does he need to ask his parents? He's a legal adult, right? Or will be soon?"

"They're claiming him on his taxes," said Kaitlyn, "and since they're in an upper-income bracket, he can't get federal aid."

"Poor little rich boy," said Jenna, intently watching a pack of wrestlers come their way in matching sweats. It was the junior varsity, and Garrett wasn't among them, to Jenna's obvious disappointment.

"It's really not fair," said Kaitlyn, annoyed by her friend's distraction. "The government just assumes your parents are going to pay all your college expenses."

"If Zachary's parents have the money, then what's the issue?" said Jenna.

"Gee, I don't know," said Kaitlyn, bumping into someone's oversized backpack. "Just that they have no idea he wants to move halfway across the country when they want him going to Wazzu."

"Wazzu?" said Jenna, as if she were referring to another planet.

"Washington State U. That's what they call it."

"The Huskies?"

"Cougars," said Kaitlyn. "The Huskies are U-Dub, as in UW.

"You really know your Washington schools now," said Jenna. "Maybe you should apply there."

"I can't be that far from my mom," said Kaitlyn. "Otherwise, I might give it some thought. It would be fun going to college out of state."

"Yeah," said Jenna, "but what if he moves all the way out here and it doesn't work out?"

"Then I guess he'll go back home and transfer to Wazzu," said Kaitlyn. Jenna was getting on her nerves.

"It just seems so far," said Jenna, as they squirmed past a gathering of band students waiting outside their music room. "I mean, going to Chicago feels like a big move, and it's only a few hours away."

Eager to change the subject, Kaitlyn asked, "Have you and Garrett decided what to do yet?" Garrett had recently been offered a wrestling scholarship at the University of Iowa, one of the nation's top-ranked programs and more than two hundred miles from Chicago.

Jenna seemed a bit sad before answering. "The drive isn't impossible, but we could only see each other on weekends, and during wrestling season, he'll be away for matches, so who knows?"

"Trust me," said Kaitlyn. "It's not easy."

"Yeah," said Jenna, looking deflated as they stopped outside her classroom.

"Have *you* considered applying to UI?" asked Kaitlyn, referring to the University of Iowa.

"I already have," said Jenna. The first bell rang and a group of freshmen hurried past.

"Still waiting to hear if I've been accepted, and still not even sure I'd want to go there."

"Well, in either case," said Kaitlyn, "time will tell if you're meant to be together."

"Yeah," said Jenna, a bit anxiously. "When will you know if Zachary's coming or not?"

"He's talking to his parents tonight," said Kaitlyn, feeling her stomach tighten. "But there's no rush. We have until May first to accept our admission offers."

"Let's hope he doesn't leave you hanging until then," said Jenna, as the hallway finally thinned out and students scattered to their respective classrooms.

"Let's hope not," said Kaitlyn, turning for her calculus class just a few doors down.

Jenna smiled and wished her "good luck."

"You too," said Kaitlyn, sincerely wanting the best for both of them.

"Iowa State?!" said his parents at the dinner table.

"What makes you want to go there?" asked Zachary's father, ignoring his steaming hot chicken wings, which were fresh off the grill.

"It's in the middle of nowhere," said his mother, distractedly holding a serving spoon as barbecue beans spilled onto her plate.

"Farm country," said his father. "Corn is all they're known for."

"They're also a leading producer of soybeans," said Zachary, "not to mention oats, hay, red clover, flaxseed, rye, and wheat. Pumpkins too, and lots of apples."

Taken aback, his mother asked, "What's that got to do with college?"

"They're the first university to offer a master's and Ph.D. in sustainable agriculture."

"You want to be a farmer?" his father said in disbelief.

"What's the big surprise, Dad? I've been talking about a sustainable garden for a while now."

"But you can have a garden without studying agriculture," said his mother.

"A greenhouse if you wanted," said his father.

"True," said Zachary, "but I want to learn as much as I can, not just for myself, but to teach others across the world. It's why I wanted to join Greenpeace instead of going to college, so just be glad I finally want to go."

"But still," said his mother, "you don't have to go all the way to Iowa, do you?"

"Wazzu has a great program in agriculture," said his father. "One of the best in the nation."

"With sustainable farming too," said his mother. "I just read about it in the alumni newsletter. They have ten acres where they grow organic fruits and vegetables."

"It's true farmland," said his father. "We even went cow-tipping once after too many beers."

"Hilarious, Dad," said Zachary, having heard the story more than once about their tipping over sleeping cows in the fields. "But male bonding through drinking and abusing animals isn't really my thing."

"I'm just saying," said his father, "that you don't need to move fifteen-hundred miles away to study farming."

Zachary didn't correct him that it was nearly eighteen-hundred miles.

"They have tornadoes there, you know," his mother worriedly informed him.

Zachary took a bite of coleslaw with a mumbled, "Mm-hm."

"Then why on Earth do you still want to go there!?" she asked.

"It's a girl," said Hailey, coming down the stairs in a studded leather jacket, her hair dyed a rebellious silver platinum.

"Who's the girl?" asked their mother.

Their dad yelled, "What'd you do to your hair?!"

"It's *en vogue*," said Hailey as she continued down the stairs. "And the girl is Kaitlyn."

"How would you know?!" said Zachary.

"She DM'd me on Instagram," said Hailey, "along with hundreds of other girls."

"Then how'd you know it's her?"

"Our walls are thin," said Hailey, "and I hear you talking to her."

Zachary felt the blood rushing to his cheeks, wondering how much she'd heard of their conversations. "You shouldn't be eaves—" he started to say, when the thundering sound of a Harley Davidson outside drowned him out.

"My date's here," said Hailey, heading for the door. "I'll be home by whenever."

"You're not getting on the back of that motorcy—!" shouted their father. The door slammed behind her, followed by the deafening roar of the Harley tearing off.

"Iowa," said his father, still trying to make sense of Zachary's choice.

"What color was that, anyway?" asked his mother, referring to Hailey's hair.

"Platinum silver," said Zachary, "but it could be a lot worse, like pink or green or bright blue."

Shaking his head in dismay, his father said, "My daughter's turning into one of those punk-disco-rapper-whatevers, and my son wants to head off to the Midwest to become Farmer Joe."

"I really need to do this, Dad," said Zachary, pleading to his father man to man.

"But son," he said, taking a close look at him, "you haven't even met this girl yet."

"I've been talking to her every day for the past two months or so," said Zachary, showing them a picture of Kaitlyn on her phone.

"Gorgeous eyes," said his father, disarmed by their striking green color.

"She's beautiful," said his mother. "But surely there are girls at your school you can go out with?"

"I know it's crazy, Mom, but she's the only one I want to be with. I think about her all the time, and lots of people go to school out of state, so what's the harm?"

"In that case," said his mother, "why can't she come to school here in Washington?"

"Her father recently died of cancer," said Zachary, "so it's just her and her mom at home."

"That's too bad," said his father, his mother nodding sympathetically. "Must be very hard on them both," she said.

"Yeah," said Zachary, "which is why she doesn't want to leave her all alone. She's already afraid of being just a few hours away at ISU."

"ISU," said his father. "You already sound like one of the locals."

Zachary nodded with a little smile.

"You know," said his father, "I wasn't much older than you when I met your mother."

"But we really need to discuss this," said his mother, scowling at his father.

"Okay, Mom, but you're not going to change my mind."

Solving advanced calculus problems at her desk was easier for Kaitlyn than waiting for Zachary's phone call. After 11:30 p.m. in her time zone, it was well past the normal dinner hour for Zachary, meaning he'd been discussing the situation with his parents for quite some time now. With every passing minute, she grew more anxious. She couldn't help but imagine his parents' reaction.

Most likely, they were desperately warning him to stay away from some crazy girl in Iowa who'd stalked him on Instagram via some weird alien connection. Any normal parent would tell him to keep a safe distance—as in 1,762 miles' worth. When his ringtone finally sounded, her chest tightened with fears of rejection. Her frantic response: "So how'd it go?!"

"You want the bad news first or the good?"

"Let's start with the bad," said Kaitlyn, her stomach sinking with dread.

"You're a true Midwest girl," said Zachary, often teasing her for saying "tough tomatoes" when things didn't go her way.

"Zach, please," she said, her nerves on edge. "What'd they say?"

"My mom doesn't want me leaving the state. I'm still her baby, and she's afraid I'll never move back."

"Oh," said Kaitlyn. She felt an awful sensation—her heart decompressing.

"But my dad stepped up and said I was old enough to make my own decisions."

"That's awesome!" she said with a surge of hope.

"But here's the thing," he said as Kaitlyn held her breath. "I never did apply to Wazzu, so I promised them I would, to at least keep my options open."

"That makes sense, I guess," she said, though not liking the sound of it.

"Yeah, they at least want me to visit the campus and meet you in person before committing to ISU."

"You mean," said Kaitlyn with rising spirits, "you're coming here *before* the summer?"

"Yeah," said Zachary, unable to contain his excitement. "I'll be flying out the day before Christmas."

"Oh, my God, oh, my God, oh, my God! That's, like, three weeks away! I can't believe it!"

Zachary, his voice filled with happiness, chuckled at her reaction. "My mom's freaking out that I won't be here on Christmas day, but Dad promised we'd celebrate the holiday before I left."

"How long are you staying?!"

"Five days. We already booked the airfare and hotel. I thought of asking to stay with you but figured your mom would—"

"Oh yeah, she would totally freak out," said Kaitlyn. The thought of being alone in Zachary's hotel room made her flush with desire.

"I can't wait to see you!" said Zachary.

"Me too! This is going to be the best Christmas ever!" she said. Then, suddenly, she felt a twinge of shame. "If only my father could be here to meet you."

"He'll be with us in spirit, I'm sure," said Zachary, speaking like someone about to finally meet the girl he'd fallen in love with.

018

While driving home from work, Kaitlyn decided to inform her mother soon that Zachary was coming to town. She'd considered not telling her at all, using her job and Jenna as cover for the time spent with him, but she didn't want to lie to her mom.

The time on the dash showed 5:25 p.m., so her mother was probably getting in the door right now after finishing another day at the feed store.

With little traffic on the county highway, Kaitlyn quickly passed a hollow stretch of cornfields, their stalks wilted bare in the gray winter dusk. Up ahead in the distance, she spotted the flashing emergency lights of a police car and an ambulance on the side of the road. A small huddle of uniformed personnel was standing by.

Getting closer, Kaitlyn saw a tow truck pulling a small red car from a ditch. The roof had collapsed on the passenger side, where it had apparently rolled, its headlight and door were bashed in, and its side mirror was dangling from wires. Suddenly, Kaitlyn recognized the make and model. It was a Ford Focus, and her heart began racing with sudden terror. Slowing down even more, she made out the familiar Iowa State U. bumper sticker, and the crumpled license plate, all confirming it was her mother's car.

The next several seconds were lost in a blur of time and motion. Kaitlyn didn't remember pulling her truck over or jumping down from its cab. "That's my mom!" she yelled, sprinting toward the cluster of paramedics surrounding the sheriff's deputy. "Is she okay? Where is she? Somebody tell me!"

"Whoa! Calm down, Miss," said the deputy, his fur-lined collar pulled up against the biting wind. "We're trying to figure that out ourselves."

"You mean, she's not in there—" said Kaitlyn, gesturing to the back of the ambulance.

The deputy shook his head. "She called for the tow truck but didn't stick around. Another deputy just went up and down the highway. She's nowhere to be seen."

"She must be all right then," Kaitlyn said hopefully.

"Normally, when people flee the scene of an accident, it's 'cuz they been drinking," said the deputy, narrowing his eyes on her. "Did your mom call you to come get 'er here before we did?"

"No, I swear, Officer," said Kaitlyn, her body tensing in the cold as she imagined her mother being in big trouble. "I was just driving home from work."

"Where do you work?"

"Daisy's Diner, just up the highway. We closed early. With the holidays and all, business was slow."

The deputy nodded, likely familiar with the diner since patrolmen often stopped in there. "Does she have any conditions that might have caused this?"

"Not that I know of," said Kaitlyn. "And I can honestly say, I haven't seen her with a drink in quite a while."

"Lots'a folks get depressed 'round this time of year," said the deputy.

Kaitlyn worriedly nodded. "What if she has a concussion? Couldn't that make her disoriented?"

"Could," said the deputy, "but unlikely she'd just wander off in that condition."

"Well, I need to go home and see if she's there," said Kaitlyn, fearing she couldn't leave the scene. To her relief, the deputy nodded. "Here's my card," he said, digging it out from his coat pocket. "Have 'er call me, okay? I need some info for my report, which her insurance company is gonna want a copy of."

Taking the card, Kaitlyn wanted to ask if her mother would be arrested for DUI but decided it would be best to remain silent, especially when she couldn't be sure if her mother had indeed been drinking. "Yes, sir," she said, racing off toward her truck.

Back in the driver's seat, she unlocked the glovebox to retrieve her phone. Turning it on, she saw that her mother had called and texted several times—even left a few voice messages. Anxious to call her back, she got her mother to pick up on the first ring. Her voice was loud and slurred. "I've been trying to reach you for the past forty-five minutes, but your—"

"Mom!" Kaitlyn shouted. "Are you okay?"

"I was in a fender bender," said her mother. "But I'm okay. I was wearing my seatbelt."

"Fender bender?!" said Kaitlyn, watching the mangled heap of her car dragged off by the tow truck. "Your car is totaled."

"Where are you?" said her mother, sounding inebriated.

"I'm here now, where you crashed," said Kaitlyn in frustration.

"Come pick me up! I'm at the gas station next to Barton's."

Kaitlyn couldn't believe she'd walked that far in these freezing temperatures. "The police are here now," she said, watching another sheriff's vehicle pull up to the scene. "They want to talk to you."

"Just come get me!" said her mom too loudly. "I don't wanna go to jail!"

"How can you be so irresponsible?" scolded Kaitlyn, as if she was the parent in charge. "You couldn't wait to get home to have a drink?"

"I stopped off at the vineyard on the way home," said her mother, struggling with her words. "I just wanted to pick up a bottle—to go—but they let me taste a couple first."

"Sounds like you did more than taste," said Kaitlyn with rising anger.

"I was doing okay," her mother said, "till one of McCormick's hogs got loose. Stupid pig came right out in front of my car. Had to swerve not to hit him."

"Had you been sober," said Kaitlyn, "you probably wouldn't've ended up in a ditch."

"Just come get me!" said her mother, bursting into tears.

"I'm on my way," said Kaitlyn. Ending the call, she stuffed her phone in a cup holder and drove off. As she nervously passed the county deputies, she anticipated them following her to their suspect, putting her mother in handcuffs, and hauling her away in the back of a sheriff's car.

Shivering at the thought, she cranked up the heat and carefully followed the speed limit all the way down the highway.

Kaitlyn picked her mother up at the gas station, where she'd been hiding inside like a fugitive, and was now driving her home. "I couldn't handle losing both parents," she said, keeping an eye in the rearview mirror for flashing blue lights. "And seeing your car, you're lucky you didn't die."

Reeking of fruity alcohol, her mother blew her nose after a long bout of crying. "I haven't been drinking the past several weeks. I swear. But the holidays without your father," she said, her voice choking up. "I just miss him so much."

"Mom," said Kaitlyn, her voice softening. "Maybe we should think about getting you some antidepressants?"

"Dr. Spalding prescribed me some already, but I never took them."

"Oh," said Kaitlyn, having no idea she'd gone back to see him. "Well, it can't hurt to try them, at least for a while, to get you through this stretch."

Still sobbing, her mother nodded. "Okay," she said, sniffling back her tears.

Kaitlyn reached over and took her hand. Her mother squeezed it in both of hers. They drove in silence until Kaitlyn's phone blared the notes of Katy Perry's "Smile."

"That boy you've been talking to?" said her mother, her speech still slurred a little.

"Actually, it's Katy Perry," said Kaitlyn, leaving her phone in the cupholder.

"Real funny," said her mother, blowing her nose with what remained of the tissue. "You already told me his name is Zachary."

"He's coming to town next week," said Kaitlyn, thinking she might as well tell her now.

"Oh," said her mother in surprise. "Am I going to meet him?"

"Of course," said Kaitlyn. "I think you'll like him."

"So long as he's safe," said her mother. "I want you to be happy, you know."

"Thanks, Mom. He's going to visit the campus while he's here."

They passed another withered cornfield, which appeared as a long black void at nightfall. "Sounds like he's serious about being with you. Do you mind if I ask his last name?"

Kaitlyn hesitated before responding. "Taylor," she said.

"Zachary Taylor," said her mother. "Why does that name sound familiar?"

Kaitlyn nervously watched the road, hoping her mother hadn't paid any attention to the news stories or remembered them if she had. "One of our presidents had the same name," she said, "sometime before the Civil War."

"Oh, yeah," said her mother, as if grappling to recall something else. "If I Google his name, will I find anything to worry about?"

"Yeah," said Kaitlyn. "He died in office, and his wife might've poisoned him."

"I don't mean the president," said her mother, snatching her phone from her purse. "You know who I mean."

Kaitlyn looked at her mother. "You're not really going to Google him, are you? After I just saved you from getting arrested? I don't think you're in a position to judge anyone."

Her mother put the phone back in her purse. "I just wish you'd tell me things. So I won't have to play detective with my own daughter."

"Fine," said Kaitlyn, knowing she was going to Google him later anyway, followed by a lengthy interrogation after she'd sobered up in the morning. "He was in the news a while back for being courageous enough to say he was abducted by a UFO."

"Dear Lord," said her mother, breathing a heavy whiff of alcohol. "I don't even know what to say."

"Then don't say anything," said Kaitlyn, following the curve in the road.

"He could be dangerous," said her mother.

"He's not dangerous!" said Kaitlyn. "He's a good student and senior class president. And not that it should matter, but he comes from a 'good family,' as you would call them. His parents own a business, and they're fairly conservative."

"Before your father died," said her mother, as if nothing she'd just said had registered, "you never had this weird fascination with aliens."

"It's not *weird*," said Kaitlyn, "and you don't even know what you're talking about. I used to watch *Ancient Aliens* with Dad whenever you weren't around."

"Your father was a good Christian. He would never watch that garbage."

"S'not true, Mom. He liked the story of Ezekiel's wheel and believed he was talking about an alien spaceship. It's in the Old Testament. You can't deny it."

"Don't tell *me* what I have to agree with," said her mother in a flash of drunken rage. "And your father was just being nice. He'd've watched anything with you."

"Whatever," said Kaitlyn, knowing that wasn't true. Her father refused to watch MTV or Lifetime movies with her.

"You've always been much easier on him than on me," said her mother.

"What's that supposed to mean?"

"Whenever he screwed up, it was okay. But if I make the smallest mistake, you treat me like a felon."

"Well, you screwed up pretty badly today. And you're lucky you didn't kill someone, which *would've* been a felony."

"I don't mean just today. You hold me to a higher standard … all the time."

Kaitlyn wondered if that was true. "Maybe you're right," she said, her headlights hitting a possum that scooted off the road. "But I'd rather remember the good parts of Dad than the bad."

"Your father was mostly good," said her mother, breaking into another sob. "But he wasn't an angel, and I don't want you judging me right now. I'm sorry I screwed up. I really am, but please don't make me feel any worse than I already do."

Kaitlyn glanced over at her mother, whose body was now shaking from tears and grief. It was agonizing to see, especially when her mother was never one to feel sorry for herself. In fact, she was the one who'd taught her to say "tough tomatoes" whenever the going got tough. "I love you, Mom," she said, giving her hand a little squeeze.

"I love you too," she sobbed.

"And I won't judge you," said Kaitlyn, "if you don't judge Zachary."

"Okay," said her mother, wiping her eyes with the back of her sleeve.

Kaitlyn turned onto the small country road that led to their house. "When we get home," she said, "let's get you a good hot meal and some coffee before you call that deputy and the insurance company."

"Good idea," said her mom in a tired voice.

"We also need to get your story straight about why you took off."

"I had to pee really badly. That's the God's honest truth."

Kaitlyn glanced over at her mother in surprise. "You walked all that way to use the ladies' room?"

"After drinking all that wine, I couldn't wait around for the tow truck driver, and I wasn't about to pee in the ditch."

Kaitlyn chuckled and shook her head. "Well, you probably saved yourself from a DUI," she said. When her mother didn't respond, she glanced over. Her mother had dozed off like a small child. Impossible to be angry with her any longer, Kaitlyn felt an overwhelming love and sorrow, making her wonder how she could ever leave for college in the fall.

Zachary was getting worried. He'd last heard from Kaitlyn when she left work. Her text message said she'd gotten off early and would call him when she got home. That was a few hours ago, and it was out of character for her not to do so. He'd texted her a few times, asking if she was okay, but heard nothing back.

Down in the basement, he anxiously surfed TV channels. Most likely, he was stressing over nothing. She probably got busy with something and hadn't checked her phone. Landing on the History Channel, he tried to focus on an episode of *Ancient Aliens* that was halfway through—something to do with aliens constructing an ancient mountaintop fortress in Peru, which contradicted the technology available to mankind at the time.

Unable to concentrate, Zachary kept watching because he needed some way to feel connected to Kaitlyn, knowing she'd probably watched this episode more than once. Perhaps it was superstition, or true cosmic energy, but the dinner bell rang on his phone, alerting him to her text:

Kaitlyn: Sorry! Crazy night. My mom was in an accident.

Zachary: What happened?!

Kaitlyn: She rolled her car into a ditch.

Zachary: OMG. Is she okay?!!

Kaitlyn: Miraculously yes. Seatbelt. She walked away with just minor scratches.

Zachary: Thank God.

Kaitlyn: You have no idea. Thought I'd lost both parents.

Zachary: Sounds terrifying.

Kaitlyn: I was really freaking out. Still am.

Zachary: Glad she's okay…You too…I was worried.

Kaitlyn: Thanks. ☺ Nice to know you care.

Zachary: I care a lot.♥♥

Kaitlyn: ♥♥Police just took a phone report. Can I call you later? Need to call insurance company now.

Zachary: Sure. I'll be up.

Kaitlyn: Thanks, sweetie. Need to hear your voice.

Zachary: Just think…we'll be together next week.

Kaitlyn: Can't wait! ☺♥ttys♥♥♥

Zachary: ☺☺☺♥♥♥♥

019

Ever since Zachary could remember, his family celebrated Christmas Eve by drinking alcohol-free eggnog, exchanging sweaters beneath the tree, and listening to Perry Como's Christmas album. Zachary had no idea when or why these family traditions began. Only this year, they'd be observed the night *before* the night before Christmas, because he would be leaving for Iowa the following day.

"We've already broken tradition," said their father, pouring rum into their glasses of eggnog, "so we may as well make the most of it."

"Honey, are you sure?" questioned their mother, looking at Zachary and his sister as if they were still in middle school.

"Please, Mom," said Hailey, her hair now bright red, which unintentionally matched the festive décor their mother had worked so tirelessly to achieve. The Christmas tree was perfectly arranged with tinsel, ornaments, and lights, and its branches were sprayed with dusty snow. "I already promised to stay home all night like a prisoner, so you don't have to worry about me driving."

"When I was their age," said their father, pouring a double shot into Zachary's glass, "I was already in the Air Force."

"Doesn't matter how drunk you get me, Dad. I'm not enlisting."

His father chuckled. "Just trying to spread some holiday cheer," he said, which Zachary understood to mean he and his sister should finally show each other some sibling love on this one special night of the year.

"Our last Christmas Eve together before you're both off to college," said their mother, a tear welling in her eye.

"Actually," said Hailey, "it's Christmas Eve Eve, which is fine by me, 'cause now I can go to a party tomorrow night. A *real* party, I mean." She took a sip of eggnog, which left a creamy mustache above her lip.

"It's not that new crowd you're hanging out with, is it?" asked their mother in concern.

"They're far more sophisticated than the people still in high school, Mom," said Hailey, who'd had zero interest in her fellow Lemley Lions since stepping down as senior class president.

"I don't want you associating with a biker gang," said their father, referring to the guy who'd picked her up on the Harley.

Hailey laughed. "Oh my God," she said. "That was Fisherman. He's an artist, and he's far more interested in sculpting me than going out with me."

"Well, that's good, I guess," said their father, likely wondering the same as Zachary. *Was she posing for a nude bust?* The answer to that neither of them really wanted to know.

"Okay, who's going first?" said Zachary, hoping to speed up their gift exchange.

"He just wants to go call his girlfriend," said Hailey. "That still sounds so weird, that you actually have one, even if she is like halfway across the country and probably catfishing you."

"I'll find out tomorrow in person," said Zachary, his spirits too high to be brought down by her petty comments.

"I know your sister's happy for you," said their mother. Setting her half-finished eggnog on the coffee table, she grabbed two identically wrapped packages, which she handed to her children. "You'll never guess what they are."

"Hmm," said Hailey, giving it a sarcastic little shake. "Matching sweat-shirts for my twin and me? How original!"

"Thanks, Mom," said Zachary, tearing his package open, which prompted his sister to do the same. In perfect timing, they held up matching gray sweatshirts emblazoned with the maroon WSU Cougar logo. Zachary exchanged a little smile with his sister. The two of them knew exactly what their parents were up to.

"Nice try, Mom," said Hailey, "but I'll be in New York."

"Your dad picked them out," said their mother, looking to him for help.

"Anything can happen between now and September," he said, raising his eggnog and downing a thick gulp.

"Well, on that note," said Zachary, snagging a gift from the pile and handing it to his sister, "this is for you."

Hailey smiled uncertainly and opened the wrapping. "NYU!" she said, holding up the purple hoodie bearing the New York University logo. "Now you're talkin'!"

Zachary chuckled. "I thought you might like that," he said.

"You even got the right size," she said as their parents happily watched.

"Three-outta-three," said Zachary. "Better quit while I'm ahead."

"Who said you're ahead?" Hailey half-joked. Reaching for another wrapped package, she tossed it to him. The weight and soft texture made him suspect clothing was inside the crinkly wrapping.

"If it's an NYU hoodie in your size, I know it wasn't by mistake," said Zachary, the family breaking into laughter, including his sister.

"Just open it, you dork," she said.

Zachary tore it open to see a University of Iowa sweatshirt with a Hawkeye across its chest. "Oh," he said, trying to mask his disappointment that she'd gotten the wrong Iowa school, but at least she'd made the effort. "It's really nice. Thanks."

Hailey smiled a bit sadly. "I have to say, it's going to be weird going to college in different states, but I'm glad you finally have a girlfriend—well, almost have."

"Thanks," said Zachary. "Are you trying to tell me you're going to miss me?"

"I wouldn't go that far," said Hailey, sipping her eggnog with a playful smile. "But I wish you luck."

"You too," said Zachary, as their mother held up her phone to take a photo. "Squeeze in, you two. I want to capture you in the moment."

Zachary slid next to his sister, and put his arm around her, which he hadn't done since the last time they'd had their picture taken together. To his surprise, he felt his sister's hand on his shoulder, the two of them toasting each other with their eggnog glasses.

"Say cheese," said their mother.

"Cheeeeeese!" they both chimed in with big smiles, the moment captured for the digital age.

"I'm glad your friend is coming," said Kaitlyn's mother, taking a Christmas ham from the freezer. "But I forgot to ask—does he eat meat?"

"It's fine, Mom," said Kaitlyn, chopping potatoes to be scalloped with peas and carrots. "We've got plenty of veggies here, and he's used to his parents' carnivorous meals."

"You say that like they're cave people for eating meat."

"I didn't mean it like that," said Kaitlyn, with a light chuckle. "He's not judgmental."

"What time can I expect him?" asked her mother, with an anxious look at the time on the stove. It was barely after ten a.m.

"Relax, Mom," said Kaitlyn. "It's a four-hour flight, and he's just leaving now. Plus, we're going to hang out for a while after I pick him up at the airport."

"Well, it'd be nice to know what time to serve dinner," said her mother.

Katy Perry blasted from her phone on the counter. "Hang on," said Kaitlyn, setting down her knife to pick up the call. "Hey, Zach!"

"Bad news," he said. She immediately felt tense. "My flight's been cancelled due to a major blizzard coming your way from the Rockies."

"What?" said Kaitlyn, peering out the kitchen window. "It's perfectly clear outside!"

Curiously watching, her mother whispered, "What's wrong?" Kaitlyn ducked past her in annoyance and fetched the TV remote from the dining room table.

"I tried getting something for tomorrow or the next day," said Zachary, "but they have nothing available."

Flipping channels, Kaitlyn stopped on a weatherwoman in front of her map. The caption at the bottom of the screen read: *Major Blizzard Impacting Holiday Travel. More Than 2,000 Flights Canceled. Storm Expected to Last Throughout the Week.* "I can't believe it," she said, knowing their winter vacation would be over by the time the storm passed.

"I'm really sorry," said Zachary, sounding as sad and disappointed as she felt. "I guess we'll have to change my visit to spring break."

"That sounds like forever," she said hopelessly.

"I know," he said, "but it's actually only a few months away."

More like four, thought Kaitlyn, a heavy silence hanging between them.

"Well," he said in a hollow voice, "tell your Mom thanks for the welcome anyway, and merry Christmas to you both."

"I will," she said, choking back a tear as her mother stood watching in concern. "Merry Christmas, Zachary."

Zachary was driving home from Sea-Tac Airport in his Chevy Volt, a car his parents had given him as a Christmas and early graduation present. A trade-in with very low mileage, it was a plug-in hybrid with enough range to hardly ever require him to gas up.

If only he'd left the day before, he'd be with her right now, sipping hot chocolate and watching the snow fall outside. Christmas music and long, slow kisses beneath the mistletoe (assuming her mother wasn't around). It was all just a fantasy, anyway, so why not make love right there next to the fireplace hung with stockings?

Driving eastbound on the 90 freeway, he considered turning the car around at the next exit and driving all the way to Iowa. On his GPS monitor, he voice-commanded "Des Moines, Iowa," the nearest major city to where she lived. Avoiding the blizzard, the map rerouted him south through Arizona, New Mexico, and even Texas, looping him back north through Oklahoma and Missouri to finally reach Iowa. Following that route would require at least three full days of driving, with the additional challenge of finding places to charge his vehicle while catching some Z's. No way could he make it there and back before the end of winter break, much less have any real time to visit with her. Missing school was an option as he saw it, but his parents would never go for it. All he could do was wait for spring break, though that seemed like an eternity to him.

So much for a white Christmas being romantic. Kaitlyn was horribly depressed, with little appetite for the glazed ham and vegetables on her plate.

"I'm really sorry he couldn't make it, honey," said her mother, pouring them glasses of alcohol-free eggnog. Since wrecking her car, she'd been taking anti-depressants, which could not be mixed with alcohol, and her mood had lifted enough to survive the holidays without it. "I really was looking forward to meeting him."

Kaitlyn barely nodded, watching the snow fall outside the window. The blizzard arrived a few hours after Zachary called, and the landscape began to white-out. She knew from science class that snow absorbed sound, yet the ghostly silence filling the house was a powerful reminder of her father's absence.

For the past several years, her father had always put a star on their tree after Christmas Eve dinner, a tradition passed down by his family for reasons unknown. Powered by two double-A batteries, the star would twinkle with colorful lights to celebrate the Star of Bethlehem. It was also a beacon to start opening presents, which brought much excitement when Kaitlyn was little. "Are we going to do the star this year?" she now asked.

Sipping her eggnog, her mother sadly smiled. "He'd be happy to know we are," she said. "Not just tonight, but in passing down the tradition to your own future family."

Kaitlyn nodded, though the future gave her little solace right now.

"I was hoping to go to church tomorrow," said her mother. Her new Ford Eco-Sport was parked in the driveway—their insurance company had considered her Focus totaled. "But even with four-wheel drive, the roads may be too difficult."

Kaitlyn barely heard what she said.

Following their Christmas Eve dinner, Kaitlyn stood on a stepladder, securing the star atop the tree. When it failed to switch on, she pried open the battery cover, only to find the compartment empty.

"I told your father to leave them in there," said her mother. "But he never—"

Pop! One of the star's tiny bulbs shattered, after which the star flashed on and off three times in a bright display of colors. Kaitlyn and her mother stood by, watching in astonishment. "I guess he heard you, Mom."

Her mother slowly nodded. Kaitlyn sensed her father had just paid a visit. She thought of Reverend Jacob, telling the story of his dearly departed sister ringing the bells on her shoelaces during the holidays.

"Here," said her mother, dragging out a large, gift-wrapped box from beneath the tree. "This was from your father. He picked it out not long after he was diagnosed."

Stepping down from the ladder, Kaitlyn curiously tore off the wrapping and opened the box. It contained a satellite dish and a bag of clamps, screws, hex nuts, washers, and many other components she didn't even recognize, all presumably to be assembled.

"It comes with a manual," said her mother, her voice a bit shaky. "But it still needs more parts. Your father was planning on getting them after he recovered."

Kaitlyn cleared a lump in her throat, her eyes misting up. "Before I dropped French class," she said, "I told him that with a satellite dish, I'd have access to many French stations, and watching them would be the best way to learn the language."

Her mother nodded. "He was really hoping the two of you could work on it together," she said, her voice breaking up with emotion. "As a science project too."

"Oh, Mom," said Kaitlyn, the two of them hugging and crying together. "I miss him so much, but he was letting us know he's okay."

"And still with us all the time," said her mother, wiping her eyes. "That's something he would do on Christmas Eve."

With a teary nod, Kaitlyn also wondered if her father, after hinting around months ago on his truck radio, was now letting her know he'd be making future contact through the satellite dish. A man who believed in science as much as his spiritual faith, he might have selected the gift for that very reason, knowing he was about to die.

Okay, Dad, she thought to herself. Looking over the assortment of parts and gadgets, she knew she had her work cut out for her.

After Hailey left for her Christmas Eve party, Zachary was home on the couch with his parents, watching their all-time favorite Christmas movie, *Elf.* Nothing could cheer him up right now, not even the sound of the dinner bell on his phone from Kaitlyn texting him: *Wish you were here.*

Up on his feet, Zachary started texting her back while heading off to his room.

"You want us to pause it?" asked his mother. Santa's sleigh was grounded in Central Park after the Claus-O-Meter dropped to zero, and the movie was nearly over.

"It's okay, Mom," said Zachary, having seen the movie a dozen times or more and not really caring if Buddy the Elf saved the day by believing in Christmas magic once again. Heading up the stairs, he texted to Kaitlyn:

Zachary: Watching Elf with my parents.

Kaitlyn: Love that movie.

Zachary: Me too, but not feeling the magic this year.

Kaitlyn: You might change your mind after you hear what happened.

Zachary: What's that?

By the time he entered his bedroom, she'd summarized her father's visit through the star on the tree. The story was too strange to be made up, yet he still had a question:

Zachary: Are you sure there wasn't a charge left behind when the batteries were taken out?

Kaitlyn: No way could there be enough juice to break a bulb. It required a massive surge of power, and the batteries were taken out at least several months ago.

Zachary: Yeah, definitely sounds like a supernatural occurrence.

Kaitlyn: I've read accounts from both psychics and physicists...how our spiritual energy is a form of electricity, and how loved ones often visit us through electrical gadgets. We truly are Light Beings.

Zachary: That's a very cool story, and I totally believe your father paid you a visit.

Kaitlyn: Thanks. I'm glad you think so.

Zachary: I'm still bummed, though. Wish I could transform

myself into a magic genie and visit you through a lamp right now.

Kaitlyn: Lol. Aladdin on Christmas? Why not? ☺ Are you going to have your shirt off?

Zachary: Is that a special request?

Kaitlyn: Sure ☺

Zachary: Only if you take yours off too.

Kaitlyn: Hahaha. I'm changing into my nightie now.

Zachary: What color is it?

Kaitlyn: If you guess correctly, I just might show you.

Zachary. Hmmm, how many chances do I get?

Kaitlyn: Lol, one.

Zachary: Give me a clue then.

Kaitlyn: It matches my eyes.

Zachary: Green!

Kaitlyn: Ta-dah!

She sent him the photo. She was wearing her black hair down, and her green eyes matched the silky jade nightgown. The sight of her round hips and bare thighs drove him wild with lust. Her cleavage was exposed in the low V-cut, and her eyes kept drawing him back to her with their seductive beauty.

Zachary: I want you so bad it's killing me.

Kaitlyn: I really want you to make love to me, Zachary.

Zachary: I want nothing more, Kaitlyn.

Kaitlyn: Let's make the most of this night.

Zachary: I'll call you on FaceTime.

Kaitlyn: Take your shirt off first.

Zachary: Okay.

020

Kaitlyn woke up in the middle of the night. As the snow continued to fall outside her window, the house was deathly quiet and a cold draft crept in through its frame. On her mind was that night's Facetime call with Zachary.

She'd never before taken her clothes off on camera, or done the things she did earlier in front of him. Not that she regretted it or felt ashamed, but she did feel a spiritual void at how superficial it all was. The only way to truly connect with someone both physically and emotionally is in-person, not eighteen-hundred miles away through an electronic device. Snuggling against her blanket, she closed her eyes and drifted back to sleep with Zachary on her mind.

Zachary wasn't sure if he was dreaming as he tried making sense of the digital code on the panel inside the spaceship. The numbers were 0000101101 00101001000101011101001011...

A blast of cold air on his face, he figured it was from a nearby generator, but suddenly woke in bed to see his window open. How strange. He couldn't remember having opened it on a freezing winter night. Outside, a strobe of lights was flashing green, red, yellow, and blue.

Stupid security fence, he thought, crawling out of bed in a groggy daze to close the window. The lights were no longer flashing outside. Even so, the sensors would need to be adjusted. To remind himself the next day, he went to his desk drawer in search of a pen and notebook. By the time he dug them out, he'd already forgotten what he had come there for.

The numbers still clouded his mind—

00001011010010100001110000010110101011101001…Decoding them into visual representations, he sketched out a series of figures resembling an ancient cave drawing.

The next morning, he did not remember putting the notebook back in his drawer. However, waking to see the window cracked open, he had the strangest sensation of having been aboard an alien spaceship. Most likely the remnant of a dream, it faded away in the coming daylight.

On New Year's Day, Iowa State was mounting a comeback against Notre Dame in the Sugar Bowl, the winner to play Clemson for the national championship. "Aren't you going to watch?" asked her mother from her seat on the couch. Their team was driving toward the end zone with less than a minute to play.

"I'm watching, Mom," said Kaitlyn. It was only partially true; she'd been working all day (and week) on assembling the satellite dish. Its many parts were scattered across the floor, her toolbox open beside her. The dish itself was a Pansat 90cm, to which she'd attached the feedhorn, adjustment flange, and mast pipe clamp. According to the manual, the feedhorn converted high-frequency signals to low-band signals that its receiver could process and decode.

Until she got more parts, however, she wouldn't be converting anything. She eagerly awaited the UPS delivery of a multi-switch device, RF modulator, amplifiers, and CAT-5 kit (to watch on a computer). If only her father were here. It would be much easier to figure out what was what, what went where, and how to piece it all together with the right tools. Highly mechanical, he understood the inner workings of the tractors and equipment he used to sell.

"Get out of bounds!" her mother yelled at the running back as he dove toward the sidelines at the five-yard line. The clock, still running, showed only twelve seconds to go.

"Oh my God!" said Kaitlyn, their team down by four as they sprinted up to the line of scrimmage to get the final play off in time. "I wish Dad could be here to see this!"

The doorbell rang. A UPS truck was parked outside their living room window.

"Just a sec!" Kaitlyn shouted as the quarterback snapped the ball. Dropping back under pressure, he rolled to his right, found an open receiver in the crowded end zone, then threw a bit too high. The pass bounced off the fingers of his tight end, leaping to make the catch. Game over. The Notre Dame players mobbed each other in celebration as Kaitlyn and her mother watched in silence, beyond disappointed.

"Oh, well," said Kaitlyn, heading to answer the ringing doorbell.

"Who won?" asked the UPS driver, a middle-aged woman with pinned-back hair.

"Not us," said Kaitlyn, dragging the heavy box inside.

"Sorry to hear that," said the driver, taking off down the steps. "But my daughter's a Hawkeye."

"Good for her," muttered Kaitlyn as she closed the door behind her.

"Maybe next year," her mother said. The Sugar Bowl was the only game she'd watched all season, mostly because everyone in the state had been talking about it.

"You never know," said Kaitlyn, tearing open the box to examine its assortment of parts. By next season, she'd be watching their games on the satellite dish, its conversion of high-frequency signals from unknown reaches of the universe. Aimed toward the heavens, it was a cosmic invitation for her father to join them.

Later that day, Kaitlyn bundled herself in a jacket, mittens, and woolly ski hat to venture out to their mailbox on the country road. A thick layer of snow crunched beneath her boots. A week after the flurry, it hadn't snowed since, but the freezing temperatures had kept the ground a solid expanse of white, save for the small circle of yellow from an apparent cat passing by. Its little clawed footprints trailed off in the distance.

Finally reaching the mailbox, Kaitlyn pried it open to see a week's worth of mail stuffed inside—mostly junk mail advertisements (and a big waste of trees). Sorting through them, she found a card from Zachary, his careful penmanship bringing a smile to her face. A car passed by on the salted highway— the sound of tires over slush—but she didn't bother looking up to see who it was. Instead, she focused on tearing open the envelope to read the card. Its cover was a beautifully illustrated Christmas tree—with a star on top beaming rays of light. Inside he wrote:

Dear Kaitlyn,

I picked out this card before you told me of your father's visit, which seems to be very serendipitous. I was planning on giving it to you in person, but the blizzard had other plans.

I can't wait to see you in April, so I guess the Universe is teaching me (and you) patience.

Time is hard to define anyway (did you ever see the movie

"Arrival?" I'm sure you did and can't believe we haven't talked about it). It shows how the aliens do not travel in linear time, but rather bend time to fit a purpose.

Someday, after you get your Ph.D. in physics, you will be able to do the same, but until then, we will meet when the time is right. I truly believe we were brought together for a higher purpose, which also explains why we were born into this world on the same day.

You are very special to me-more than I can possibly express in words. In fact, I still can't believe that someone like you can even exist, which makes me want to meet you even more, to prove in person that you're not a dream (but if so, the best dream I've ever had).

Merry Christmas and Happy New Year!

Love, (if I can say that already) Zachary

PS - I hope you like the small gifts I picked out (taped to the back of this card). I don't really know how to shop for a girl, but I think they will look really beautiful on you (but what wouldn't?). I picked them out to match your eyes.

Kaitlyn started crying halfway through his note, and her tears nearly froze on her cheeks. "Zachary," she said, turning the card over to see a pair of jade earrings and a matching necklace taped to the back. Putting them on, she traipsed back to her house. The cold prairie wind smacked her face, yet she didn't feel any of its sting as she read Zachary's card again and again.

Zachary was reading the same dystopian teen novel (*Beyond the Maiden Dawn*) that he'd taken to the river the day he'd skipped school a few months ago. Strange how much his life had changed in the short time since then. No longer was he absorbed in these dark, hopeless tales of a future human race fighting for survival against an army of robotic zombies after disease and climate change left them with a dying planet. Not that he didn't fear for the future of mankind, but he could no longer feel hopeless and depressed because Kaitlyn had entered his life.

In fact, his only reason to open the book again was to reconnect his thoughts with that day he'd fallen asleep on the riverbank. This past week he'd been recalling bits and pieces of his dream aboard the spacecraft. The dream felt so real, he couldn't help but wonder if he really *had* been abducted, his memory erased by the aliens, and fragments of the experience lingering in his subconscious.

If so, that might explain why he blurted out what he did in Mr. Klausen's office, and why that brief episode was now resurfacing in his dreams. Months ago, Kaitlyn had predicted that might happen. She'd even suggested hypno-therapy to achieve a more significant breakthrough. Back then, he'd shied away from the truth, but now he wasn't so sure what that truth even was.

Even if he hadn't been abducted, he considered the possibility that the aliens had channeled their message into his thoughts so he'd become their spokesper-son for reducing carbon emissions on planet Earth, especially if it affected other life forms in the galaxy. Or maybe there was indeed a connection to Kaitlyn's father and why she was brought into Zachary's orbit. It all sounded crazy, he knew, but he felt as if, in time, all the pieces would somehow fit together.

Or maybe he was just starting to believe his own lie after retelling it so many times.

021

The more she went through the manual, the more Kaitlyn realized she needed more parts for her satellite dish, and some of them would be quite expensive, even online. That led to a treasure hunt to garage sales, flea markets, and finally a scrap yard, where she'd been lucky enough to find an RG-6 cable, coaxial cable cutter, and crimper.

Still, she needed a receiver, the most important (and expensive) component, along with a low-voltage tester to ensure its signal strength. Dragging Jenna along for company, she now searched the aisles of a wholesale electronics store in Des Moines.

"What *exactly* are we looking for?" her friend asked.

"A Dreambox UHD receiver with Wi-Fi, dual tuner, and automated channel scan. So far, the cheapest one I could find was nearly three hundred dollars on eBay." Passing one aisle of electronics, Kaitlyn recognized many of the gadgets she couldn't have named a month before.

"May I ask *why* you are doing this?" said Jenna, hurrying to keep up with her.

"I know it sounds strange," said Kaitlyn, "but it's like my dad is still sort of with me. He got me the dish and planned on building it with me."

"I hear what you're saying," said Jenna, "but I'm worried about you, never having fun with a so-called boyfriend a million miles away."

"Seventeen-hundred miles," said Kaitlyn, "and he'll be here in exactly eight weeks."

On the shelf, she found a refurbished Dreambox DM-920 for sixty dollars. So long as it worked, it was a steal. She carried it down the aisle, her friend hustling after her.

"If I had to wait nearly two months to see Garrett," said Jenna, a little out of breath, "I think I'd go crazy."

Down the next aisle, Kaitlyn picked out a low-voltage tester on sale at half-price. "Are things still hot and heavy between you two?"

"My mom wants me to go on the pill," said Jenna as they headed for the cashier. "But my dad has no clue."

Kaitlyn gave her a teasing smile. "So, I guess she didn't fall for his 'teaching you self-defense moves,' huh?" The week before, Jenna's mom had come home early from work to find Jenna and Garrett entangled on the floor, their music thumping too loud to hear her arrival.

"Oh, my God, that was embarrassing," said Jenna, lowering her voice to nearly a whisper. "But thankfully, we still had most of our clothes on."

"I won't ask who pinned who," said Kaitlyn. The girls stifled their giggles as they approached the cashier, a middle-aged woman with a grumpy expression. Paying with cash, Kaitlyn suddenly felt a horrible sense of loneliness. The thought of eight more weeks seemed a lot longer than it had just a few minutes ago.

After finally making up his mind to see a hypnotherapist, Zachary had to wait several days for a session. He now waited in her lobby, which was actually the living room of her Victorian house. He was already nervous about coming here, and the burning incense and meditative music did little to help. Neither did the walls, which were covered with New Age artwork: an eye peeking through the clouds to transmit golden rays of truth; a diamond prism of light that reminded him of his grandfather's Pink Floyd CD covers; a Hindu goddess with several arms reaching out in a psychedelic display of colors. He tried remembering her name when he heard someone crying in the therapist's office.

It sounded like a man, which made Zachary even more uneasy. The last thing he wanted was to start blubbering like a child in front of a complete stranger. Not that he was ashamed to cry, but he was more afraid of the hypnotic powers she might have over him. Reminded of a Las Vegas stage act, he feared clucking like a chicken to complete strangers in the street, or robbing a bank in the nude if she had a twisted sense of humor (and bills to pay off).

Looking at a horned deity on the wall, he could even picture her performing satanic rituals on him, a much older woman preying on his sexual energy. That might turn him on, so long as she didn't feed off his blood. His anxious thoughts raced out of control.

The man's sobbing grew louder. "No, Mommy," he cried, "I'm afraid of the water!" Hearing enough, Zachary stood to go, the smell of incense nauseating him in the confined quarters. With lightened footsteps, he made his way to the door, an old floorboard creaking beneath him as he slipped outside into the cool, refreshing air.

On the way to his car, he wondered what he was truly afraid of. If he *had* been abducted, it would be a frightening experience to relive, to say the least. But far worse would be the confirmation that he'd simply blurted out a lie in the school principal's office.

Driving off, he decided it was better not to know. This way, he could continue believing he wasn't a fraud. And this seemed the only way to preserve his relationship with Kaitlyn.

022

Valentine's Day was supposed to be the most romantic day of the year, but so far, Cupid had gone AWOL on Kaitlyn. As of the final school bell that day, she hadn't heard from Zachary, yet she was still hoping—if not expecting—to receive a heart-filled text message.

Meanwhile, her best friend Jenna was lavished with Godiva chocolates and two dozen roses (which appeared to be redder and fuller than the ones Garrett had ambushed Kaitlyn with nearly five months before). "Get a room," she wanted to say, sneaking past the couple as they made out in the hallway.

Driving home a little faster than usual, she was hoping to be surprised with flowers and chocolates delivered to her doorstep, a card from Zachary expressing how deeply he cared for her (plus, even better, a cheesy poem that rhymed). No such luck.

She spent the next few hours working on her satellite dish project. "Damn it!" she muttered, trying to prep the ends of her RG-6 cable with a stripper.

"What's the matter?" asked her mother, coming into the living room.

"Nothing," Kaitlyn said testily. "The guy on YouTube makes this look a lot easier than it really is."

Watching her expression, her mother said, "This wouldn't have anything to do with Zachary, would it?"

With a frustrated sigh, Kaitlyn inserted the cable into the hole of the stripper to try again. "No text, no email, no card in the mail. Not even a simple phone call to let me know he's thinking of me today, of all days."

"That's odd," said her mother, "since you guys text and chat non-stop almost every day."

"Guess he forgot about me," said Kaitlyn, turning the dial of the rotary stripper. "Or found another girl to 'be his valentine.'"

"I highly doubt that," said her mother. "Something must've happened."

"Like what?" said Kaitlyn, suddenly horrified that he'd been in a tragic accident. "Maybe I should text him—make sure he's okay."

"If it makes you feel better," said her mother. "But I think you're worrying about nothing. I really do."

Kaitlyn nodded, removing the cable from the stripper to find a perfect cut. The conductor was perfectly exposed as she removed the loose strands of shielding. According to her YouTube instructor Big Bob, a jovial baldheaded guy in overalls, it was ready to be crimped to its F-connector. "Let's go make some mac and cheese," she said, seeking a needed break. "With something super chocolatey for dessert."

Zachary looked at the time on his phone with a growing sense of anxiety. Kaitlyn still hadn't called or texted to thank him for his roses, card, and chocolates. They were supposed to be a surprise, and the reason why he hadn't called or texted to ask if they'd been delivered. It was possible she hadn't gotten home yet if Daisy had called her in right after school, which sometimes happened when another waitress called in sick. But if she had gone straight home and nothing had arrived, then she probably thought he was the biggest jerk in the world right now for going the entire day without a word. *Happy Valentine's Day*, he finally texted her, with a cupid emoji shooting little hearts in the air. *You at home?*

"Your father's taking me out to dinner," said his mother, appearing in the living room with his father. The two of them were dressed to go somewhere upscale.

"If you and your sister want to order a pizza," said his father, thumbing some cash from his wallet and handing it over.

"Thanks, Dad," said Zachary, setting his book facedown to hide its cover: *True Accounts of Alien Abductees*, from which he hoped to gain some valuable insights.

"I think Hailey prefers gluten-free crust," said his mother.

A door burst open upstairs, and his sister screamed, "How do you know what I want?" The door slammed, as if to make an exclamation point.

"I hope she's okay," their mother said. "She's been sulking in her room all afternoon."

"Probably a boy," said their father, looking as if he wanted to strangle the culprit.

"Valentine's Day," said their mother. "It can be heartbreaking."

"It's not a stupid boyfriend!" said Hailey, storming down the stairs. "It's him!" she declared, pointing at Zachary.

"Me?" he said, the dinner bell ringing on his phone. He wanted to check Kaitlyn's message but didn't dare do so with his sister on the warpath.

"You're the reason I didn't get accepted to NYU!" she said. "I had the grades and the SATs, but thanks to you, I was no longer senior class president!"

"Oh, honey," said their mother. "I'm so sorry, but you can't blame your brother for that."

"Yes I can!" said Hailey. "He screwed everything up for me!"

Zachary felt horrible, and tried to assuage his guilt by saying, "I'm sorry, too, but even if you *were* still class president, there's no guarantee you'd've gotten in."

"BS!" she argued. "They look at extracurricular activities! Leadership abilities! And student government is the best thing to have on your application!"

I never made you quit, Zachary wanted to say, but seeing how angry Hailey was, he decided against it.

"I know you're upset, sweetie," said their mother," but you can still go to Wazzu."

"I don't want to go to that cow-tipping school in the middle of nowhere!" said Hailey.

"It may not be New York," said their father, "but your mother and I had a blast there."

"Plus, you'll be much closer to family," said their mother, "and people who love you."

"I never even applied," said Hailey, huffing off.

"Wait!" said their father, calling after her. "You mean you're not going to college!"

"No shit, Sherlock," she said, tromping up the stairs. "I hate you all!"

Zachary sat facing his parents in silence, the door slamming hard enough upstairs to rattle the walls. "She'll be okay," he assured them, though with little conviction.

His mother stood awkwardly with her jacket draped over an arm. "We should probably cancel that reservation," she quietly said.

His father somberly nodded. "I'll give them a call." He took out his phone, which reminded Zachary to check his own. Kaitlyn had responded to his text with a curt *Yeah*, letting him know she was home and clearly upset for having gone the entire day without hearing from him. *I guess you didn't get my surprise*, he texted back, as angry thrash metal blared from Hailey's room. It was the type of music she never listened to.

The only surprise was not hearing from you, Kaitlyn texted in response.

189

Zachary didn't think the day could have gotten any worse, but then a KIRO news van pulled up outside.

"He still should've texted or called," said Kaitlyn, joining her mother at the table for homemade mac and cheese, "before waiting until the cows came home."

"Maybe he was afraid of spoiling the surprise," said her mother, eating with far more appetite now that she was regularly taking anti-depressants. In fact, her weight was almost back to normal. "Which is actually quite romantic."

"He still could've sent me a text, wishing me a Happy Valentine's Day."

"He said he was sorry, didn't he?"

Kaitlyn nodded, taking a bite of the creamy pasta. "Jenna got two dozen roses and a box of Godiva. I had to watch her parading them around all day, when she wasn't sticking her tongue down Garrett's throat in the hallway."

"Don't forget," counseled her mother, "you're the one who chose to be in a long-distance relationship when you could've been the one dating him instead."

"True," said Kaitlyn, "but he's still not my type."

Her mother carefully watched her expression. "Do you think you chose a boy you can't be with because you're really afraid of being in a real relationship with someone?"

Kaitlyn hadn't even thought about that. "I dunno," she said, mulling it over. "Maybe, I guess, but I would hate to think I'm one of those masochistic women."

"Dr. Spalding said it's quite normal to avoid intimacy after the loss of someone so close to you."

"Don't tell me that he wants you to start dating again," Kaitlyn said bitterly.

"No," her mother sharply replied. "It's way too soon for that. I'm still grieving for your father, as you well know."

"Then how did the subject even come up?"

Sipping her sparkling water, her mother said, "We were talking about you."

"Well, I'm none of his business!" said Kaitlyn. "So, if you have something to say about me, do so to my face!"

Her mother stayed patiently calm. "I think you need therapy, but since you won't go, I've been trying to go for the both of us."

Kaitlyn set down her fork. She no longer had an appetite for dinner. "Didn't know you thought I was such a freak."

"I don't think you're a freak at all," said her mother. "I think you're a remarkable young woman who's dealing with a lot of pain, just as I am."

Overcome by emotion, Kaitlyn's eyes filled with angry tears. "I hate Valentine's Day," she said. Her mother reached over to console her with a hug.

More news vans arrived at the Taylors' home, including a mobile satellite vehicle from CNA. A growing crowd of reporters and their crews gathered mob-like outside the family's security fence.

"What do they want?" his mother nervously asked, their intercom buzzer ringing incessantly.

"I dunno, Mom," said Zachary, anxiously watching them on his phone's iSentry app, which showed various angles from their security cameras. "But I'll go find out." Heading out the door, he was greeted by the shouts of reporters beyond the fence.

"Zachary! Can you comment on your sister's post?"

"Is it true your abduction was a hoax?"

"To help your family sell electric vehicles?"

As they hurled more questions, Zachary quickly realized that his sister had sought revenge on social media. "I haven't had a chance to see her post," he responded. The reporters were barely visible through a space between sections of their driveway gate.

"She says you're a fraud!"

"That you made the whole thing up!"

"That your parents first told you to admit it was a hoax!"

"A cheap excuse for skipping school!"

"But selling cars is all that really matters in your family!"

"That's not true!" Zachary retorted. "We made bigger profits from maintenance and repairs on gas guzzlers, while EVs don't require nearly as much." He kept from saying that their car wash, charging stations, and convenience store were showing significant profits.

"Do you deny your sister's allegations?"

"She's had a very bad day," said Zachary. He turned and retreated inside the house, the reporters shouting after him. As his stomach churned with anxiety, he wondered if Kaitlyn had seen the post yet, and what he was going to tell her.

Kaitlyn was doing homework in her room when Jenna texted *OMG did u see this??!*

Curious, she tapped open a post from Hailey on Instagram:

My brother Zachary is a lying disgusting fraud. He was never abducted by a UFO.

Taken aback, Kaitlyn felt as if someone had just sucker-punched her. Catching her breath, she dared to keep reading: **It was a stupid excuse for skipping school. My parents knew it. They initially told him to confess to the media. But when my idiot brother continued the BS story, they went along with it to sell cars (and stuffed alien dolls). I no longer want my family's dirty money and think the public should know the truth.**

Sincerely (and I sincerely mean that), Hailey.

Overcome by shock, Kaitlyn thought *it can't be true.* As the room began feeling much warmer than it truly was, in came the annoying blare of Taylor Swift. Jenna had sent another text, and another, the message tone repeating itself. Hands trembling, Kaitlyn started typing on her phone. It wasn't in response to her friend, but a message to Zachary: *Call me.*

When the dinner bell rang on his phone, Zachary could barely hear it over his father, who was yelling at his sister through her bedroom door. "Thanks to you, somebody just threw a brick through our storeroom window and vandalized several cars on our lot!"

"You're lucky nobody was hurt!" shouted his mother. Just minutes earlier their sales manager had frantically called to report the damage.

"Lucky for *you*!" screamed his sister. "You're the ones who lied, not me!"

Slipping out of his room, Zachary headed downstairs to call Kaitlyn, as her text message demanded. Overwhelmed by dread, he still had no idea what to say to her. In the quiet refuge of the basement, he made the call. Her phone rang twice before she answered in a hollow tone: "Hey."

"Hey," said Zachary, an awkward silence hanging between them. When she still said nothing, he realized she was waiting for him to go first. "I guess you saw my sister's post?"

"Yeah."

"And you're wondering if it's true?"

"Come on, Zachary," she said in frustration.

Zachary took a deep breath and started from the beginning. "I don't know why I said what I said to the school principal, but I never meant it to become a big media story. The school secretary told her daughter, and the next thing you know, all these reporters and news cameras were outside my house."

"Oh my God," said Kaitlyn, her voice barely above a whisper. "I was hoping you'd tell me your sister was a lying bitch."

"I was trying to help the planet," he pleaded, "by getting people to drive EVs and switch from fossil fuels to solar energy. I had no idea I'd end up with thousands of followers on social media, including you."

"Including me," she said tersely. "Another one of your bimbos."

"I never said that," said Zachary. "You're the only girl I'm talking to. I swear!"

"Like I would believe anything you say right now."

"Listen, I've been having these dreams, and I'm starting to wonder if I really *was* abducted or at least had contact somehow with the aliens. The dreams feel so real. They might explain why I said what I did. Nothing else makes sense!"

"More like you want to believe your own lies," said Kaitlyn. "And your so-called dreams are a manifestation of your guilt."

"I really don't think so," he said unconvincingly. Her theory made perfect sense to him.

"You fooled a lot of people, but I don't blame you."

"You don't?" he asked, with a sense of relief.

"I only blame myself," said Kaitlyn, "for committing to someone I never even met when I could've been dating someone local and having fun my senior year."

"It's my senior year too," said Zachary, "and I've turned down chances with the hottest chicks in school."

"Do you even know how pathetically shallow you sound right now?"

"If you knew how I felt about you, you wouldn't say that."

"My mother was right," said Kaitlyn. "I cut myself off from other boys to deal with my grief."

"I'm sorry you lost your dad, but what if my dreams are a connection to—"

"Don't even talk about my father, you lying, disgusting fraud," she said, repeating what Zachary's sister had called him.

"I'm sorry," he said, feeling her slip away. "I really am."

"Me too, Zachary," she said in a distant tone. "You have no idea."

Desperately afraid of losing her forever, he stupidly asked, "Did you get my flowers?"

She chuckled bitterly. "I think it's a little late for that, but I wish you the best of luck. I really do." Ending the call, she left him sitting in the quiet darkness, talking to no one.

023

It might have been a magical winter night if not for Kaitlyn bawling her eyes out in her truck, which she'd parked outside Jenna's house. Her friend was in pajamas and seated next to her. "I hate to say I told you so," Jenna said, "but I knew this guy was weird."

"I'm such an idiot," Kaitlyn sobbed. "How could I be so blind?"

"You've been through a lot," said Jenna, "and he took advantage of your sweet vulnerability."

"I don't deserve this," said Kaitlyn, her words choked with emotion. "I know I'm far from perfect, but I could never do what he did to another human being."

"I know," her friend said softly, reaching over to comfort her.

"I'm never going to trust any boy again," said Kaitlyn.

"Shh, don't say that," said Jenna. "You're going to meet so many guys at college, and once you find the right one, you'll appreciate him that much more."

"I thought I loved him," said Kaitlyn, with an aching sob. "In fact, I still do, which makes this even harder."

"I know," said Jenna, "but time will heal your broken heart, as clichéish as that may sound."

"It sure doesn't feel like it right now," said Kaitlyn.

Jenna quietly held her. "I'm always here for you," she said, "no matter where we go to college next year."

"Same here," said Kaitlyn. "You're like the sister I never had, only better, 'cause I never have to share a room or clothes with you."

Jenna smiled, her curls a brighter blonde in the moonlight. "I'm way too messy to share a room with," she said.

"I know," said Kaitlyn, her sobbing mixed with a cathartic chuckle. "But I still love you."

"I love you, too," said Jenna.

Hanging on to her friend, Kaitlyn cried without shame. Love had betrayed her.

By the time Kaitlyn got home from Jenna's, her mother had already gone to bed. The house was so quietly still, she felt swallowed up in its void. Afraid of making a sound, she softly closed the front door behind her and turned on the light. On the dining room table were a dozen roses, a box of chocolates, and a Valentine's Day card from you know who.

Stopped in her tracks, she gathered herself before approaching the table to read a note left by her mother: *Mrs. Stottlemeyer brought these by. They were mistakenly delivered to her house on County Road #3. PS – I told you so.* :) Not that it mattered any more, but the delivery driver had mistaken their *Country* Road #3 for *County* Road just a few miles away, and her mother had no idea that Kaitlyn had already expelled Zachary from her life. Gathering his offerings, she marched them outside to throw them away, a thorn pricking her hand as she crammed the long-stemmed flowers into the bin. His unopened card was buried in a pile of junk mail to be recycled.

Heading back inside, she found herself curious as to what he had written, but not enough to surrender what remained of her dignity. Unfazed by the freezing night temperature, she was done with his lies, once and for all.

Cold and gray outside, the morning brought a horrible sadness. "One day at a time," Kaitlyn told herself, picking out her clothes to wear to school. If she could get through the day, one classroom period at a time, then she could ultimately persevere in her ordeal with Zachary. The days ahead would not be easy, but she had to keep going or surrender to depression and self-pity, and the latter was not an option. If she could survive the shock of her father's death, then certainly she had the strength to bounce back from a romance turned sour.

Stepping into the shower, she knew the first obstacle would be to somehow forgive Zachary. Not that she would ever accept what he did or let him back into her life, but if she were truly a Christian, she had to find forgiveness in her heart. As Reverend Jacob had once said in a Sunday sermon, everyone sins against others, but holding onto angry grudges only weighs us down and plunges us into darkness. She hated herself for being so foolishly naïve. In the clarity of the morning, with the warm water rinsing over her, she realized it might be an even bigger challenge to forgive herself.

Knocking on his bedroom door, his mother called out, "Zachary! Are you going to school?"

"I'm not feeling well," he faintly responded from bed. The smell of bacon cooking downstairs made him want to upchuck.

The door opened a crack, and his mother peeked in. "Your sister's gone," she said, stepping into the room. "She packed up most of her clothes, threw them in suitcases, and left."

"Am I supposed to be concerned?" said Zachary, his sister having destroyed his entire life. Not only had he lost the girl he loved, but now thousands of people were posting horrible things about him on social media. Worse yet, his Instagram account was filled with hateful threats and messages. Around the country—if not the world—his reputation had been destroyed. Yet the worst of it, he knew, would come right here in Lemley—that is, if he dared go back to school.

"She's still your sister," said his mother, "and I know you don't want her harmed."

"Don't worry, Mom. I'm sure she's staying with some stuck-up friend of hers."

"I hope it's not that guy with the Harley Davidson," his mother said worriedly.

"At least she would have somebody," said Zachary, choking back a tear.

"Oh, sweetie," said his mother, coming toward the bed to sit beside him. "Is it that girl in Iowa?"

Zachary nodded sadly.

"She'll come around," said his mother, in a firm yet gentle tone, "once she has time to process everything that's happened."

"You have no idea," said Zachary, his voice trembling with emotion. "She thought her father was taken by a UFO the night he died of cancer, like Ezekiel's wheel of lights in the Bible, and I let her think we had that connection."

"Oh," said his mother, her face expressing bewilderment.

"She's not crazy, Mom, I swear. A little religious perhaps, but also super smart with a strong belief in science."

"Midwest girl," said his mother. "They're far more conservative, but I'm sure she's very nice or you wouldn't feel so passionately about her."

"Doesn't matter now," said Zachary, feeling wet warm tears on his cheeks. "She seriously hates me now and wants nothing to do with me."

"Oh, sweetie," said his mother, leaning over to give him a hug. "Things'll get better. I promise."

A door slammed down the hall. "I just got off the phone with our lawyer!" yelled his father. "Some crackpot agency that calls itself Truth in Advertising has filed complaints against us with the FTC and state regulators, alleging deceptive marketing practices!"

"Oh my God," said his mother under her breath.

"Delores!" shouted his father, a door bursting open across the hall. "Where are you?"

"I'm in here!" she called back. "In Zach's room!"

Zachary quickly sat up and wiped his eyes before his father barged in. "We could be facing major fines and the revoking of our business license," he said.

The color drained from his mother's face, and her wrinkles showed more than ever. "What are we going to do?" she asked.

"I don't know," said his father, his posture unusually stooped. "I really don't know."

Seeing his parents nearly broken, Zachary felt like pulling the blankets over his head to stay hidden for a long, long time. But knowing he was the original source of his family's problems, he climbed out of bed to face the coming storm.

The day at school began in the darkened chambers of the principal's office.

The shades were pulled shut, as if Mr. Klausen couldn't bear the sunlight. "I'm sorry to hear what your family is going through," he said, twitching his pointy eyebrows like Count Dracula.

"All because Hailey couldn't get into the college of her choice," said Zachary, wondering if his principal had a hangover, because it was highly unlikely that a true vampire would lobby for solar energy. "And now she's left home. We don't even know if she came to school or not."

Mr. Klausen picked up his phone and dialed an extension. "David, could you please check and lemme know if Hailey Taylor came to school today?" Hearing back after a lengthy pause, he thanked his attendance clerk and hung up. "She didn't show," he reported to Zachary, "but I'm sure she's just upset still."

"Yeah," said Zachary, feeling zero compassion for his twin.

"Happens every year," said Mr. Klausen. "Students traumatized by rejection letters from universities they dream of going to. Years ago, a boy here committed suicide after Princeton turned him down. Straight-A student. Had a brilliant future ahead of him." Mr. Klausen sadly shook his head. "It's why we should have a peer support group. Other high schools do, especially at this time of the year."

Zachary showed little enthusiasm for the idea. "I'll propose it at our next student government meeting this Wednesday."

"Actually," said Mr. Klausen in a gentle tone, "I was thinking you might want to step down for a while as class president. With everything going on, I'm sure you could use a little break."

Zachary nodded, feeling more relief than disappointment.

"Aliens or no aliens," said Mr. Klausen, "you accomplished something that nobody else could have dared. You changed this school forever by bringing us renewable energy."

"Both of us did that," said Zachary, "and I'm sorry for any embarrassment I may have caused you or Lemley High."

Mr. Klausen gave him a nurturing look. "Some of the greatest people in history have gone through far more controversy than what you're experiencing right now. Nikola Tesla, for example. He pioneered the idea of free energy for the world."

"He died in poverty," said Zachary, feeling little encouragement, "after his reputation was slandered by the corporate establishment."

"But he inspired future great minds," said Mr. Klausen, "like Elon Musk, who named his cars after him."

"So, what are you saying?" said Zachary, with a horrible sense of dread. "That I'm going to suffer the rest of my life, but a hundred years from now, they might put a statue of me in our solar student lounge?"

"I see great things ahead for you," Mr. Klausen assured him, "so long as you don't let others bring you down."

"Easier said than done," said Zachary, thinking of the thousands of hateful posts on social media, not to mention the endless jeers and taunts from class-mates on his way here to the office. His locker had been graffitied once again, this time with a cartoon depicting his face as a giant penis named "Lying Dickhead."

"'Civilization is man surviving man,'" said Mr. Klausen. "It's one of my favorite quotes from Ayn Rand, and something to carry with you."

Zachary somberly nodded. "Thanks, Mr. Klausen," he said, getting up to leave the office.

For the rest of the day, he thought about the quote and its meaning. It was true, he realized. The world was advanced by innovators who took chances while the rest of humanity tried to drag them down. Why? Fear of progress, perhaps, or simply being left behind.

As he passed the crowded solar lounge, he was heckled and jeered by the very students now enjoying free Wi-Fi and cappuccino, both of which he'd made possible.

"Loser!"

"Dickhead!"

"Screw you and your family!"

Someone threw a cardboard pint of chocolate milk, which splattered against his head. Everyone laughed except Camila, who pretended not to see him. His very existence was way beneath her. He felt like giving them all the middle finger salute but thought it more appropriate to say, "You're welcome."

"The State of Iowa may have been named after the Iowa or Ioway people," said Mr. Jankowski, at the front of the history class in his trademark bow-tie and round-framed glasses. "But they never called themselves that. Can anyone tell me what their real name was?"

Seated near the front, Kaitlyn normally would have raised her hand with the answer. Thinking of Zachary, though, she wondered why she hadn't pressed him harder to prove his story of being abducted.

"The Baxoje," said a tall, gangly boy named Gavin, who always turned red whenever he answered questions in class.

"Bah-Kho-Je," said Mr. Jankowski, supplying a slight correction in his pronunciation. "You've been doing your reading."

"Yes, sir," said Gavin, the redness creeping to his ears.

Mr. Jankowski turned to the rest of the class. "Can anyone tell us how they became known as the Ioway?"

Barely hearing the question, Kaitlyn realized she didn't want to know the truth about Zachary, because deep down, she had always known he was lying. Now, she regretted not pushing him for answers.

"Kaitlyn!" her teacher said in a raised voice. "Earth to Kaitlyn!" As everyone laughed, she suddenly realized he'd been calling on her. "Oh," she said, feeling her face flush hotter than Gavin's. "Sorry, what was the question again?"

"Can you tell us how the Ioway got their name?"

"It's what the Sioux called them," she said, having read the assigned chapter. "Iowa means 'Sleepy Ones.'"

"Ayuhwa," said Mr. Jankowski, giving the exact pronunciation. "Was this even a word in the Bajoxe language?"

"No," said Kaitlyn, "but when the white settlers arrived, they heard them called that, and the name stuck."

"Correct," said Mr. Jankowski, giving her a smile. He paced to another side of the classroom. "Can anyone tell me what Bajoxe actually means?" he asked.

Kaitlyn already knew the answer was "gray snow" before a girl named Celia responded. Sadly, the Iowa tribe no longer existed in the state named after them. Driven from their lands, they were placed on reservations in Kansas, Nebraska, and Oklahoma. Considering how an entire race of people had been lied to and deceived, she couldn't complain too much about being played by a stupid teenage boy.

Between second and third period, Zachary checked his phone, mostly out of habit. After months of texting Kaitlyn back and forth, it was strange to think he would no longer be getting her friendly hellos and updates about her day's doings. He got little consolation from his mother, whose missed calls and string of texts let him know that Hailey would be staying with a friend they'd never heard of. She would not be returning to Lemley High but completing her GED instead. As the phone buzzed in Zachary's hand, he saw it was his mother calling again.

"Hey, Mom," he said, ducking into a stairwell to avoid a cluster of students passing by in the hall.

"How did I fail you as a mother?" she wailed. "Please tell me! I really need to know!"

"You didn't fail us," he said, unaccustomed to hearing his mother in tears. Last time he'd seen her cry was at her father's funeral.

"Did you not see my texts?" she said. "Your sister's dropping out of high school."

"But she's getting her GED," said Zachary, "which is the same as a diploma."

"Maybe so," sobbed his mother. "But she's not going to college. If she can't go to NYU, she said she'd rather join the Marines."

Zachary nearly laughed out loud at the thought of his sister crawling through the muck and barbed wire with an M-16. "She'll never join the military, but if she did, it might be good for her."

"They do have the GI Bill," said his mother, "which is how your father paid for college."

"College isn't everything," said Zachary. "Hailey is smart, and people generally like her for some reason, so she's going to do fine no matter where she goes."

"I hope so," said his mother. "I still can't believe everything that's happening to our family."

"Me neither," said Zachary, feeling the unspoken blame in the silence that followed. "Well, I gotta get to class, Mom."

"Okay, Zachary. I love you."

"I love you too, Mom." Ending the call, he remained in the darkened stairwell until the last trickle of students passed by.

After school, Zachary was sweeping glass off the showroom floor. The broken pane itself was now covered in cardboard and duct tape, and would remain so until it got replaced. The family's auto center was officially closed for the day, with hired security guards stationed around its perimeter. In the back office, his parents were arguing in muffled voices.

"We're not selling," he heard his father say, to which his mother responded, "It's not safe for us to stay here." Reaching with his broom, Zachary swept out a pile of shards beneath the salesperson's desk. Its metal surface bore a massive dent where the brick had ricocheted and landed on the floor a few yards away. Horrified by what could have resulted in death or a serious injury, he was highly relieved that the salesperson hadn't been struck in the head. It would have been blood on Zachary's hands.

Retrieving the brick, he headed outside to dispose of what seemed like a murder weapon. On his way to the dumpster, he passed a row of cars with their windshields and doors bashed in, the hood of a silver Mustang crumpled from the force of an apparent baseball bat. On the side of a white Mach-E, someone had spray-painted in bright red letters: LIARS BURN IN HELL.

Finally reaching the dumpster, Zachary dropped the brick inside. It landed with a violent thud. Maybe his mother was right. Maybe it *was* time to sell the family business, before someone got hurt.

024

Two weeks had passed since her last conversation with Zachary. Driving home from Daisy's after a Saturday afternoon lunch shift, Kaitlyn tried remembering the very last thing she'd said to him. She couldn't recall telling him to never call her again, but that was probably quite obvious by how the conversation had ended. Even so, she felt some disappointment that he hadn't even tried to win her back, not a single message or phone call since.

She hadn't blocked him on her phone or Instagram because she at least wanted him to try. To think he'd forgotten her already was hard to accept. Even harder was the possibility he was now with another girl. Then again, Kaitlyn *was* the one who broke up with him, and part of her was relieved that he'd been leaving her alone.

As she watched the sunset over the countryside, she missed not telling him the little things that happened throughout her day. She missed their constant exchange of little flirts, hellos, and funny tidbits that always brought a smile to her face. If he ever did call or text again, she wasn't sure if or how she would respond.

Turning on the stereo, she hoped to take her mind off him completely, when the voice of Katy Perry filled the cab with "Smile," the song Kaitlyn had dedicated to Zachary's ringtone. Quick to change the station, she looked at the parting clouds and wondered if the heavens were toying with her.

With her mother away in Nebraska to visit her sister (Kaitlyn's Aunt Theresa) and Jenna spending the weekend with Garrett, Kaitlyn used her free time to work on her satellite dish. Despite her father's prior "visits" via the FM truck radio and the Christmas tree star, she no longer expected him to make some grand appearance on the airwaves. She'd been fooled by Zachary, and was opening her eyes to her own delusions, which were nothing more than lies to herself. In fact, she was seriously starting to question if there had ever truly been a flying saucer over her house.

Perhaps her mother was right all along. She'd been a sleepwalker as a child and was probably doing the same the night her father died. Plus, the influence of television was quite obvious—she'd watched an *Ancient Aliens* episode about Ezekiel's wheel just a week or two before her father's passing. On a subconscious level, it was likely a way of coping with grief—to believe her father might someday return in a spaceship coming down from the sky.

Regardless, she could still finish the satellite dish project in her father's honor. In her living room workspace, she was getting much better with tools, and the YouTube instructors were proving to be a big help (Big Bob was still her favorite). Learning to use the crimper, she'd assembled the F-connectors to the RG-6 cable, thus securing the airwave inputs to the receiver, dish, and amplifiers. On the playback device, she connected her speakers, headphones, and TV by simply plugging them into the USB and HDMI ports. With her CAT-6 cable, she linked the internet modem to the receiver.

Because their house was already wired for cable reception, she'd installed a four-point multi-switch on the junction box to convert it to satellite. In the digital age, she realized she wouldn't need the RF Modulator, which the clearly outdated manual referred to as the way to connect a DVD player to an analog TV. Unfortunately, she didn't realize that until *after* her 30-day return policy had expired. Oh well. She'd bought a used one on Amazon for $9.99, which she might be able to resell for the same price.

The next major task would be to mount the dish on the rooftop where the cable fed to their old antenna. Only one problem: shingles slick with ice on the roof's steep slope. Far too dangerous still, she'd promised her mother to wait until spring. With the thaw coming soon, she hoped her feelings for Zachary would melt away with the bitter frost.

Waking up in the middle of the night, Zachary realized he was no longer having the same abduction dreams. He did have to pee very badly, however. As he groggily made his way to the bathroom, he realized that Kaitlyn was right—his dreams were nothing more than a manifestation of guilt, his subconscious tricking him to believe he'd made contact with the aliens. That way, he could better live with the lies he'd told her and everyone else.

Any psychologist could probably tell him that, yet it still didn't explain how his window had been left open that night weeks ago. It was possible he'd crawled out of bed half-asleep—much as he was doing now—and forgotten about it by the time he'd woken up. Chilled by the cold night air, he wondered why he would do so in the middle of winter unless he was covered in too many blankets. While relieving his bladder, he decided that was the only logical explanation.

Back in bed, he couldn't sleep now as he contemplated where he would be in the fall. Just a few weeks ago, he had planned on moving halfway across the country to the picture-perfect campus of Iowa State University, strolling hand-in-hand with his raven-haired girlfriend. Now, he would likely become a Washington State Cougar, a university three-and-a-half-hours from home. Beautiful country indeed, yet he felt zero excitement about attending his parents' alma mater.

"Just wait until the end of summer," his father had counseled. "Once the disappointment of that girl wears off, you'll be counting the days to start college there." He said the words "that girl" as if she were a third-grade crush he upset on the playground during recess.

After setting his mind so strongly on Iowa State, Zachary still considered accepting their admissions offer. Regardless of Kaitlyn, he was truly inspired by their sustainable agriculture program, and with thirty-thousand students there, she might not even know he was one of them—until they ended up in the same prerequisite class together or ran into each other at the library, bookstore, or cafeteria. An awkward moment to say the least, or worse: She'd think he was psychotically stalking her.

That's why he hadn't texted Kaitlyn since their "breakup" call, even if he didn't recall her saying to never contact her again. She obviously hated him, and he was afraid of pissing her off even more by messaging her. The last thing he needed was a restraining order, but even if he wanted to risk that kind of humiliation, she might have already blocked his number.

He wasn't sure, though, since she hadn't blocked him on Instagram. The week before, she'd uploaded a video of Jenna's birthday party. Jenna's boy-friend was there, cheering her on as she blew out the candles on her cake. He was some muscle-headed guy who seemed far more interested in Kaitlyn, at least judging by the way he was sneaking glances her way and laughing at every little thing she said. Garrett, if he recalled correctly, was his name, though for some reason Kaitlyn rarely mentioned him.

Zachary wondered why she hadn't blocked him on social media, unless she still wanted him to know what she was up to. Perhaps that was a sign she wanted to hear from him as well, or at least wasn't totally freaked out by him.

If only he knew what to write, he might take the chance, but he could think of nothing that would change her mind. After several minutes of rehashing the same thoughts over and over, he finally dozed off into the early stages of REM sleep.

Like a message in a bottle, the words floated up from somewhere deep in his subconscious. Half-awake, he reached for his phone and texted a message to Kaitlyn. Short and sweet—it was all he needed to say. Fumbling to set the phone down, he quickly submerged himself into a deep, peaceful slumber.

Arriving on campus, Kaitlyn parked in the student lot, took her phone out of the glovebox, and powered it on. After hitting the snooze button twice that morning, she hadn't had time to check her messages. Not surprisingly, Jenna had texted her a few times, asking if she wanted to meet one of Garrett's friends or that counselor from Blossoms she wouldn't give up on. *Go date him yourself*, she wanted to text back, *if he's so great*. She truly wondered if Jenna had a crush on the guy.

Then, as she spotted the message from Zachary, her heart took a leap off a high dive and plummeted into a pool of stomach acids. Daring to open it, she read:

Before I met you, I did not believe in a higher power, but only God could create someone as beautiful as you and save me from the pain I am suffering without you in my life.

Eyes stinging with tears, Kaitlyn tried to swallow the lump in her throat. It was just another BS lie, she told herself, a way of exploiting her faith to manipulate her emotions. She couldn't let him break her, no matter how badly she wanted to believe him.

Taking a deep breath, she knew she had to cut him out of her life for good. So, on her phone, she blocked his number, then his username on Instagram, followed by her lesser-used social media apps: Facebook, Twitter, Snapchat. No longer could he see her posts or contact her in any way.

Seated in the cab of her truck, she watched a crowd of students approaching the school building. Not only did she feel empowered, but she got a strange high from knowing he hadn't forgotten her.

Without warning, a sudden hailstorm sent the students running inside. In fact, the pelting balls of ice came down so hard on Kaitlyn's windshield that she feared they would crack the glass or riddle her father's truck with dings. In a matter of seconds, the pounding storm was over like a thrash metal drum solo coming to an end.

Getting out of the truck, she headed for the school in the eerie silence that followed. If nature was being poetic, she wasn't sure what exactly it was trying to tell her.

Zachary might have forgotten about sending the text if not for seeing it on his phone the next morning. It was something he could write only in the twilight hours, when the soul is wide awake and the conscious mind at rest. Not that he didn't mean what he said, but he wondered if he scared her away by exposing too much of his inner self.

When a week had passed and he still hadn't heard back from her, he knew he'd received his answer. Meanwhile, his parents were constantly at odds, their arguments becoming more intense—like the one they were having downstairs right now.

"I'm not selling the business I worked so hard to build!" shouted his father.

"That *you* built?!" yelled his mother. "You mean that *we* built!"

"I didn't mean it like that. You were always far more than just the accountant."

"*Just* the accountant? That's obviously what you think!"

"No, it's not, Delores! You're twisting my words now!"

"I'm not twisting anything! Right out of college, I could've worked as a CPA at any big firm in Seattle, and by now, I'd be making three times what I do at some stupid car dealership!"

"Well, I'm sorry you married a loser like me!"

"I never said that!"

"Not in those words, but you still did!"

"You should be far more concerned about your daughter living with some guy we don't even know!"

"She's a legal adult! What am I supposed to do?"

"You're her father! You tell me!"

"You want me to go beat the guy up like some kind of gangster?"

"It'd be better than watching you do nothing!"

"I'm trying to save our family by saving our business!"

"Oh, give me a break, Russ!"

Inserting earbuds, Zachary tuned them out with music on his phone, a new indie band from Wisconsin named Antonym. He'd downloaded their album on Spotify after hearing them on the local college station. They sounded way different than what anyone at Lemley High was listening to. If this is what they played in the dorms at college, he might actually make some cool friends there and enjoy himself, whether in Washington or Iowa. Assuming, that is, that people had forgotten his story by then, and he was no longer that weird guy involved in that UFO hoax.

"It's not *your* decision!" screamed his mother over his music.

"Well, you tell me a better plan!" his father shouted back.

A door slammed as they took their bickering voices into another room.

Pausing the track on his phone, Zachary thought he'd heard his name mentioned. He really wanted to move out, but that would have to wait until after he graduated from high school. Alone in his room, he really needed someone to talk to. That someone was Kaitlyn.

Deep down, he didn't believe he'd ever hear from her again, but just to be certain, or possibly to torment himself, he called her number, which went straight to an automated message from AT&T. The sound of chimes preceded a pleasant voice saying, "We're sorry, but the wireless customer you're trying to reach is not accepting calls at this time."

She'd blocked him, and now he felt totally humiliated. No way on Earth could he go to Iowa now. He was going to be a homegrown Washington State Cougar. His heart had been clawed out by his former friend.

025

In the middle of March, it was still too cold to sleep outside, which is why Blossoms Troop #276 was given the opportunity to pitch their tents inside the East Plains Middle School gymnasium after a full day in the wilderness. Glad to have joined their outing, Kaitlyn used her camping skills to teach the kids how to start a campfire, bait a hook on a fishing pole, watch for poison ivy and rattlesnakes, and provide basic first-aid to those not watching carefully enough.

"Thanks again for coming," said Jenna, as she and Kaitlyn braved it outside in sleeping bags so they could watch the starry sky. "You were a big help, and the kids really love you."

"Not as much as you," said Kaitlyn, keeping her voice quiet so they wouldn't wake those asleep in tents. "I should've known you'd become a teacher someday."

"It all started with babysitting my neighbor's kids," said Jenna. "The couple was surprised how well I got the kids to behave and to do their homework. It's weird because I have a hard time concentrating on my own studies, but when I'm instructing kids, I'm totally focused. Plus, it's a lot of fun reading them stories and taking them on outings like this."

"Sounds like it's your calling," said Kaitlyn.

"I think so," said Jenna, gazing up at a waxing gibbous moon.

Kaitlyn, the cold stinging her lungs, inhaled a crisp breath of air. "This reminds me of those camping trips with my father."

"You were always much better at roughing it than I was," said Jenna.

Kaitlyn smiled, recalling her friend bringing battery-powered everything, from a blow dryer to an electric toothbrush to battery packs for her phone to recharge. "You are definitely more suited for glamping than camping," she teased.

"I just hated feeling skuzzy," said Jenna, "especially when we ran into boys by the lake."

"Don't have to worry about that now," said Kaitlyn, since it was an all-girls retreat. The boys were headed off on a separate venture.

"Too bad," said Jenna. "You could've finally met Joe." She was still harping on that camp counselor guy.

"No rush," said Kaitlyn. "I'm not shopping for a boyfriend quite yet."

"Who said anything about a boyfriend? I'm talking about a date. How long has it been since you've even been out on one?"

"A while," said Kaitlyn, not wanting to think about the time she wasted on Zachary. "How 'bout you and Garrett? How're things going?"

Jenna turned silent, a faint glow of moonlight on her somber face. "I don't know," she said. "He's been acting kind of strange lately."

"How so?"

"Like last week, after I was accepted to UI, he told me not to make any college decisions based on him."

"Well," said Kaitlyn, unsure what to make of that. "Maybe he's just trying to be fair to you."

"He and I both know that if I go to Chicago, our relationship will be over. So, he's basically telling me he doesn't care whether we break up or not."

"That, or he doesn't want you making sacrifices you might regret later, especially if he's the one to blame."

"Yeah, I've thought about that too," said Jenna, her words trailing off. "I don't know what to think."

"Have you straight-up asked him what he wants?"

"He says he wants me there with him, but I'm not so sure. Being on the wrestling team, he can get tons of girls and probably doesn't want his old high school girlfriend hanging around everywhere he goes."

"Have you discussed dating other people in college?"

"He says he's not into that, but I don't think he really knows what he wants."

"We're eighteen," said Kaitlyn. "It's hard to imagine being with anyone right now for the rest of our lives." She already felt stupid for believing Zachary was *the one* for her—the guy with whom she'd have kids and grow old together.

"It's not just that," said Jenna, her voice tensing. "I think he might still be into you."

"Oh, come on," said Kaitlyn in total disbelief. "There was just this weird sentimental crush, which was really more about my dad than me."

"How's that?" said Jenna, sitting up in her sleeping bag.

Kaitlyn never did tell her what Garrett had written in the condolence card. "On a chance encounter," she finally confessed, "my dad made a big influence on his life. Outside the Walmart, Garrett was selling candy bars for his Little League team and was about to quit on a cold day, knowing his parents would buy the rest. My dad told him to stick it out, that quitting destroyed a person's character, and it stayed with Garrett for years to come. He says it's what made him a better wrestler."

"Why didn't you tell me that?" said Jenna, looking painfully surprised.

"I just did," said Kaitlyn, hoping the nighttime hid the guilt on her face.

"I mean back when you first found out."

"I don't know," said Kaitlyn. "It was right after my dad died, and you two weren't even dating yet."

"It's okay," said Jenna, settling back into her sleeping bag. "It really wasn't my business."

"I'm still sorry," said Kaitlyn. "I should have said something, later, after you became a couple, but I wasn't sure how to bring it up. And the more time that passed, the more awkward it became." They lay in silence, gazing up at the thousands of brightly burning stars in the far expanses of their galaxy.

"I'm sorry I didn't believe you," said Jenna, "when you told me about the UFO over your house the night your dad died."

"You were probably right," said Kaitlyn. "I was probably just sleepwalking."

"Real or not, you saw what you saw," said Jenna. "So, no matter what, it's real to you."

"Thanks," said Kaitlyn, with a grateful smile at her friend. For the rest of the evening, she couldn't help but watch for those mysterious lights in the sky. As her eyes grew tired, she finally dozed off in the cozy warmth of her sleeping bag.

When Kaitlyn returned from her weekend retreat, her mother had news for her. "My sister called," she said. "Checkers ran away from their house."

"Really?" said Kaitlyn in surprise. "When?"

"Two days ago."

"I thought he was happy there," said Kaitlyn, wanting for some reason to blame her Aunt Theresa and Uncle James.

"He seemed to be," said her mother, "when I was there to visit just recently."

"Maybe he missed you after you left," said Kaitlyn, "and wanted to come home."

"I wondered the same, but I sure hope not," said her mother. "It's over two-hundred miles from Beatrice." Beatrice was the town where her sister lived in Nebraska.

Kaitlyn thought about the dog all alone out there without anyone to feed him. If he wasn't hit by a car or frozen to death at night, he'd be lucky to survive by eating scraps from trash cans and drinking water from puddles. "Well, let's hope he just wandered off."

Her mother nodded, her face showing the same worries. "My sister and James have gotten pretty close to him."

He's still our dog, Kaitlyn thought, but was instantly ashamed for letting that cross her mind. In fact, if he was anyone's dog, he was her father's. All that mattered now was Checkers being safe from harm.

"We're selling the family business," said Zachary's father at the breakfast table. Still in pajamas, he looked sadly defeated, his face covered in atypical stubble.

"Your father and I agreed," said his mother. Her eyes gleamed with victory to match her "dress for success" attire—a power business suit with pinstripes.

Zachary looked down into his bowl of cereal, feeling too much shame to face his parents. "I'm really sorry, Mom and Dad. I really don't know what came over me, to say those things I said in front of those news people outside our house." If there were, in fact, aliens who could travel through time, he'd give anything right now to go back to that night and admit, in the school principal's office, it was all a stupid joke, even if it meant his parents continued selling their gas-guzzling SUVs. Better to save his family than the entire human race, which had quickly turned against him anyway.

"Don't look so down," said his mother. "It's not like your father and I really believed you were abducted."

"I kind of cornered you," said Zachary, "by announcing our Blowout EV Sale to the entire nation."

"*Kind of* cornered us?" said his father. "You bent our arms behind our backs and hogtied us. We had no choice but to play along."

"Oh, come on, Russ," said his mother. "You loved the attention far more than he did. Not to mention the money rolling in."

"It was your idea to sell those little alien dolls," said his father, "and T-shirts with flying saucers advertising our business."

"With your last name, not mine!" said his mother, referring to Taylor Automotive Sales.

"Last I checked," said his father, "you took on my name when we got married twenty-three years ago."

"Twenty-four, and I'll be going by Phelps again," she said. Phelps was her maiden name.

Zachary suddenly felt ill, the sight of his soggy cereal making him want to hurl. "You're not divorcing Dad, are you?"

His father, just as curious for an answer, looked to his mother.

"Not that I'm aware of," she said, "but I'm going to a job interview today, and it's better they don't associate me with your former business."

"My former business?!" said his father. "I thought it was *our* business, remember?"

"I should've hyphenated my name when we first got married," she said. "But since it's not Phelps-Taylor Automotive, there's no reason for them to know I ever played a part."

His father closely watched her as if trying to figure out who this stranger was at the table. "Where is your interview?" he finally asked.

"The Boeing plant in Seattle."

"Seattle?" said his father. "That's way too far to commute."

"Which is why we need to move," said his mother. "To start anew in a new place, where no one knows who we are. Wherever we go in this little town, people will be gawking and whispering about us. Our reputations are soiled forever."

His father sat there dumbfounded. Unable to argue, he asked, "So what am *I* going to do? Sell used cars at some two-bit dealership?"

"I think you'll do better than that," said his mother. "Once we put this thing behind us, every business needs a good sales manager. Doesn't have to be selling cars."

His father slowly nodded, more in surrender than agreement. "We can put the house up for sale once Zachary heads off for college in the fall."

His mother smiled, putting her hands over both of theirs. "It's a new lease on life," she said, speaking as if she were still an auto finance specialist, even if it was their future, and not cars, that she was trying to sell to them.

Looking at his parents, Zachary couldn't imagine them doing anything else. His father's expression was that of someone lost in a blizzard.

In the late afternoon, business at Daisy's Diner was very slow, so Kaitlyn was stocking napkin holders and wiping down tables. Hearing the jingle of the front doorbell, she headed for the register to greet their customer. She was taken aback on seeing it was Garrett, his head hung low as if deeply troubled by something.

"Garrett? What's wrong?" she asked.

"It's Jenna," he said, giving Kaitlyn a sudden jolt of terror that something tragic had happened to her. "She just broke up with me."

Kaitlyn sighed in relief. At least her friend was okay. "I'm sorry," she said, grabbing a menu and leading him to a back-corner table—the same one he and Jenna were cozying up at just a few months before. "I'm really not hungry," he said, taking a seat.

"Did she say why she broke up?" Kaitlyn wondered why her friend hadn't told her at school that day what she was planning.

Garrett grimly shook his head. "She decided on Chicago and figures we may as well break up now since a long-distance relationship won't work."

Kaitlyn nodded, thinking that's not quite everything her friend had told her.

"Doesn't make sense, though," Garrett continued. "We still have a few more months till graduation, and just last week, we talked about staying together at least until the end of summer before making the big decision."

"I'm really sorry, Garrett," she said, a bit awkwardly.

"What did she tell you?" he asked, looking up at her with a pleading expression. "I know she tells you everything."

Kaitlyn hesitated. Her first instinct was to protect her friend, but it was difficult seeing Garrett so desperate for answers. "Well," she cautiously said, "she's not really sure you know exactly what you want, and she doesn't want to become that clingy girlfriend you don't really want around."

"Bullshit!" said Garrett, pounding his fist on the table loud enough to draw Daisy herself out of the kitchen.

"Everything okay out here?" she asked, a chef's knife in hand.

"He'll be having your meatloaf, with a side of mashed," said Kaitlyn, remembering what he'd ordered last time.

Sizing Garrett up, Daisy returned to the back with a slight frown.

"Sorry," said Garrett, getting a hold of himself. "But she's the one who doesn't know what she wants, so she's putting it all on me."

A bit puzzled, Kaitlyn inquired, "Is that all she said? For why she's breaking up?"

"She thinks I might be interested in someone else," said Garrett, glancing down at his menu. It was the first time, Kaitlyn suddenly realized, without a single peek at her breasts.

"Is that true?" she dared to ask.

Garrett gazed up at her, his blue eyes filled with intense certainty. "Maybe a bit of a crush still, but I'm in love with Jenna." He broke down in tears, asking, "How come nobody I love wants me? What's wrong with *me* anyway?"

"Nothing is wrong with you," said Kaitlyn, leaning over to give him a hug, his massive shoulders shaking from the force of his emotions. As he sobbed against her, she couldn't help but wonder if she'd let the right one get away.

SPRING

026

The roof was no longer covered in frost, its shingled slope less dangerous than before. Kaitlyn angled the ladder against the house and climbed up its rungs with the satellite dish slung over her shoulder. "Don't worry!" she called down to her mother, who was standing careful watch below. "It's really not that heavy!"

"Watch out for those shingles!" warned her mother. "They break loose sometimes!"

"I know!" said Kaitlyn, reaching a flatter portion of the roof, where she set down the dish next to her toolbox and instruments. She was a little out of breath, it being her fourth trip up and down the ladder to carry everything up.

Finally, ready to begin, she removed the plate cover on the roof, exposing the RG-6 cable, which ran through a tightly sealed hole from inside the house. Bolting down the mast, she attached the cable and dish, keeping the screws a bit loose to adjust the angle. But first, she wanted to test the signal and noise meter, so she grabbed her low-voltage reader to see if she had a strong output.

"Is everything okay up there?" her mother called out.

"Yes, Mom! Now please stop asking, 'cause you're making me nervous!"

"Okay!" she said, the worry carrying in her voice.

Kaitlyn knew that for a satellite to work, it had to orbit our planet at nearly seven thousand miles per hour to stay on a parallel path to the Earth's rotation. Geostationary orbit was the scientific term. It required the dish to be aimed as close as possible to the satellite's direction from which she was hoping to receive a transmission—in her case, the Starburst2000, which relayed and delivered over 260 TV stations from across the globe.

A precise angle was required, and she'd done the mathematical calculations for its magnetic azimuth, elevation, and LNB (low noise block) skew, all of which were measured in spherical degrees from zero to 360. Using a level, she made sure the mounting pipe was vertically straight and perpendicular to the horizon before setting the elevation at 49.3 degrees. Next, she gathered her compass to align the azimuth, a certain number of degrees along the horizon to the satellite's vertical plane, which happened to be 201.4 degrees. To mark a perfectly straight line from her vantage point, she set up stakes and string like a map surveyor.

The final step was to align the LNB contained in the feedhorn—its antenna needed to be perfectly in line with the polarized signals from Starburst2000. Without the LNB, the signals would not be converted to the receiver inside the house. A little off-kilter, she turned the screw clockwise in its mounting bracket, then measured it with a protractor device she'd made herself. After several minor adjustments, she finally had the perfect skew at 22.3 degrees.

"We did it, Dad," she said, tightening the screws into place. The dish was now aimed perfectly at the sky above. Nearly three months after Christmas, she had completed their project all by herself. Straightening up, she could see the cornfields to the north stretching for miles in all directions. To the west was Barton's pumpkin orchard, and the Whitmore ranch filling the landscape with rustic colors. Southeast gave view to a rolling prairie, its tall grasses swaying in the breeze with hypnotic beauty.

Lost in the moment, Kaitlyn enjoyed the warmth of the sun on her face. Far away in the fields, a four-legged creature came trotting into view, its scrawny silhouette appearing to be a coyote, but as it got closer, it turned out to be a dog. Must be one of the Whitmore hounds on the loose again, she figured, until she noticed its fur was too long for a hound, and its coat so filthy that she could barely make out its golden color and white patches. *No, it can't possibly be*, she thought to herself when she spotted the familiar red collar.

"Mom!" she cried out in disbelief.

"What's the matter?!" asked her mother, craning her neck to squint up at her.

"It's Checkers!" said Kaitlyn, watching their dog come trotting closer, his ribcage a lot leaner than she last remembered, his tail wagging regardless. "He's coming home!"

They found some dog food in the garage and mixed it with some chicken dinner leftovers from the night before. Hovering over his meal, Checkers devoured the meal with such fervor that he pushed his dish completely across the kitchen linoleum. "You're a hungry boy, aren't you?" said Kaitlyn, trying to wipe him down with a warm wet towel. "And stinky too. You're getting a bath as soon as you're done eating."

On the phone nearby, her mother was talking to Aunt Theresa. "We're just as shocked as you are. Yes, he's way too skinny and filthy, but other than that, he's fine. I know, I know. I feel horrible that you and James took such good care of him, only to see him run off like this. Thank you so much. I just hope he doesn't get separation anxiety all over again once he realizes that Roger's not coming back."

"You know that, right?" said Kaitlyn, the dog looking up from his empty dish to lick her face. "You know your daddy's not here and never coming back?" It pained her to say this, but Checkers wagged his tail and barked excitedly. Perhaps he understood.

"You, too," said her mother on the phone, "and thanks again." Ending the call with a sigh, she turned to Kaitlyn. "I can tell my sister's upset, but she's being a great sport, as always."

Done with his meal, Checkers went to lay down on the carpet next to the TV and went straight to sleep. So much for the bath.

"That's weird," said her mother. "He never used to sleep there."

Kaitlyn thought about it. His favorite spot had always been near the front window looking out. "Maybe he came for the free satellite stations."

Her mother laughed, and Kaitlyn joined in, the dog twitching his ears in his sleep. It felt almost like a normal Sunday in their house, before her father had died.

The next day, Kaitlyn sat on the couch with Checkers in her lap, his fur still damp from the bath she'd given him. Remote in hand, she checked out her new satellite stations on TV: a Turkish news channel, an Indian cricket match, a Mexican soap opera, a Japanese cooking show, an Australian rugby scrum, a German financial report, a Croatian game show, and a Norwegian reality program about modern-day adventurers tracing the ancient routes of Vikings in replicated longships.

Finally landing on the French spy film *Dossier 5*, she was surprised to understand the dialogue a lot better than she'd anticipated. With viewing and practice, she'd catch up to where she'd been before her father's illness, with hopes of becoming fluent in college. That would make him proud since he hated her dropping her French class to care for him.

The front door opened, and her mother came in wearing a tracksuit. Her face was flushed from a jog in the countryside. "I hope we still get the Weather Channel," she said, watching Kaitlyn flip past a Ukrainian news report showing tanks in the street.

"Channel Three-Hundred," said Kaitlyn, turning to see its weather map of the USA. In late March, they were still a couple of months before tornado season, though the first could happen anytime, and with little warning.

"Easy to remember," said her mother, kicking off her running shoes in the foyer.

"How was your jog?" asked Kaitlyn.

"Beautiful sunset," said her mother, walking into the living room in her socks. "But I wish I had your father's discipline to get up first thing every morning to run."

As the dog slept in her lap, Kaitlyn said, "Well, you'll have a jogging partner once he catches up on some rest."

Her mother smiled. "With enough exercise, I'm hoping to get off the meds completely." Dr. Spalding had already cut back her dosage of anti-depressants, recommending both physical and social activities instead. In recent weeks, her mother had joined a book club, signed up for a painting class, and was volunteering at the church as a grief counselor, sharing her own experience to help others. With everything going on, she seemed to be in much better spirits.

"I'm glad to see you doing so much better, Mom," said Kaitlyn.

Her mother gave her a loving smile. "I hope you know how proud I am of you," she said, "and constantly praying for what's best for you."

"Thanks, Mom," she said, feeling her chest swell with emotion. "I think we're going to be okay."

027

It was the day before spring break and, for Zachary, it could not begin soon enough. Every day brought a new form of taunts. His locker had been graffitied so many times the custodian had stopped removing and painting over it. This morning, someone had written in black sharpie: "Travis Walton Jr." *Whoever that was,* he wondered, spinning the combination lock to grab his biology worksheets for first period.

"Travis!" shouted a voice passing by, followed by a group of boys sarcastically calling out, "TRAAAA-VIS!" A few lockers down, Camila appeared in a pair of jeans that made him question how he had ever turned her down in the first place. "Yo, Travis!" said some punk little freshman passing by, popping his gum with a stupid smirk. Ignoring him, Zachary turned to Camila grabbing her things. "Any idea who this Travis guy is?"

"Pff," she said in disgust, banging her locker closed. "Have you ever heard of Netflix?"

As she departed, Zachary took out his phone to Google him. Travis Walton appeared in too many articles to count. *The Hollywood Reporter* featured a documentary series about him that was trending number one on Netflix. Reading more, Zachary learned he was a former lumberjack who claimed aliens abducted him in 1975, following a five-day disappearance from a national forest in Arizona. At the time, his abduction became a wildly popular news story. The media gave his story credence because of UFO "experts" agreeing with law enforcement officials that the details of his account added up. He'd even passed a lie detector test.

But as the years passed by, many skeptics began to question the validity of his story. Upon closer inspection, his so-called details were extremely vague, and the polygraph machine was likely not calibrated, but even if it was, he could have cheated by tensing his body and holding his breath. Many accused Walton of pulling off a major hoax so he could financially profit from his best-selling book, the rights of which were sold to Paramount Pictures to become the movie *Fire in the Sky*.

Thirty years later, he was put to the test on the game show *Moment of Truth*. Asked if he had really been abducted by aliens, Walton responded, "Yes," to which the polygraph showed he was lying. Even so, thousands of people still believed (*or wanted to believe*, thought Zachary) that he'd been abducted.

According to *The Hollywood Reporter*, the Netflix doc juxtaposed both possible theories, leaving the viewer to decide if it was just a hoax or if he'd really gone aboard an alien spaceship. Given the similarities of their stories, Zachary was surprised he'd never heard of Walton before today, even if Walton's so-called encounter had been nearly half a century ago.

"TRAAAAVIS!" called out another pack of boys passing behind him.

Nearly half a century, Zachary thought to himself, making Travis Walton at least seventy-years-old today. It suddenly dawned on him that not only would he would never be able to escape this public scrutiny, but he was destined for unending humiliation and ridicule. Fifty years from now, he'd be watching a documentary about himself, and his family would still feel shamed and haunted by his foolish stunt.

On his way to class, he lost all interest in going to college the following school year. If he had any future at all, it would have to be in a job dealing with technology rather than people. With robots taking over anyway, he could learn how to program them through online courses, or so he hoped.

"TRAVIS!" shouted another voice down the hall.

Sad to say, but a robot might be the only companion that didn't make fun of him.

While some of the wealthier kids at East Plains High were heading off to Daytona Beach for spring break, Kaitlyn was over at Jenna's house for a Netflix and pizza night. Scrolling the menu for something to watch, they saw the Travis Walton docuseries still trending at number one. "Anything but that!" said Kaitlyn, her body tensing at the movie poster design of a small figure shadowed in bright lights shining down through the trees, the spacecraft unseen, as if left for the viewer to decide if it was really there or not.

"A lot of people still think he's telling the truth," said Jenna, scrolling past it to land on the newest *Enola Holmes* movie, the comic-adventure series about Sherlock Holmes's perky younger sister, whom they both loved. "Oh my God, I didn't even know this was out!"

"Me neither," said Kaitlyn, her limited time for television recently dedicated to her new satellite stations. "Let's watch it."

Starting the movie, Jenna grabbed a slice of pepperoni. "It's nice hanging out again, just the two of us."

Kaitlyn smiled at her friend and asked, "Are you doing okay?" As much as Jenna loved to talk, she'd been unusually quiet about her breakup with Garrett. "Is there anything you want to talk about?"

"I'm fine," said Jenna with a quick smile, cranking up the volume as the opening credits began over music.

"Time out," said Kaitlyn, taking the remote and hitting pause. "Just for the record, Garrett is totally over me, and he's in love with you, so I hope that's not the reason why you dumped him."

Jenna gave her a curious look. "How would you know?"

"He came into the diner the day you ended it," said Kaitlyn. "I was his shoulder to cry on—nothing more."

Jenna looked at her in anguished disbelief. "Oh my God," she said. "I thought you were done withholding secrets from me. I *thought* you were my best friend."

"I am your best friend," said Kaitlyn, "which is why I'm telling you this. I don't want this kept between us, especially when it's not even true."

"What did he tell you?" said Jenna, her expression as demanding as her voice.

"Just as I said. He was over me and in love with you."

"There had to be more to it than that. Don't tell me he was just blubbering like a baby the whole time."

"He wanted to know why you really broke up with him. That *you* were afraid of committing, not him."

Jenna looked a bit stunned. "He really said that?"

"Yeah," said Kaitlyn. "Why is that so shocking?"

"I-I'm not sure," said Jenna, a sudden realization coming over her. "Maybe 'cause it's true, I guess."

Watching her friend, Kaitlyn could see how conflicted she was. "I can totally understand why you'd be afraid of committing to someone going to a different college than you."

"He says it's only a few hours away," said Jenna. "But it's really seven hours round-trip. That's a full day of driving, meaning we could only see each other on the weekends, which would be impossible during wrestling season. So we wouldn't really see each other for at least three months. Meanwhile, there'd be a ton of girls he could go out with."

"Not to mention plenty of cute guys at the University of Chicago," said Kaitlyn. Her friend seemed to flinch at her bluff being called.

"Okay," she admitted. "I want to *experience* college. I don't want to be sitting in my dorm room, waiting around for my boyfriend to text or call, while everyone else is out having fun. If I wanted to become a nun, I'd join a monastery. But yeah, there will be a ton of guys to go out with, so why lie to myself?"

"You shouldn't," said Kaitlyn. "But Garrett deserves the truth as well. The full truth." *And not making me your excuse,* she wanted to add.

Jenna thought about it. "I didn't think he could handle it if we agreed to date other people, but it's the only way to really find out whether or not we're right for each other."

"You should talk to him about it," said Kaitlyn.

Jenna nodded. "I do miss him a lot, and seeing him in the hallway at school nearly breaks my heart every time."

Kaitlyn felt relieved. "Okay," she said, grabbing a slice of pizza, "let's watch Enola kick some butt."

Spring break had just begun, and Zachary was already restless and bored in his room. The latest novel he was reading about a virus wiping out the human race did little to cheer him up. Since Hailey's vengeful post, he'd done his best to stay off the internet to avoid what people were saying about him. He'd also deleted his Instagram account after Kaitlyn blocked him.

No matter how hard he tried to hide, he was still hounded by reporters. Daring to peek outside the window, he saw a photographer lingering outside their security fence, a scuzzy-looking guy who quickly raised his camera and took aim. Quick to duck, Zachary was likely a second too late. He felt as if a piece of his soul had been snatched away, as had his privacy.

To leave the house, he'd tinted the windows of his Chevy Volt. In recent weeks, he'd been driving it to school and coming straight home to sneak through their security gate. As sad and lonely as he felt right now, he still preferred the isolation of his room over going to school. When he heard a pinging text alert on his phone, he figured it was another pesty reporter. Reflexively, he went to delete the text when he saw a message from the last person on Earth he expected to hear from. Make that second to last. It wasn't Kaitlyn, but his sister Hailey. *Hey,* she'd written. Their mother most likely gave her his latest number. *We need to talk.*

Saturday morning, Daisy's was packed with a noisy breakfast crowd, and the place smelled of greasy fried bacon and sausage. Hopping from table to table, Kaitlyn was, without a second to exhale, taking orders and bringing plates of food from the kitchen. "Here you go," she said to a youngish couple with three small kids bouncing around in their booth. "I'll be right back with your side of hash browns."

"Can I get some more ketchup, too?" said the dad, whose hair was starting to gray prematurely.

"Daddy-Daddy-Daddy-Daddy!" screamed his three-year-old.

"Sure thing," said Kaitlyn, grabbing the empty bottle from the table and speeding back to the kitchen to refill it.

"Can you get table six?" asked Daisy, flipping her specialty blueberry pancakes on the grill. "Fiona's behind on her orders." A sweet-faced junior at Kaitlyn's school, Fiona was the new waitress, and she was struggling to keep up.

"Okay," she said, a little annoyed. Daisy had never been so soft on her, even right after her father died. "More tips for me, right?" The ketchup bottle refilled, she whisked out into the dining section, when a pair of truckers waved her down from their booth.

"Miss, we're out of syrup over here!"

"Your waitress will be right with you," said Kaitlyn, looking across the diner to see Fiona flirting with some guys on their high school football team. She felt like throwing a dirty, wadded-up napkin to get her attention, but forced a smile instead as she continued toward the family waiting for the ketchup. "There you go," she said, setting it down to grab the bottle of maple syrup. "Are you done with this?"

"Yes, they've had plenty," said the mother with a tired smile. Her kids were still bouncing around in the booth, their barely eaten pancakes in a puddle of syrup.

"Thanks," said Kaitlyn, taking the bottle to the pair of truckers on her way to table six. Its sole occupant sat behind the cover of an open book titled *Seven Brief Lessons on Physics* by Carlo Rovelli. Highly curious to know who the reader was, Kaitlyn said, "Hi there. May I take your order?"

Lowering the book a few inches, a young man peered up at her with inquisitive hazel eyes. "Two eggs, over medium," he said in a well-mannered tone. "Two slices of toast, preferably wheat bread if you have it. Side of hash browns, please."

Kaitlyn didn't need to write it down. "I'm going to start as a physics major next year at Iowa State," she blurted out, though she still hadn't confirmed her admissions acceptance, much less declared a major.

"Really?" said the young man, lowering his book some more to reveal his face. His brown hair, cut short, brought out the sharp angles of his nose and cheekbones. "I'm a freshman there now but still undecided on a major."

Taken aback by his bold features, Kaitlyn decided he was handsome in a very unconventional way. "Well, you must have some interest in physics," she said, excited to be talking to someone already on campus.

"I do, but I'm not that strong at math, which explains why I'm reading this," he said of the book.

Kaitlyn had never heard of it, though its cover advertised *NY Times Bestseller*. "I bet it's interesting," she said, a little nervously.

Nodding, he said, "It breaks things down in layman's terms, from Einstein's theory of relativity to quantum mechanics. That way, I can sound really smart at the dinner table without really knowing anything."

Kaitlyn chuckled. "Isn't that why people go to college? To sound smarter than they really are?"

"Exactly," he said, his smile revealing a crooked front tooth, which somehow made him more attractive.

"I'm Kaitlyn," she said, keenly aware of demanding customers behind her.

"George," he said, reaching out to shake her hand.

"You from around here?" she asked, knowing most of the faces that came in.

"Marshalltown," he said, which Kaitlyn knew was about twenty minutes away. "On my way to Des Moines when I stopped off to get some gas and saw this place."

Kaitlyn smiled, sensing a mutual attraction. "Glad you found us," she said as Fiona flitted by with a steaming pot of coffee in hand.

"I had to refill your customers at table nine," she scoldingly said to Kaitlyn. So much for that sweet face of hers. Kaitlyn wanted to remind her that she was covering her table right at this moment but couldn't complain because she was more than happy to be chatting with this cute college boy.

"I'll be right back with your order," she told him, turning and retreating for the kitchen. Along the way, she assumed he was checking out her backside, and she self-consciously regretted not wearing her other pair of black pants.

After George was done eating, and she brought him his check, she noticed he'd wiped off his table—his crumpled napkin was in the middle of the plate so she wouldn't have to touch it. "Would it be okay if I got your number?" he politely asked.

She smiled and set down the check. "It's already on there," she said.

028

Zachary waited a few days to respond to his sister's text message. She wanted to meet at the bar where she now worked in Seattle's Broadway District. Traffic being worse than he'd expected, it took him nearly two hours to finally get there and find a metered spot to park at. Two blocks from the bar, he walked the busy sidewalk, passing an indie coffee shop, hipster tattoo parlor, LGBTQ bookstore, and vegan café. A group of homeless teens gathered outside with their boombox blaring punk rock from the 70's. Their cardboard sign asked for "Donations." Next to it was a cup filled with change.

"Hey, Burb!" they called out, whatever that meant. Probably short for "suburbs," he realized, and wondered if he was really that obvious.

"How 'bout a dollar, Burb?" said a woman with a purple Mohawk and studded lip.

On his way past, his body language giving away his awkwardness, Zachary wasn't sure if he should ignore them.

"Come on, Burb!" shouted a punker guy with green hair. "Help the cause, bro!"

Zachary wasn't sure exactly what their cause was but felt trapped either way. If he gave them money, he'd feel punked and naïve. If he didn't, he'd be proving them correct that he was a bourgeoisie suburbanite.

"Just a dollar, bro!" pleaded a girl with a shaved head covered in tats. "Before you go back to the burbs!"

As a form of compromise, Zachary scooped fifty cents from his pocket and dropped it in their cup, the group cheering and jeering, "Thanks, Burb!"

Down a darkly lit stairwell, he entered a lounge with no name, the music playing over speakers a sound he couldn't describe: hypnotic, primitive, unapologetic. In the middle of the day, the crowd consisted mostly of college students and alternative young people. Lots of wildly colored hair and facial piercings. Their T-shirts ranged from Seattle U to indie rock bands he'd never heard of.

Making his way to the bar, he didn't recognize his sister at first, her hair now bright blue as she filled a cup of draft beer with her back to him. When she finally turned his way, she showed little recognition, coming toward him as if he were any customer off the street. "What can I get you?" she said.

Taken aback, Zachary replied, "I didn't know I could legally buy alcohol or that you could legally serve it."

"If anyone asks," said Hailey, "I'm a server, not a tender, so yes I can."

"You wanted to talk," said Zachary, not caring what the legal differences were.

"Yeah," said Hailey, the music just loud enough to give them privacy. "I wanted to say thank you, but I will never forgive you."

"Okay," said Zachary, having no idea what that was supposed to mean.

"Thank you for ruining my life," she said, "because it was the only way to destroy my old self. I'm finally free to find out who I really am and who *I* want to become instead of following the blueprint our parents drew up for us when we were in diapers."

"I never cared about the blueprint," said Zachary.

"Obviously," said his sister, "which is why you destroyed our family's business."

"You're the one who did that with your Instagram post."

"Sooner or later, you were going to be exposed, and the damage would've been worse to Mom and Dad."

"Don't give me that," said Zachary. "You don't have a crystal ball to foresee the future."

"True," said Hailey. "But I couldn't keep playing along. So now I'm free."

"You're welcome, I guess, so now you can stop hating me."

Hailey, showing some spite in her smile, looked at him. "This will follow you forever, you know. Just like Travis Walton."

"Maybe not," said Zachary, looking around at the self-absorbed crowd. "Nobody here even recognizes me."

Just then, a college-aged girl came up to him, her pretty face covered in heavy eyeliner and black lipstick, and her hair dyed Gothic black, when its natural color was probably blonde or sandy brown. "I know you," she said.

"I don't think so," said Zachary, watching his sister roll her eyes.

"You're Zachary Taylor," said the girl.

"What'd I tell you?" said Hailey, heading down the bar to serve some waiting customers.

"So that's it?" he yelled after her. "You had me drive all this way just to tell me that?!"

Pulling a spout to fill a beer mug, she glanced his way to respond. "I thought you'd be happy for me! To see me moving on."

"Thrilled," he said. "I'll tell Mom and Dad you're doing great."

She pretended not to hear, sliding the mug of beer to a skinny young guy with a long, bushy beard that made him look like a lumberjack.

"Families are such a drain," said the girl with black lipstick. "I'm Venus, by the way."

"Venus," said Zachary, turning to face her. "You may think you know me, but you really don't."

"So then let's get to know each other better," she said, leaning toward him, her hot breath in his ear. "My apartment's nearby if you wanna talk in private."

Feeling her breast against his arm, Zachary saw she was even prettier than he'd first noticed. Her Gothic appearance, including a black leather miniskirt over fishnet stockings, was like a sexy Halloween costume. "Okay," he said, pulling his shirt down over his growing erection. The thought of going back to a college girl's apartment gave him a total rush of excitement.

As they left the bar together, he felt his sister's bitter stare and savored every second of it.

Venus' apartment was bigger and nicer than he'd expected—with a living room view of Elliot Bay looking out toward downtown Seattle's skyline. Its Space Needle was so perfectly centered, it might as well have been a postcard. "You're really in college?" he asked, as he sat down next to her on the couch with a lemon drop martini. It was her drink of preference, and she'd made it for both of them.

"Marketing major," said Venus. "My parents want me to go on for my MBA, but I want nothing to do with running their business."

"What kind of business is it?" Zachary asked.

She hesitated, a bit theatrically, he thought. "They're a private vendor," she said, "contracting with Weyerhaeuser to produce timber for their manufacturing."

"I thought Weyerhaeuser was already in the business of cutting down trees for profit?"

"You can never have enough, though, right?" she said, giving her glass a little shake to rattle the ice cubes. "Who cares about the ecosystem? Wildlife can go to hell. Farms can flood. Landslides, soil erosion, streams destroyed with sediment. I want nothing to do with that. I'm sorry."

Zachary looked around at her upscale apartment and its expensive furnish-ings—clear evidence she had no real objections to taking her parents' money. As if reading his mind, she nuzzled against him. "Which is why I admire you so much, Zachary. You stood up to your family's business to make it better."

"Not really," he said, having lost his erection despite the sensation of her breast pressing against his arm. "They're going *out of* business."

"Even better!" she said. "No more selling gas-consuming SUVs!"

Zachary seriously doubted she'd want to put her own family out of busi-ness if it meant giving up this life of luxury. In no mood to argue, he awkwardly sipped his drink. *Way too sweet,* he thought. *I can barely taste the alcohol.* The ice cubes rattled in his near-empty glass.

"Let me make you another," she said, taking his glass to head off for the kitchen.

"That's okay," said Zachary, his stomach a bit queasy. "I've got a long drive ahead of me and should probably get going." Thinking of Kaitlyn, he wondered if she ever still thought of him. The memory often left a painful void which he didn't know how to fill.

"You can pull up here," said Kaitlyn on the gravel road leading up to her house. A light was on in the window, indicating her mother was still up. Safe from view, George stopped and killed the headlights, his old Corolla parked in perfect rural darkness.

"I had a nice time," she said, having enjoyed the way he listened to what she had to say, rather than trying to impress her with his life ambitions and accomplishments like most other boys.

"Me too," said George. He wore cheap cologne that was a bit too strong, but smelled nice on him. "You're far more mature than most of the girls already in college."

She smiled. "You're just saying that because you want to kiss me."

"No, I mean it," he said, his face moving closer to hers.

"So, then you don't want to kiss me?" she teased.

"What do you think?" He kissed her softly, their mouths parting and tongues clumsily wrestling until they found a rhythm. It'd been a while since she'd made out with anyone, and her body felt a need to be touched. Eyes closed, she thought of Zachary and tried pushing him out of her mind. In her mind, the hand gliding over her breast belonged to him, not to George.

"No!" she said, pulling away.

"Sorry!" he said, catching his breath. "I'm really sorry—I thought it was okay."

By his expression, she could tell she'd freaked him out. "You're really sweet," she said, "but I—forget it."

"It's someone else, isn't it?" he quietly asked.

She nodded, but was hesitant to admit it. "I thought I was getting over him. I mostly am, and I really enjoyed spending time with you tonight."

He started the car, his expression more disappointed than angry. "Figures," he said, flicking on the headlights as he put the car in drive. "I really like you."

"I like you, too!" said Kaitlyn. "So, call me, okay?"

He pulled to a stop in her driveway, waiting for her to get out. "Why don't *you* call me?" he suggested, "once you're no longer thinking of that other guy."

"I barely did tonight. I swear!"

He looked her in the eyes and somberly nodded. "I should probably be getting back. I've got to get up early tomorrow."

Taking the hint to leave, Kaitlyn choked back tears while opening the passenger door. "I think you're being kind of a jerk."

"I wasn't trying to be. I was just—"

Kaitlyn slammed the door after getting out. She huffed off to her front porch, his headlights on her back as he waited for her to safely get inside.

"How'd it go?" asked her mother. She was watching the news on TV.

"Great, Mom," she said, hearing George's car drive off. Making a beeline to her room, she broke down in sobs while texting Jenna on her phone: *Hey.*

Jenna: Hey! How'd it go?!

Kaitlyn: Great...until I effed it up.

Jenna: What happened?!!

Kaitlyn: We were making out...and I freaked out, thinking of you know who.

Jenna: No way!

Kaitlyn: Yes.

Jenna: UFO boy?? WTF? He's such a loser.

Kaitlyn: I know. I must be attracted to psychos.

Jenna: Ugh! Was this George guy a good kisser?

Kaitlyn: Very + super smart, mature, thoughtful, sweet...

Jenna: And NORMAL?

Kaitlyn: Yes, whatever that really means.

Jenna: As in someone who doesn't say he was abducted by aliens.

Kaitlyn: If he was, he forgot to mention it.

Jenna: Lol. It's okay to be happy, you know.

Kaitlyn: I know.

Jenna: Do you really?

Kaitlyn: .....yes.

Jenna: Then promise me you will call this guy back.

Kaitlyn: I don't think he wants me to.

Jenna: Yes he does.

Kaitlyn: Only when I'm totally over you know who. He said so.

Jenna: Then get over him already!

Angry at herself, Kaitlyn couldn't understand why she still felt anything at all for Zachary. Even if it was nothing more than hatred and resentment, it was more passion than he deserved.

029

In the silence before dawn, Zachary awakened to an overwhelming feeling of loneliness. More than ever, he needed to talk to Kaitlyn, but she had blocked him from her life—by phone, text, and social media. If only he could send up a smoke signal, showing his true spirit through some shaman magic. In hopeless desperation, he suddenly realized he still had her home address, to which he'd mailed the Christmas card a few months back. It was saved on his phone, which he quickly found in her contact listing.

Out of bed, he went to his desk and dug out a notebook to write her a letter. As he thumbed through its pages for a blank set of lines, he came across a bold set of drawings that caught his eye. At first, he didn't recognize his own hand as the artist, but only he could've sketched a flying saucer over an egg-shaped moon. The cornfield below was crudely depicted, as if his parents had been playing Pictionary. At the picture's margins was a curious string of zeros and ones—binary code, he realized.

A sudden chill crept over him and made the hair on his arms stand up straight. He must've done this in the middle of the night, in that twilight hour between sleep and wakefulness. On his phone, he Googled "Egg Moon," which, he learned, got its name for the time of year when birds laid their eggs, which was the first full moon after the spring equinox. The Christians renamed it Passover Moon, with Easter being celebrated the following Sunday. That was two days from now, and the first stages of a full moon were appearing outside his window.

Tearing out the page of drawings, he grabbed his duffel bag to pack for a road trip.

With no school, work, or homework, it was one of the rare mornings that Kaitlyn got to sleep in. Still in bed, she'd been texting Jenna for the past hour. Jenna and Garrett had decided to continue their relationship until the end of summer, giving them five full months before leaving for separate colleges. By then, they hoped to have a better idea of how committed they wanted to remain to one another while in different states. *That's a good plan,* Kaitlyn texted in agreement.

"Kaitlyn!" her mother called out. "I'm making sandwiches. Do you want one?"

Kaitlyn looked at the time on her phone—it was 11:55 a.m. *OMG*, she messaged Jenna. *It's almost noon. I gotta help my mom with spring cleaning.*

"Kaitlyn!" her mother repeated. "Did you hear me?"

"Yeah, Mom! I'll take one, thanks. No tomato!"

Signing off with Jenna, she spotted a tabloid news alert on her phone. *Venus Aligns with Zachary: Can their Romance Save Planet Earth?* Highly curious, Kaitlyn opened the photo of Zachary with some Goth-looking chick wearing black lipstick and heavy eyeliner. Hand in hand, they were about to enter an upscale apartment building, the Goth chick looking back at the camera as if expecting the photographer to be there. Overcome by intense jealousy, Kaitlyn quickly read the article.

SEATTLE, Wash., March, 29—Teen heartthrob Zachary Taylor may have never been abducted by aliens, but he certainly had a recent encounter with Venus—Venus Wilcox, that is, whose billionaire father, John Wilcox, is founder and CEO of JW Timber, the logging company facing heated protests from environmental groups. "I totally support whatever it takes to save the planet," Venus confirmed in a press conference today. "It's what Zachary and I agree on. In fact, he was a huge inspiration to me, the way he challenged his parents to sell EVs instead of carbon-producing and polluting SUVs. Now I'm calling on my parents to stop destroying the ecosystem for timber production." Wilcox did not yet reveal her alternative plan for lumber, which she hopes to promote in a reality TV series. "I'll be pitching to Netflix tomorrow," she said. "Ironically, my father plays golf with an executive there, and I sometimes go clubbing with his daughter."

What a phony bitch, thought Kaitlyn, who wanted to wipe the smile right off her face. And what was with the Goth look? Spoiled little rich girl didn't even know how to rebel without looking ridiculous. She wondered how long Zachary had been seeing her—probably the whole time they'd been chatting. God, she was such an idiot to ever believe a single word he'd said.

"Did you want mayo?!" her mother shouted from the kitchen.

"Yeah, fine!" she snapped. How infuriating that he was now being celebrated as an eco-warrior when he was nothing more than a pathetic con-artist. The truth no longer mattered, so long as you were good-looking and people were dumb enough to fall for your BS.

"Melted cheese okay?" asked her mother. "I'm toasting the bread!"

"Whatever, Mom!" Glaring at the couple's photo, she had completely lost her appetite.

Zachary had been driving on 90-East for the past five hours, passing through Spokane into Idaho, and crossing its narrow wedge into Montana. A road sign welcomed him to Mineral County, its river rapids twisting through the rolling forest mountains, whose peaks were still covered in patches of snow. If he had the time, he might dare to go whitewater rafting as advertised on a billboard. "Next Exit."

The phone rang over his speakers, cutting off the music, which he'd forgotten was even playing. Seeing his father was the caller on the infotainment screen, he tapped the Bluetooth button to answer, "Hey, Dad!"

"Where the hell are you?!"

"Just crossing into Montana."

"Montana?" said his father in surprise. "What on Earth are you doing there?"

"I was planning on calling you," said Zachary. "To let you know I'm heading to Iowa."

His father's sigh was projected over the audio system. "You have school on Monday, you know."

"I know, Dad, but I have to see her. It's just something I need to do."

As he followed the winding road, he could hear his father thinking out loud, letting him know he was being foolish and irrational, and not thinking of the consequences. To his surprise, he said, "You must think this Kaitlyn is pretty special."

"Yeah," said Zachary. "I think I'm in love with her."

A brief silence followed. "I'd have done the same for your mom," said his father. "Still would, in fact, but just promise me one thing."

"What's that?" said Zachary, passing a deer crossing sign.

"That you pull over when you start feeling tired."

"I will, I promise."

"I mean it," said his father. "It's much too dangerous to fight off sleep."

"I know, Dad. I've got twenty more hours of driving, so I was planning on stopping after dinner to spend the night in a cheap motel."

"Okay," said his father, his voice sounding relieved. "Call us once you're checked in. You know your mother will be worried sick."

"Will do," said Zachary, ready to end the call.

"One more thing, Zach."

"Yeah?" he said, a bit impatiently.

"I'm proud to have you as my son."

"Thanks, Dad," he said, a lump forming in his throat. "And I'm proud to say you're my father." After awkward goodbyes, he continued down the road in tears. Up until this very moment, he never fully realized how much he and his father truly loved each other.

If the day hadn't started badly enough, seeing Zachary with that Goth chick, Kaitlyn was now helping her mother clean out her father's side of her parents' bedroom closet, putting his clothes into bags for the Salvation Army.

"Dr. Spalding said I needed to do this," said her mother in tears. "That it's part of moving forward in the grieving process."

"I know, Mom," said Kaitlyn, taking a blue dress shirt off its hanger and carefully folding it like a sacred relic. "I got him this for Father's Day," she said, breaking into a sob.

"Oh, sweetie," said her mother, turning to give her a hug. Even with the weight she'd put back on, she still felt frail in Kaitlyn's arms. "Mom?" she said, her voice filled with emotion. "If I leave for college in the fall, are you really going to be okay here all alone?"

"Yes, of course," said her mother, wiping her eyes with her sleeve. "I've got plenty to keep me busy, and I made a new friend in my therapy group. Frannie's a retired schoolteacher and also a widow."

Kaitlyn nodded. Her financial aid had been approved by the university. "I have to let them know by May first if I'm coming."

Her mother held her at arm's length to face her. "The real question here is," she said, "are *you* going to be okay away from home?"

Kaitlyn suddenly realized how afraid she was to leave the only home she'd ever known. All her memories were of growing up here, including the ones of her father—even buying him a tie for Christmas, which she clutched tightly in her hand. "I don't know," she said, her voice choking up.

"Come here," said her mother, pulling her close to comfort her. Kaitlyn felt as if she were a small child again but strangely didn't mind. "I'm really scared, Mom."

"I was just as scared leaving for college," said her mother. "I think most people your age are, but they would never admit it. But it's only a couple hours away, and you can always come home on the weekends for a homemade meal and to do your laundry."

"And to see you," Kaitlyn said, breaking into another sob.

"This will always be your home," said her mother with a teary smile. "No matter where you are."

Holding on to her, Kaitlyn felt so much love for her mother that she drenched her shoulder with tears. Come fall, she was going to Iowa State University to become a Cyclone just like her parents before her.

Zachary couldn't believe how big Montana was. After several hours of driving, he wasn't even halfway through the state, which totaled nearly six hundred miles across. To keep his mind occupied, he tried remembering the names of the towns he passed by. Many of them sounded as if they were named in the days of the old Wild West: Bearmouth, Goldcreek, Deer Lodge, Racetrack, Three Forks. There was also Manhattan, which he guessed was named by a New York prospector in the 1800s. He pictured a guy in a tweed suit with muttonchops.

Right this second, he just wanted to know where the nearest gas station was. He desperately needed to pee, and his fuel gauge showed he was nearly empty. On his GPS monitor, he was directed to the Town Pump Food Store in Bozeman, which was coming up in a few miles. As he followed the exit, he lowered his visor to block a glaring sunset.

Minutes later, he pulled up to the fuel pump, something he rarely had to do owning a hybrid vehicle. Not only did he hate consuming fossil energy, but thought it to be horribly hypocritical. Unfortunately, he couldn't spare the time to charge his Chevy Volt, much less find places to do so in the middle of this last frontier (or so it felt). Out of the car, he set the nozzle lever in place and hurried off to find a restroom, his legs stiff from driving and his bladder about to burst.

Following a long whiz (as his father liked to call it), he entered the store to buy some snacks. The smell of hotdogs on the grill made him feel incredibly hungry. To his surprise, they had vegan dogs as an option. He grabbed two to go, a bag of chips, a Monster energy drink, and as many bottles of water as he could cradle in his arms, and headed toward the register.

The cashier, a heavyset woman in her early twenties, looked up from her phone. She gave him a curious look, then glanced outside to see the Washington plates on his car. "You're that boy who got abducted, or *said* he was, aren't you?" Without taking her eyes off him, she robotically scanned his items.

"Uh, yeah," said Zachary, nervously watching a family enter the store, the kids running off for the soda machine.

"I knew it!" said the cashier. "You're with Venus now!" She held up her phone to show a picture of them together. Taken aback, Zachary quickly figured out that Venus had played him for publicity.

"Not quite," he said, anxiously inserting his credit card to pay.

"I can't really see the two of you together," said the cashier, bagging his goods.

"Thanks," said Zachary, snatching the bag and heading out. On his way to the car to remove the fuel nozzle, he wondered if Kaitlyn had seen him with Venus. Of course, she had; it was popping up on everyone's phones. Horrified by the thought, he at least hoped it made her jealous. In fact, he kind of liked to believe it had.

With a bit of a gloating smile, he got back into his car and hit the road again.

In need of some time alone, Kaitlyn sat outside on the porch swing, the moon glowing across the fields like a big yellow Easter egg. On the deck beside her, the bags of her father's clothes were ready to be picked up by the Salvation Army the next day. They would *not* be taking his Cyclones' sweatshirt, which remained in her truck, a keepsake nobody could ever take from her. In fact, she planned on wearing it on campus next fall, the perfect way of keeping his memory alive while preserving their family tradition.

Strange to think how much things would be changing after high school. After years of being spoiled with her own large bedroom, she'd be sharing a small dorm room with another girl—one with whom she'd hopefully get along. She'd better not be a slob, leaving dirty, smelly clothes and food wrappings about. Or even worse, a total neat freak expecting the same of her.

With enough on her mind already, she kept thinking of Zachary. To see him with that poser Goth chick was too much to stomach, and it had to happen just when she was starting to get over him. If Travis Walton was any indicator, she would be tormented by Zachary for years to come, or at least until she fell in love with someone else—someone who made her see how ridiculous her feelings for him had been in the first place. But given her date with George, the kind of guy she *should* fall in love with, she clearly wasn't ready to open her heart to anyone just yet.

Gazing out at the moon, she silently prayed for the right guy to come her way when the time was right.

The Monster energy drink carried Zachary the next few hours on the highway, his headlights penetrating the darkness and reflecting off another deer crossing sign ahead. Through a clearing of trees, the sky came into view—a great expanse of brightly burning stars in all directions. Montana truly was the Big Sky State, as motto'd on the license plate of a pickup truck passing by.

Even the moon was bigger and bolder here, or at least appeared to be. In science class, he'd learned that a full moon lasted for only an instant, but to the naked eye on Earth, it lasted for three full days. Its gravitational pull affected the tides and even our moods. In fact, the term "loony" was a reference to that lunar force, which drove some people to madness. He had to admit: He felt energized by the moonlight pouring down through his windshield.

On the passenger seat beside him, he'd placed the page of drawings in hopes of better deciphering what they meant. The cornfield was obvious, and the Egg Moon would still be in effect by the time of his arrival on Easter the next day. However, the string of binary numbers was way too bizarre, and his subconscious writing of code didn't make any sense. It was just a dream, he reminded himself. He also knew how crazy it was to follow a dream.

Blazing the highway at night, he felt like a time-traveling astronaut, the stars surrounding him as he continued toward his destination, which was a person more than a place—Planet Kaitlyn. He wondered how she would react upon seeing him. She might totally freak out and call the police, or she might see the truth in his eyes and know he'd never lied about the way he felt about her. Various scenarios played in his mind, ranging from a door being slammed in his face (with pepper spray in his eyes) to Kaitlyn running across the prairie grass to throw her arms around him in a swooping embrace.

After another hour on the road, he finally stopped to eat at the Big Horn Hotel. He hoped to cross Montana before bedtime, but after a large dinner— soup, salad, fresh trout, and baked potato—and thirteen hours of driving already, he was slammed with exhaustion.

Checking into a room upstairs, he barely had the energy to floss and brush his teeth. As he crawled into bed, he suddenly remembered to call his parents to let them know he was okay. Glad to hear their voices, he said good night and instantly crashed into a heavy slumber. 0101010001100010101000010000001 00100000101101010100001011010000...

Go to her no matter what forces try to stop you.

□∋□

The church was packed on Easter morning. Seated next to her mother, Kaitlyn was glad to be back for the first time since her father's funeral. Looking out the window, she saw the pawpaw tree in bloom, its reddish-purple flowers so small they needed to be seen up close to truly be appreciated.

"It's no coincidence that Jesus' resurrection occurs in the spring," said Reverend Jacob at his pulpit. "It's a time of rebirth, to start anew with enlightened spirits. It's also a time to find our faith once again, no matter how bleak and hopeless we may have felt in the dead of winter." He was looking right at Kaitlyn, which made her squirm.

"But what is faith," he continued, "if not listening to our inner voice, which some may call a conscience or moral compass telling us what to do? But isn't that voice really the voice of God, which we can choose to listen to or not?"

"Amen!" shouted several brethren in the pews. Seated behind the organ, the reverend's wife Faizah looked more striking than ever in a violet dress.

"If you build it, he will come!" said Reverend Jacob. "Does anyone know what I'm referring to?"

Kaitlyn nodded with the rest of the congregation as several hands shot up in the air. Just about everyone in Iowa knew the movie *Field of Dreams*. Its story took place in their home state, and even was filmed on location in Dyersville. More than thirty years later, the ballpark was still a favorite tourist attraction for people across the country.

"If you build it, he will come," said Reverend Jacob. "That was Ray Kinsella's inner voice telling him to build a baseball diamond instead of planting corn that year. Only he could hear that strange and magical whisper which kept telling him to do so. And while everyone thought he was crazy, he trusted that voice and risked losing his farm to build that field."

Kaitlyn shared a smile with her mother. The movie was one of her father's all-time favorites—something they had watched together as a family many times. Her mother carried a long-time crush on its star, Kevin Costner, as her father often teased.

"But who's going to play on that field?" asked Reverend Jacob. "'Why nobody!' said Ray's best friend, telling him he was going to bankrupt his family for no apparent reason. That same friend who couldn't see some of the greatest old ballplayers brought back to life, like Shoeless Joe Jackson, who finally got redemption to play the game he loved."

The audience's nods grew more fervent.

"What caused that friend's blindness was nothing more than a lack of faith," preached the reverend. "But once he opened his eyes, he witnessed that miracle on the field."

"Hallelujah!" shouted old farmer Red in the back. The congregation broke into laughter, including Kaitlyn, who felt lighter than she had in a long while.

"If you build it, he will come," said Reverend Jacob with a smile. "But who was the *he* the voice was talking about? It wasn't Shoeless Joe Jackson after all, but Ray Kinsella's father, who died before they could make amends."

Kaitlyn was choking back tears, thinking of watching that final scene with her own father, when Ray plays catch with his dad. It sometimes made her wonder if he might have preferred a son, but they did so much together that she knew he couldn't possibly have loved a boy more than her.

"Yes, I know what some of you might be thinking," said Reverend Jacob. "That it's just some Hollywood film, and not from the Testament. But I still like its message—that if we have faith and listen to our inner voice, we might find a small patch of heaven right before us here on Earth. You see, God gives us beauty all around, but we often fail to see it because we're far too focused on the problems in our lives."

Kaitlyn saw her mother dabbing at her eyes, as many in the audience were. After so many months of darkness and doubt, she felt her spirit lifted like the stained-glass image of Christ ascending from the cross.

Reverend Jacob gave her a smile from the pulpit. "Happy Easter, everyone."

Zachary woke up an hour later than he'd wanted to, his body still operating on Pacific Standard Time. Grabbing a coffee to go, he skipped the complimentary hotel breakfast to get back on the road. The time on his dashboard showed 8:35 when it was really 9:35. The day before, he hadn't even realized he'd crossed into Mountain Standard Time.

According to his GPS monitor, he still had four more hours of driving before he would finally exit Montana. With a state speed limit of eighty miles per hour, he could do so faster than most other places, but still set his cruise control for sixty-five. Saving fuel might also save his life. Better to reach Iowa an hour or two later that evening than risk a fatal crash. If his GPS was correct, he would reach East Plains at 10:23 p.m. Their Central Time Zone was another hour ahead.

Out on the highway, a pickup truck went tearing past him, and he noticed a shotgun rack and fishing poles in its cab. Though he never wanted to go hunting, he would love to try fly fishing sometime. Seeing it on TV, it looked to be very meditative, angling a reel back and forth in the flowing stream. He'd even read somewhere it was called the "contemplative man's recreation," but that could wait for another time.

He had a girl to go see.

After church, her mother waited in the car so Kaitlyn could have a minute alone at her father's grave, while the crowd of churchgoers trickled out of the chapel. "I finished building the satellite dish," she said, reading her father's name engraved for eternity: *Roger Stokes: Beloved Husband and Father.* "I think you'd be impressed."

A rumble of thunder in the sky preceded a cluster of storm clouds passing overhead.

"So far, the reception is great, but we'll see how it does in this storm. I'm watching those French spy movies we used to rent on Amazon—the ones Mom never liked—and I'm already catching up on my French. I'm going to take it at Iowa State next year, so I can someday become a French-speaking physicist. I hope that makes you proud."

A light drizzle began, bringing back a memory from years past. "April showers bring May flowers, right, Dad? I remember you telling me that when I was a little girl and didn't want to go to school in the rain." The raindrops were cold but refreshing on her face. "I miss you a lot, and wish I could've said goodbye before you went." The drizzle turned into a downpour, requiring an umbrella which she didn't have. "Well, Mom's waiting, so guess I'll see you soon."

Hurrying back to the car, she'd meant that promise as a figure of speech, though the charge of electrons in the atmosphere gave her a strange indescribable sensation.

"Welcome to Wyoming" read the billboard displaying their trademark Bronco and Rider silhouetted over a jagged mountain range in the background. Finally departing Montana, Zachary entered Crook County, where he envisioned outlaws on horseback, their guns ablazin' as they chased a long line of covered wagons. Across the rolling, grassy plains, he saw herds of cattle and endless bales of hay in neatly bundled rolls. The landscape, seemingly untouched by modern times, was so beautiful it made him feel something he couldn't express in thoughts or words. To see it alone somehow felt wrong. If only Kaitlyn were in the passenger seat beside him, he could share this experience with her, their hands joined together as they silently gazed out the window.

Farther down the 212 Highway, he caught a glimpse of the Devil's Tower National Monument, a jutting rock formation that was perfectly named. Its looming presence felt almost supernatural. Little did he know that many believed it was an alien landing post.

Less than twenty minutes later, after cutting across the northeast corner of Wyoming, he was already in South Dakota. The next state to the east was Iowa. Back on the Interstate 90, he planned on stopping for lunch in Sturgis as a group of bikers roared past him on Harley Davidsons.

A sudden patter of rain hit the windshield. His wipers smeared a thick layer of dirt and grime, which he finally washed away after several squirts of wiper fluid. Peering into the distance, he saw the sky turning black. Then he saw the storm alert on his GPS.

If the bikers could tough out the wind and rain, so could he. The road dared him onward.

Following an Easter dinner of roasted chicken and buttery mashed potatoes, Kaitlyn and her mother were watching the Weather Channel on TV. The
satellite reception sputtered in and out because of a heavy downpour. Their dog
Checkers hunkered beneath the davenport, asleep.

"Severe storm alerts throughout the Midwest," said the weatherwoman in
front of her map. She pointed to a collision of cold air (blue) from the Rockies
with warm air (red) from the southeast to form a violent swirl of purple over
their region. "Tornado warnings in South Dakota and northern Iowa."

"At least a hundred miles away," said Kaitlyn as the raindrops hammered
their roof, the sky pitch black outside the window.

"We should be safe here," said her mother, both of them knowing that
tornadoes rarely stayed on the ground for long. In very rare cases did they
travel a hundred miles or more.

"Just in case, I stocked the storm cellar," said Kaitlyn, having supplied it
with bottled water, packaged food, and a battery-operated lantern.

"Let's see how it's looking in a few hours," said her mother. It was too
early for bed, and neither of them wanted to sleep in that dungeon-like darkness, their pillows and sleeping bags smelling of mildew in the cold, dank air.

Kaitlyn nodded, watching the satellite coverage on TV. "I feel sorry
for all those people right now," she said, their homes getting battered by
hurricane-like winds and torrential hail and rain. If they hadn't already fled
for safety underground, they were racing off in their cars for the nearest
community shelter.

"They could use some prayers," suggested her mother.

A thundering blast made them jump and the dog bark. A flash of lightning gave them a glimpse of the windswept rain against the windows.

"It's okay, Checkers," said Kaitlyn, as the dog came toward her with a nervous whine.

Grateful to be safe indoors, she silently prayed. *Please, dear Lord, watch over any poor soul who might be stranded out there…*

Driving through the stormy night, Zachary could barely see the road ahead, even with his wipers on the highest setting, swiftly sloshing back and forth against the heavy rain pounding his windshield. More than an hour had passed since he'd last seen another vehicle, and its driver had raced off toward the nearest exit.

Eerily alone on the highway, he knew he should've listened to that radio report back in Rapid City, warning everyone to get indoors immediately after the South Dakota governor closed the highways. "We might even see tornadoes" was the last thing Zachary heard before he lost reception completely. Across the AM and FM dials, he got nothing but static, while his GPS monitor advised of a *Severe Storm Alert!*

If the roads were truly closed, he questioned why he hadn't encountered any barricades, or police cars pulling him over. He wanted to believe that was a positive sign, but realistically, he suspected the cops had taken cover indoors themselves—no need to sacrifice their lives in a wasted effort to save idiots like him. *Idiot*, that was. The right word was singular.

Blasted by a sudden gale, he flew out of his lane, his car shaking and rattling as he tried to steady it against the battering winds. With rain slamming down like Niagara Falls, his windshield wipers seemed more of a distraction than a help.

Terrified for his life, he saw an exit coming up on his GPS monitor. Squinting into the dark, he finally spotted it through the slashing downpour. If he pulled over now, he might be lucky enough to find a motel still open. If not, he would find an overpass or tunnel to shelter him from any twisters, as he'd learned to do from a segment on CNA News.

The exit lane was now on his right, and he was about to turn off, when he suddenly whipped the wheel to continue onto the highway. He had to stay the course for Iowa, even if it was the last thing he ever did.

Asleep in her bed, Kaitlyn was having strange dreams—even stranger than the one she'd had of flying through the school hallways in her underwear. Alone in the church (fully dressed, thankfully), she prayed for her father's soul, his coffin open near the pulpit but no longer containing his body. She prayed for her mother, and Jenna, and even Zachary, who, outside the window, was galloping on horseback across the open plains, which looked far more like Wyoming or Montana than their actual church grounds.

Her prayers transmitted to the heavens above, they were quickly answered and sent back like a satellite signal. A string of binary numbers scrambled her thoughts, her subconscious working hard to decode them: 1000001011110101 0101101110100111000001010100010001...

You already built it, whispered a voice in her head. *Now he's coming.*

Popping with static, the Rolling Stones came over the airwaves. It was the first broadcast he'd heard since the AM news station in Rapid City more than a few hours ago. Classic rock wasn't really Zachary's thing, but he was thrilled to hear Mick Jagger's voice if it meant he'd passed the eye of the storm.

It even stopped raining, though curiously, the road was less visible, and the looming darkness quickly swallowed up the beam of his headlights. Slowing down, he heard a low rumble, and the music sputtered out in a high-pitched hum. As the rumble grew louder, he could no longer see a thing in front of—

Whoosh! A thundering roar filled his ears, the unseen force throwing him into a violent spin. The seatbelt twisted around his neck as he quickly unbuckled it to escape the driver's seat. Too late—his car was lifted into its whirling vacuum. *This is how I'm going to die* was the last thing that raced through his mind.

The windows burst all around him, the intense pressure nearly breaking his eardrums. Sucked through the windshield, he was taken by the cyclone, his body tossing about with the other flying debris.

Something banged against his legs. It felt like a lawn chair. A newspaper slapped him in the face before peeling off, and a cloud of dirt and dust pelted his eyes. He might have screamed but couldn't hear himself over the sonic boom of this black monster whipping around him, taking him higher and higher into the sky.

Just let me die, he pleaded, when a beam of light appeared at the end of the funnel cloud. Bright and shining with a peaceful glow, it beckoned him toward safety and warmth.

Sorry, Mom and Dad. I'm going to a better place now.

Kaitlyn suddenly awoke to the flickering screens on her phone, computer, and iPad. Sitting up, she saw the same broadcast on all three devices; it looked to be a live feed from a NASA space station. The distant reception was filled with static. *That's weird*, she thought. She had no idea how all three devices came on, much less how they ended up on NASA Television, one of the hundreds of stations available through her satellite dish.

Grabbing her phone from the bedstand, she watched with curiosity. It wasn't NASA TV after all, but a channel number that didn't normally come in. At closer view, its signal was coming from inside a spacecraft. Nobody in sight, as the camera showed a large oval room with various corridors branching off. The walls, floors, and ceiling were all a sterile white.

Along a semi-circular panel, various space-age computers churned out digital codes on their monitors. 001001011010101100101001000001011001110101001001010101010100010...

Far down a tunnel-like passageway, a portal slid open and a figure came through, the door zipping shut behind him. Though his face was not yet visible, something about him seemed familiar.

Wearing her pajamas, Kaitlyn quickly stepped into a pair of shoes and grabbed her jacket. Phone in hand, she hurried out of her room, watching the figure grow closer on her screen as she bustled down the hallway. As she neared the living area, she heard the family china rattling in its cabinet. A book plummeted off the shelf and hit the floor with a thud. The family photos clanked against the trembling walls, but she didn't notice that one of them had tilted sideways.

"Kaitlyn," said her father, his face emerging through static on her phone. Their dog leapt up at the TV on which he simultaneously appeared. His voice faintly reverberated from all the devices in her room. "Meet me at Bart—" he said, then the screen filled with snowy gray as his image dissolved. Barton's Pumpkin Patch—she knew it had to be. Checkers was already at the front door, scratching and whining to get out. As she opened it up, a gust of rain pelted her face, and the dog sprinted off in the direction she'd assumed.

"Kaitlyn?" her mom called out from her bedroom down the hall. "What was—"

"Everything's fine, Mom!" she said, whipping the door shut behind her. She didn't have time to explain, knowing her mother wouldn't believe her anyway, and would try to stop her from going out in the storm. Heading straight to her truck, she fired up the engine and tore off down the road. Up ahead, she caught Checkers in her headlights, the dog dashing through a field across the way. She considered following his shortcut but feared her wheels getting stuck in the mud.

Out on the county highway, she raced ahead. Peering through the downpour, she didn't see the swamp-like puddle until she smacked right into it, her front end dragging through water spraying up over her windshield. Blinded for a moment, she adjusted her wipers to clear it off. Several miles to the north, she saw flashes of lightning where the peak of the storm did its damage.

A few minutes later, she saw Barton's farmhouse on her right. There, a single light was on in an upstairs window. Just after passing it, she skidded to a stop on the side of the road. Out of the truck, she climbed over a short wooden fence and ran out onto Barton's field, where endless rows of pumpkin seeds had been planted in small mounds of dirt.

Checking the sky in all directions, she saw nothing but black, and heard only the sound of Checkers barking to her right. Straight above him, the lights descended through the storm clouds, and the spacecraft hovered into view.

It was just as she remembered—a Ferris wheel on its side, its edge lights flashing in a mystifying pattern of blue-yellow, blue-yellow, red-red, green, yellow...Kaitlyn could almost hear the notes of a symphony accompanying the strobing colors, their perfect orchestration transmitting some type of message which she could not decode. At the center of the wheel, the blades of a mechanical iris door fanned open, through which a bright beam of light shone downward.

As Kaitlyn squinted through its blinding glare, she made out her father's silhouette, the dog barking frantically. Just as quickly as he appeared, he vanished into the beam, which transported him in a flash of blue to the ground below. Stepping forward, he remained a being of light, his face and body no longer decimated by illness. "Kaitlyn," he said with a loving smile.

"Dad!" she cried, running toward him, the dog leaping up at his chest, only to be stopped by his energy field.

"Hey, boy. Good to see you!" said her father, scratching between Checkers' ears.

"Tell me I'm not dreaming," said Kaitlyn, feeling his radiating warmth as she wrapped her arms around him.

"This is real," he said, hugging her back. "But we don't have long."

"Okay," she said, overwhelmed by the moment and everything that was happening.

"This planet's going to need people like you and Zachary to slow down its destruction, so future generations can learn ways of surviving through more advanced technology."

"Zachary?" she said in disbelief. "You mean—"

"He wasn't lying," said her father. "We made several visits in his sleep, and that's why you two connected after our message was delivered."

Too stunned to speak, Kaitlyn numbly stared at her father. All this time, he'd been playing matchmaker from outer space.

"You each have separate skill sets," he continued, "which totally complement each other for what needs to be done."

Kaitlyn took a second to absorb this. "You mean like soulmates?"

"Together, you can do great things," he said with a smile. "Without love, technology can't save anyone. And love is what the planet needs more than anything right now."

Kaitlyn felt her chest tighten, wishing Zachary were here right now so she could tell him she'd been wrong. "What about Mom?" she asked. "Is she going to be okay?"

"She's always been strong," said her father, his eyes shining with compassion. "In time, her heart will heal, and she'll be ready for the right man to come along."

"But Dad," said Kaitlyn, feeling a horrible sense of betrayal, "you can't be replaced. I want us to be a family for eternity."

"We will," he assured her. "But if you truly love her, you'll want to see her happy for the rest of her time on Earth."

Kaitlyn nodded, shamed by her selfishness.

Overhead, the spaceship's lights blinked faster—green, red, yellow, blue. The colors reflected on their faces in an urgent pattern. "I have to go now," said her father, the beam of light moving over him. "This was my final mission here on Earth."

Kaitlyn held onto his glowing warmth, wanting to always remember how this felt. "I love you, Dad!" she said, breaking down in tears.

"I love you too," he said, his body dissolving into the beam of light. "And I never got to tell you how proud I am of you." In a flashing streak of blue, he ascended to the spacecraft, their dog barking in confusion.

"It's okay, boy," sobbed Kaitlyn, her tears mixed with rain as she clung to Checkers. "We're going to be okay. I promise." She expected the spaceship to take off, but it still hovered overhead, its beam of light shooting a red bolt down its center. A patch of dirt flew up where the laser struck the ground. "Dad?" she said, hoping he was coming back after all.

Stepping out of the light was Zachary, as Checkers ran forward to sniff his human flesh. With the rain pouring down on him, he looked at Kaitlyn in the darkened pumpkin patch. "Are we in heaven?" he asked, patting the dog on the head.

Kaitlyn smiled, her wet hair plastered to her face. "No, you're in Iowa," she said, thinking it was as close to heaven as anywhere else on Earth right now.

The spaceship lifted off above, the beam of light sucked through its iris portal and whirling shut. Looking up, they watched it lift off into the horizon, a streaking trail of neon left behind.

Checkers barked a couple of times but didn't bother chasing it.

"I thought I'd died," said Zachary, watching the sky. "Last thing I remember, I saw this bright warm light which brought me here. I had no idea it was…" He stopped from saying "aliens." His gaze was now on Kaitlyn.

Kaitlyn smiled, the downpour drenching her jacket over her pajamas. "I want to hear all about it, but let's get out of this rain!"

They ran for her truck across the field, their hands joining together as they fell into stride. Right behind them was Checkers—tail wagging, happy to be going home.

031

A few days later, Zachary's car was found on its side in the shallow waters of the Cheyenne River by two South Dakotan kids playing on its banks. By then, his UFO "abduction" had gone viral after Emily Barton, an eighth grader at East Plains Middle School, recorded the flying saucer over her family's pumpkin patch. Captured on her phone from her bedroom window upstairs, the video was dark and blurry because of the rain. Even so, Zachary was clearly visible in the spaceship's beam of light.

More than 40 million viewers (and counting) watched the video on her YouTube channel. It had to be a hoax, the doubters posted, a clever piece of filmmaking with the latest software. Skeptics demanded some real evidence that Zachary had even been driving to Iowa in the first place and sucked into a tornado which nobody could possibly survive. The twister destroyed homes and farms for several miles in its wake. A Denny's restaurant was completely lifted off its foundation, a storage shed facility reduced to scrap metal, and a Kohl's department store turned to rubble.

"It's definitely Zachary Taylor's car," announced the Pennington County sheriff to the Cable News America crew on site. "We matched his VIN number with his Washington State registration." Towed out of the river, the car was totally demolished, its interior flooded with water that poured out through a missing door, and its license plates ripped away.

"There's no faking this," confirmed Sheriff Wyman. "It's a miracle he's still alive."

"I won't argue that," said Zachary, responding by live video feed to the CNA anchor, a serious-faced woman with short brown hair and librarian eyeglasses.

"Do you feel vindicated?" she asked. "That you finally have proof of your alien contact?"

"All I feel is blessed," said Zachary. "Just to be alive and starting college next year with Kaitlyn. Also, for my parents and all they've done for my sister and me."

"Is it true they're starting another dealership?"

"Yes, they'll be selling EVs to a bigger market of consumers, with plans to build solar charging stations across the state. Hi, Mom and Dad, if you're watching!"

The news anchor smiled, a faint twitch at the corners of her lips before she turned serious again. "Thanks for joining us, Zachary. We'll be going to commercial now."

"Okay," said Zachary. "Go green, everyone!"

"They forgot to ask about your sister," said Kaitlyn, coming into her living room, where Zachary had just been interviewed via Facetime on his phone.

"Believe it or not," he said, standing up to embrace her, "she's asking for my endorsement now." Taking advantage of his recent popularity, Hailey was running for the Lemley City Council, adopting his platform to save the planet for future generations.

"I hope she wins," said Kaitlyn, their faces inches apart.

"Me too," said Zachary, giving her a kiss. Tonight, he would be catching a flight to Washington to finish high school there. That would give him a few months with his family before returning to Iowa. Now that his sister was talking to him, he hoped to actually miss her when he left again in the summer.

"Your last night in town," said Kaitlyn's mother, entering the room. "What do you want for dinner?"

"Anything is fine, Mrs. Stokes," said Zachary, clumsily releasing Kaitlyn from his embrace.

"Please, call me Carol," she said, having taken a quick liking to Zachary and his good manners.

"Yes, ma'am," he said. "I mean, okay, Carol."

"Jenna will be joining us," said Kaitlyn. "She's dying to meet Zachary before he leaves."

"I bet," said her mother, with a smile at Zachary. "You're a real celebrity now."

Zachary shrugged it off. "I didn't do anything to deserve it, other than being dumb enough to drive into a tornado."

"But at least my mom finally believes in UFOs," said Kaitlyn.

"Is Garrett coming, too?" asked her mother, still uncomfortable with all the attention the story was drawing—reporters were calling the house non-stop.

"They broke up," said Kaitlyn.

"I thought they just got back together?"

"They did, but all they did was argue about what was going to happen next fall when they both left for separate colleges."

"I'm sorry to hear that," said her mother.

"She's taking it better than Garrett, but I know he'll be okay."

"One day at a time," said her mother. "It's the only way to ever be happy."

As the doorbell rang, Kaitlyn suspected it was Jenna, and headed over to answer.

"Hey, you!" said her curly blonde friend, giving her a little hug.

"Hey!" Kaitlyn said cheerily. "Come on in and meet Zachary."

"Oh, my God," said Jenna, as Zachary came over to greet her. "You're really real!"

"I sure hope so," he said, as everyone laughed.

Gathered with the people she loved, Kaitlyn knew her mother was right. One day at a time, and right now, she was grateful for this moment with everyone together.

SUMMER

032

Summer vacation was nearly over. Since her father's spacecraft visit, she'd stopped having nightmares about his corpse floating up in its coffin. Kaitlyn now dreamt of him as he existed before his illness—when he had that same warmth, love, and light as during his final appearance on Earth.

On starry evenings like tonight, she still found herself watching for that wheel of lights, even though she didn't expect to ever see it again. It had taken her father to heaven, much like the wheeled chariot that transported Ezekiel to visit with God. Whether its pilots were aliens, angels, or our future selves would remain a mystery—one of many questions that science might never answer.

What she did know for certain was that things in motion stay in motion. It was the fundamental law of the universe, and why hanging on to what she couldn't control would never stop things from changing for the better or for the worse. Earlier that day, she and Jenna had said their teary goodbyes after packing her friend's car for the University of Chicago.

"Everything okay?" asked Zachary, parking his new Chevy Bolt in a cornfield dappled with moonlight, the sound of crickets chirping into the night.

Kaitlyn nodded, her smile filled with sadness. "She texted me a little while ago, letting me know she got to Chicago okay, and how they have the best pizza anywhere."

Zachary gave her a look as if sharing her thoughts. "It's still weird not waking up in my old room, hearing my parents making breakfast downstairs and talking way too loud for the early morning. All those things that used to drive me nuts, I'm actually going to miss."

She watched him closely, feeling the burden of taking him from his family. "You sure you made the right decision, coming all this way just for—?"

"I've never been more sure of anything," he said, holding her gaze with a calm certainty that made her want to kiss him. Putting her hand on his chest, she was happy to finally be alone with him, this strange, magical person brought into this world on the same day as she. All summer long, they'd been hounded by reporters or complete strangers coming up to them to say, "Hey, I know you!"

While Zachary was thrilled to have a voice to promote clean energy, it wasn't the ideal situation for a budding romance. To add to their frustrations, he'd been sleeping in their spare bedroom down the hall. Kaitlyn promised her mother they wouldn't "do the deed" in her home. It was a promise she and Zachary painstakingly abided by and respected.

Finally alone, in the middle of a cornfield on a perfect summer evening, Kaitlyn opened the passenger door and got out, her bright green eyes reflecting the lunar rays. Like beacons in the night, they signaled him to follow. Venturing into the field, she reached back and found his hand in the darkness.

ACKNOWLEDGMENTS

First and foremost, I'd like to give a big shout out to Bruce Bortz, my publisher and editor, for believing in the work and making me appear to be a much better writer than I am with his savvy editing skills. Jennifer Medrano, his assistant editor at Bancroft Press, fixed my teenage vernacular throughout the novel and made some fine editing suggestions and improvements of her own.

I would also like to thank the following:

My parents, Larry and Judi, for raising me with the discipline needed to sit down every day and write. Despite the passion I had for the story, there were days on which I struggled to stay motivated. Fear of having the novel rejected, exhaustion after a long week, and the temptation of vegging out on Sunday football games were ongoing obstacles to overcome (though I still watched the hometown 'Hawks).

Roya, for her constant optimism and Buddhist chanting, which have proven to be magical. My sister Nikki, bro-in-law Brad, and nephews Jake and Jordan (memory of). Clem Edwards, former HAB leader and AFSCME director, who turned down an offer from the Washington Senators but accepted his draft card to Vietnam. LeMont Davis, Jeanne Roccapriore, Jasmin Brown, John Michalski, and Roger Gray (in rank of serial numbers) for taking the stand on my behalf in a heated labor board hearing. I could never write characters as courageous as you, and your actions will never be forgotten. Barrett Stuart, for keeping me up to date on climate change issues with his series of op-ed letters (when he's not producing movies). Stanley Paez, for bringing me up to speed on the genius of Elon Musk, when I was naively following the media-smearing campaign against him and Tesla. Ken Atchity, producer and literary manager extraordinaire, for investing his time in various projects we've developed together. Phillip Rosen, my longtime entertainment lawyer, who kept me on his client list even during the cold spells (and always returned calls).

The University of North Alabama, where I first began writing and received a lot of encouragement from Dr. Foster and his English Department faculty, especially Lynne Burris-Butler and Dr. Ron Smith. My lifelong UNA friends, Dr. Steven Murray, who is now a professor at Cal-Berkeley, and Scott Erickson, whose family in Philly will always be a second family (even though I still think Cheese Whiz on a sandwich is disgusting). Jacqueline Rainwater, who miraculously awoke from a coma after a tree crashed down on the car we were in (bad first lunch date, but we're both here to tell about it). And last, but far from least, the Alguard family: Ches, Wendy, Harry, Norma, and her infamous picnic ham. Eyes go wide as saucers!

In writing *Kaitlyn's Wheel*, I drew from various sources, mixing scientific and biblical theories in a work of fiction. When Kaitlyn is building her satellite dish, much of her "knowledge" is gained from Dennis C. Brewer's *Build Your Own Free-to-Air (FTA) Satellite TV System* (McGraw-Hill, 2012).

I was also greatly inspired by Hari Kunzru's novel *Gods Without Men* (though I could never dream of writing on his level), and Steven Spielberg's *Close Encounters of the Third Kind*, which left a powerful impression on me as a child that remains today.

And special thanks to everyone who read this novel, especially if you made it this far through the Acknowledgments. Keep an eye on the sky for that big spinning wheel.

ABOUT THE AUTHOR

Chris Halvorson grew up in the Pacific Northwest. In fifth grade, he skipped a day of school to attend the Seattle Sonics championship parade. After dreaming of playing in the NBA himself, he soon realized he was too short and slow, so he followed his passion for books to become an author.

He majored in Professional Writing at the University of North Alabama and received an MFA in Film Writing at Columbia University in the City of New York.

He currently lives in Los Angeles, where he's adapting *Kaitlyn's Wheel* for a television series.